Shocks & Bar-B-Q

© Primordial Press
A division of Uprising Communications Group
P.O. Box 490
Laguna Beach, CA 92652

Copyright © 1992 by Michael Panno
Cover design by Studio Productions
Library of Congress Catalog Card Number 2007927943
ISBN: 0-9677859-1-X

First Edition

UPRISING

Shocks & Bar-B-Q
Michael Panno

Primordial Press
Laguna Beach

In the land of the blind, the one-eyed is king.
Apostolius: Paroemiae VII.xxiii.

…can we all get along? Can we get along?
Rodney King

For my son Sean,
who lets me steal his ideas (or so he says).

Also by Michael Panno

Animal Rites

AUTHOR'S NOTE

One evening, many years ago, I was watching Larry King, whose guests that night included two gay men who had started a controversial magazine, the primary function of which was to "out" famous heretofore "straight" individuals as gay.

Listening to these two men rattle on about their calling, I was struck by their arrogance. It was their duty, they said—for the sake of every self-loathing gay still in the closet—to expose these celebrities, thereby making it easier for all gays to not only feel better about themselves, but to find their rightful place in society. To me, they were the quintessential tattle-tales, tugging at society's sleeve, polished apple in hand, messing in peoples' lives with absolutely no concern with the consequences of their behavior.

I asked myself a question: What if one of their liberated victims wasn't quite ready, for whatever reason, to have his (or her) sexual proclivity exposed to the world? What chain of events might follow this sort of intrusion into another's personal life?

It was this question that led me shortly thereafter to this novel, and while I readily admit my total loathing for these two gentlemen and for anybody who meddles in the lives of others, I do owe them a debt of gratitude for giving me the idea for this book. Life is full of little ironies.

The book was written in 1992, dusted off and polished up in 2010 and finally published and presented for your approval in 2011. Thanks for your patience.

Summer 1992

ONE

Martin Sheppard shuffled up the short path to Vern Melnick's trailer. It was a warm, breezy summer afternoon, the offshore winds depositing a thin sheet of orange smog along the eastern shoreline of the distant Catalina Island. Martin had a few pieces of mail tucked under his left arm and he was in the process of removing a letter from its envelope. A gust of wind tore at the paper and Martin stopped shy of Vern's door, grabbed the letter with both hands and slowly digested the contents. He shook his head in disgust, stuffed the letter into his back pocket, and gave a turn to the knob on Vern's front door. It was unlocked (as usual) so Martin let himself in without knocking.

"Vern. You in here? It's Martin."

Martin thought he heard his friend's voice coming from the kitchen but he wasn't sure, and of course Vern was not about to accommodate Martin or anyone else by shouting, for it was of no concern to him if he were heard or not, if he had visitors or not, if he ever saw another human being. He'd come back to the World in seventy-two, short one leg, his stomach splattered with raw pink tissue where the shrapnel had been removed—it looked like an unfinished puzzle of flesh—and spent six weeks in that God-awful V.A. hospital planning for the future, glad to be alive. They had given him the prosthesis and once a week the shrink had come by to try and get him to talk about his experience, but each time Vern would just shake his head in disbelief and say something like, "It's just meat, Professor, let's not get too hung up over it."

So he shut it all away, put on the phony leg and hobbled out the door. Now, here he was, twenty-plus years later, alone, cut off from the outside world (well, he had his bugs), his prosthesis stuffed away in the back of a closet, given up long ago for the wheel chair—he'd put on so much weight that even walking on two real legs would be a challenge. Martin was the first person in years he had taken a liking to, had actually allowed to penetrate his little enclave, but he was not about to holler, even for him.

As he approached the kitchen from the hall, Martin could see Vern's huge body enveloping his wheel chair. The grey baggy sweats drooped over the seat, causing Vern to appear even larger than his three hundred pounds and giving his one good leg a loose, flabby contour; not that Vern had what one might refer to as muscle tone. Only his arms—which had received a workout with his manual chair—had any real definition, and surely that would all change now that his battery operated wheels had arrived.

"Here's your mail." Martin tossed the letters onto the table. "I got another rejection slip," he added, gazing over Vern's shoulder.

"Yeah, in a minute." Vern was hunched over his kitchen table, the brakes set on his wheelchair, a small cylinder of light encircling the half-dozen empty mayonnaise jars before him. Along with the jars, but just outside the circle of light, were a bottle of cooking oil, a slice of white bread, some paper towels, and an open jar of peanut butter. Vern had removed the crust from the bread, cut the doughy hearts into one-inch squares, and covered them with peanut butter. He licked the peanut butter from his fingers then carefully dropped the squares into the jars, peanut butter up.

"Vern…"

"One minute." Vern soaked a paper towel with oil and rubbed it along the inside edge of each jar. "Terrific," he added, as he grabbed two of the jars and handed them to Martin. "Put one in the bathroom in the corner behind the john and one in my bedroom. Make sure you put them in a corner."

"Yeah, I know the routine. How much longer is this gonna last?"

"Until I complete my census." He grabbed two of the jars and wheeled himself across the room.

"Couldn't you just do it by mail?"

"Oh, Martin made a joke."

"Why don't you just get some of those hotels, or whatever they are, you know, 'roaches check in—'"

Vern did a half-turn in his chair and glared at him. "I never figured you for the malevolent type. Perhaps you think the little Blatta Americana just waltzes into your hotel and passes out. I assure you it's a far more sanguinary event. First they rip their legs off trying to escape—they're very free spirited, you know—then they just plop down on their bellies and slowly starve to death. And what is accomplished by all this suffering? Absolutely nothing. The cockroach as a species is here to stay my friend."

"They're just bugs, Vern," said Martin as he reached the bathroom. "And I didn't say I wanted to watch." He set the jar in the corner and spent a minute studying the pictures and articles on the walls. On the one directly across from the toilet seat was a large blown-up picture of a snail; he had never seen this one before today. The other walls contained similar shots of various insects: bees resting on flowers, two flies copulating, a wasp feeding on whitefly larvae. The larvae enlargement was a little too graphic for Martin and made him feel a bit queasy. He placed the second jar in Vern's bedroom and returned to the kitchen. "I want to show you this letter."

Vern placed the last of the baited jars under the sink. "Did you see my new poster?"

"Yeah, it's great, a real piece of art."

"That's the docollate snail. Fascinating creature, bit of a cannibal, it eats common garden snails."

"Oh. You planning on growing a garden?"

"Unless I am mistaken, that would require my presence out-doors, an experience I long ago rejected as both unnecessary and, most importantly, unpleasant."

Martin looked around the old trailer. It was a clutter of books and manuscripts, dirty dishes, various newspaper arti-cles scattered about the floor. All the shades were pulled down tight, allowing only narrow slits of light through at the edges. Martin had done the purchasing and the installation of the shades to Vern's exact specifications. "I don't want any of those transparent models," he had said. "It's important that the room be kept in a perpetual state of caliginosity. A palpable obscurity, if you will."

"Would you mind if I open a shade and let a little of the outdoors in here?" asked Martin.

"If you must. But only one."

Martin reached for the shade above the kitchen window.

"Not that one!"

It was too late. The shade snapped out of Martin's hand and a beam of light shot across the room and onto Vern's face. He reached down for the wheels of his chair and then, realizing he was in his new powered one, reached back up for his con-trols, only to hit the wrong button and send himself backwards against the wall. Little beads of sweat began forming on his brow and Vern went into a slight panic. "Shut it! Jesus. Shut the damn thing." There was a look of desperation on his face, like a convict caught half way up the wall.

Martin reached up and lowered the shade as Vern scrambled to the far side of the room. There was a small table in the corner with a bottle of bourbon on it. Vern snatched it up and took a huge gulp.

"Vern, are you okay?"

"Jesus, you know I hate light."

"I knew you hated it, I didn't know you were afraid of it. Is there something you're not telling me?"

4

Vern took another swig of whiskey. "Just keep the damn thing down, okay? Make yourself useful and put on a pot of coffee. Something I'm not telling you. Yeah, I'm a vampire, a fucking vampire in a wheelchair."

Martin poured them more coffee and added a shot of bourbon to each cup. Vern had calmed down considerably from earlier.

"I got another rejection slip today."

"Yes, so you mentioned. Well, at least somebody's thinking of you."

"Not exactly good thoughts. I'm running out of room for them all. I've papered most of my coach and I've got boxes stacked up; you should see my place."

"So tell me. What did it say?"

"It was from that Sci-fi magazine, Planet Earth. I sent them the story about the man giving birth. Did I show you that one?"

"First Borne, I believe was the title. Very clever. And I mean that in the best way."

"I'm sure you do. Anyway, the editor sent me this scathing letter."

Martin reached into his pocket and retrieved the crumbled letter. "Listen to this. 'Dear Mr. Sheppard.' At least she spelled my name right. 'Dear Mister Sheppard. Thank you for sending me First Borne. I'm afraid this story has a major problem: believability! Nothing in it can convince me that a character like the male you depict would (in a million years) agree to carry a child for his wife.' I like the way she adds the 'million years' bit, like she's got some lock on the future. Jesus Christ, we could be walking on one leg by then."

"You think?" said Vern

Martin glanced over at Vern's missing leg. "You know what I mean."

Vern took a swig from the bottle of bourbon. "I remember now. Your protagonist, J.T., was a bit of a chauvinist, right?"

"In the beginning, but he changes by the story's end. He gets in touch with the feminine side of himself."

"Well, that gives me the creeps. Anyway, you assumed that because this woman is the fiction editor of a slick magazine, that she would get it."

"A fucking baboon should be able to get it!"

"There's no need to disparage the poor baboons. Why are you sending your stories to those rags, anyway?"

"Well, Vern, they have a magazine that publishes stories. I write stories. Are you following me here? I'm trying to make some money, maybe start some kind of a career. I'm almost forty years old. I haven't sold a thing, not one story. My wife's gone. I live in a broken down piece-of-shit trailer..."

Vern gestured with both arms, offering his surroundings as an example. "Well," he said, "you could always fix your place up."

"I'm serious, Vern. I've got nothing going."

Vern took a deep breath and glanced toward the partially open shade, then back at his friend. Martin looked more like thirty than pushing forty, well built, no grey in his hair.

"You've got both legs for starters, a youthful face, a neighbor that knows more about insects than probably any other person alive, and..." He abruptly stopped, quite aware of his preachy tone. "Drop the resentment, Martin," he said in his most Buddha-like voice. "Now, let me ask you something; something more important. Are you still having the vision?"

Martin sank into his chair. Whenever he thought of the vision, he thought of June, and whenever he thought of June, it was of those last three months together. Was it the vision that finally drove her away or was it her withdrawal from him that brought it on in the first place? The line seemed very fuzzy.

She had complained of being bored for a long time. Martin never wanted to go anywhere, do anything, except sit in his room and write. That was bad enough. Then he went dry, couldn't write a paragraph, not a word. He would sit for hours staring at his computer screen, waiting. He tried drugs, alcohol, drugs and alcohol, sleep deprivation. Nothing was working.

He got depressed, then angry, then (according to June) downright mean. When she suggested they go to Sea World one Saturday afternoon, he went crazy. "I'm fighting for my God damn life here, June! Are you blind? Sea World! God. They're holding all these fish hostage, forcing them to jump through hoops for a bunch of idiot tourists from Bumfuck, Nebraska! They come out here and start smelling the salt air, they're liable to wake up and realize how miserable their lives are and before you know they'll be packing up and moving out here. Is that what you want, huh? More people? More congestion? Would that assuage your boredom?"

He had gotten up from his chair and made a move toward June—a move she later said was wrought with violence—but all the booze and adrenalin was too much. He passed out. When he woke up, June was asleep on the couch, and it was later that night that the vision first appeared. He paid it little attention. After all, it had been a long drunken day, and there had been the fight. Had he really passed out? But when it returned the following night he got excited. His block was over, he was sure of it. It must have been the big fight. Sure, that was it. He just needed to blow off some steam, release all his stress and anger. He thought about telling June but decided to wait. She was still pretty angry.

For the next week he didn't so much as look at a bottle of booze and each night he climbed into bed eagerly anticipating the revealing of his new story, but each night was the same. He would turn out the light, close his eyes and it would appear: an un-cocked double-barrel shotgun, suspended in pitch-black space. He felt that if he reached out he could easily touch it. A few seconds would pass and then a hand would appear, load two shells into the barrels and cock the gun. He could hear the barrels snapping shut, a sound so unique to a shotgun, very deep and hoarse, a sound full of anger and serious intent. And then, silence, as the rifle hovered in space, loaded, cocked and ready. But for what?

Martin would try to force the story along, imagining different scenarios that might put a shotgun in his hero's hands. One night he imagined a world in the near future, a revolution had broken out, the government had become fascistic and Martin's hero was part of an Underground. In his fantasy his hero—perhaps his name is Buck—grabbed the shotgun as a group of faceless men gathered around him, their chosen leader. And then what, thought Martin, knowing already it was false, that he was forcing the vision in the wrong direction; he had no interest in revolutions, or guns for that matter. No, there was something else, some other purpose behind this vision. It would come, he was sure of it. And with this acknowledgment, the rifle would vanish and Martin would drift off to sleep.

"I'm waiting," said Vern.

"What?"

"The vision. Are you still having it?"

"Every night. I used to think there might be a story there, but now, I don't know. Maybe it's just symbolic."

"Well, perhaps a psychiatrist is in order."

The irony was not lost on Martin. "Well, Vern, it's possible. It's been over six months and nothing's happened. It's probably just some manifestation of my psychosis. The shotgun could be my desire to blow up my old life and start over. In fact, I wish it were that easy."

Vern wheeled himself to the open shade and pulled it shut. "If I'm going to allow you to come into my house and disrupt my lifestyle by opening windows and entertaining notions of cockroach genocide, you must promise never to say things like that again. It makes me feel bad, like maybe I misjudged you."

Then he cruised over to his desk, grabbed a slide and stuck it under his microscope. Martin knew this signal only too well. It was Vern's thinking time. He was capable of sitting for hours squinting into his microscope at sections of caterpillar legs or dragon fly wings, or any number of fragments, without uttering a word. It wore Martin down; it drove him crazy. He felt like he was under the glass, himself, that Vern could see inside him, could probably tell him everything, was sitting there right now sizing him up like one of his bugs. Why couldn't he just spell it out for him?

The silence was brief, maybe five minutes, then, Vern spoke.

"Buy a gun."

"What?"

"Buy the shotgun and see if the vision goes away, or if it changes. It's the only way to make anything happen. You have to get involved with the dream. You're waiting for it to do all the work."

"I don't like guns, Vern. There are too many of them in the world already, and even if I did get one—which I'm not about to do—just what exactly would you suggest I do with it?"

"Well, I suppose you'll have to wait for the next episode, but I would assume you would shoot something; or someone." Vern was on a roll now; Martin could see it in his eyes. "In fact, that may very well be the answer to your writing problem."

"Oh, really."

Vern chuckled. "Well, you couldn't just shoot anybody. It would have to be some type of potentate, a celebrity maybe, or politician."

Martin grimaced and took a quick shot of bourbon. "How about the President. Why not go all the way to the top?"

"That would work. In fact, I think he's coming out here in a few weeks. You'd get your name in the paper. You could go on Geraldo or Oprah. And, you would be upholding an age old tradition."

"And what might that be?"

"Regicide, of course."

"Regicide? More like suicide."

"Listen, it was very common in Africa. In Russia, the Khazars put their kings to death after a set term, or even after some calamitous event like a drought, or a flood; anything that might indicate a demise in their powers. Talk about accountability."

"This isn't exactly a monarchy."

"King, President, what's the difference? Considering the state of affairs in this country I'd say our leader was due to leave."

"Well, not by my hand."

"You said you wanted fame."

"As a writer, Vern, not a killer."

Vern didn't let up. "Famous people sell books. It's not the other way around. You think if Lee Harvey Oswald were alive today and wrote a book he'd have a hard time finding a publisher? If it's really fame you want, it's there for the having. Speaking of Oprah, what time is it?"

Martin got up from the table. "Time for me to go home. Thanks for the rotten advice."

"My pleasure. By the way, you haven't mentioned my new chair."

Martin laughed. "Yeah, I noticed you're quite adept with it. When did you get it?"

"Yesterday. The VA's been promising me for six months. Bunch of assholes."

"Maybe you're the one needs a shot-gun."

"I've already done my share."

As he was leaving the room, Martin noticed a cockroach sticking its head into one of the jars. Its feet hit the oil and it quickly plopped down to the bottom of the glass prison. Martin pointed to the jar. "Got one."

"Alive and well. If it were up to you, he'd be dying right now."

Martin smirked. "Yeah, I guess I'm a killer at heart."

Vern put his left arm down in his lap and began scratching at his sweats where his left knee would have been if he had a left knee. "Well, you're only human."

The dizziness from the bourbon was now replaced by a dull headache as Martin prepared for bed. His conversation with Vern brought a smile to his face. One good thing that had come from his separation from June was his moving to the trailer park and meeting Vern. He drove Martin a little crazy but he was always entertaining, and (even more to the point) smarter than Martin. His intellect, his perceptions, could be trusted, even if his spin was a little askew.

It was almost ten o'clock. In another seven hours he'd be up and out the door, making the dreaded drive to L.A. He could hear the surf crashing pretty hard and figured there was a new swell coming in. He would have liked getting one of the units right on the beach but he had seen the damage done in the past by the combination of a high tide and a large west swell. Having a six-foot wave break through his front window was something he could live without. He counted himself lucky finding anything in Laguna Beach at these rates, even though the place did belong to one of June's friends; it wasn't the first time he'd had to swallow his pride.

There was a knock on the door, but before he could get to it, she came in.

"Martin?"

He came out of the bedroom, dressed only in his white jockeys, or as June had referred to them "old man underwear." June was studying the rejection slips tacked onto the living room wall. The one she was reading was only four words long. It read: 'You gotta be kidding.'

"What are you doing here?"

June turned away from the wall. She took one look at his attire and shook her head. "God, I hate those."

"What's with the heavy coat, June? On your way to Aspen?"

June had on a full-length grey winter coat with a fur collar. When she bought it, she thought the collar was mink but it turned out to be synthetic, which didn't stop Martin from attacking. "Mink is for minks to wear, June, not vain women."

"I just came by to show you something," she said. "Just because we're not married anymore doesn't mean we can't still be friends."

Martin sighed with impatience. "We were never exactly friends, June, and if you want to see me, and I don't know why you would, you could call first. What if I had company tonight?"

The thought that another woman might be interested in Martin would of course never occur to June. She was the one who had always turned eyes (from men and women), had gotten all the attention when they were out together, had men lining up to get next to her. Martin, well, he wasn't bad looking, but he was always so…disheveled. He just didn't care one way or another what anybody thought about him. They'd go out for dinner and he'd put on some old Levis—they might even have holes in them—and a t-shirt and sometimes wouldn't bother to comb his hair, while June would be dressed to kill. Was it any wonder he rarely got any play from other women, why people said they were so mismatched?

They had met at a party, June was encircled by men and Martin was doing his best to ignore her until he finally couldn't stand the scene anymore and walked right up to her and made some remark about taking a number for his turn, which, to Martin's surprise, brought forth tears from June, and had him feeling like a complete heel. There was an apology, some self-deprecating humor on his part, a glass of wine and an arrangement to get together.

"Yeah, what if," said June. "Anyway, I did call, Martin. I left a message on your machine. In fact, I've left a lot of them in the last few weeks. I thought maybe you were dead or something. Are you going to ask me in, or not?"

"My machine isn't working, hasn't been for months." He reached over and closed the door. "You're already in. You can't stay long. I have to get up early."

Feeling uneasy, Martin went into his room and put on a robe. He knew all he had to do was brush up against June, and her smell, her feel, would take control of him, and in those flimsy underwear his weakness would be all too apparent. The robe was his safety net.

"Martin, why do you tack all these rejection slips up on your wall like this?"

He came out of the bedroom. "I can't afford wallpaper. Now, what did you want to show me?"

She turned to face him and removed the coat. She was wearing nothing but white panties. Martin wished his robe were made of steel.

"What do you think?" June cupped her perfect breasts in her hands. Martin figured them at about 34Cs.

"Only three thousand for the pair. It's part of a package."

Martin tried to speak but his tongue wouldn't work. He tried to move toward June but his feet felt like anchors. His head was throbbing. He'd had much too much bourbon, but not enough to handle this.

"Well? Do you like them?"

"This is what you came to show me?" he said, his mouth working again.

"I wanted you to be the first."

Martin plopped himself into a chair. He couldn't keep his eyes off her. She'd lost some of her usual tan, but she actually looked better without it; her skin seemed purer now, her hazel eyes more prominent. Her hair was the same as before, a soft canary yellow—okay, it was bleached, but it was a good job; it looked natural—but longer than he'd ever seen it, the ends curling just above her nipples. He felt his hand start to reach out for her, as though it had a will of its own, but he quickly reined it in.

"You didn't have to take off your pants to show me your tits."

"I wanted you to see the whole perspective," she said. "Do you think they're too small for the rest of my body?"

"Do I think they're too small? Why don't you ask your boy-friend? Why are you here, June? Why are you doing this to me?"

She started to cry. "I thought you would tell me the truth, if I made a mistake or not."

Martin took a deep breath, raised one hand up to his forehead and began massaging it. Why did she have to cry? He was angry; he had a right to be. And not just about tonight, but everything. She'd kicked him out, given up on him when he needed her most. For better or for worse, you bet. Now all she had to do was turn on the water and he was supposed to just let it go—just like that? Boy, could she work him. "Stop crying. Look, they're perfect. What do you want me to say? I'm happy for you. I just don't get it. I liked them before."

"They were too big, before. I mean, you know, they were okay for dancing, but I've got this new agent now and he's sending me out for modeling jobs and, well, smaller breasts are in now. Martin got up from his chair, picked the coat up off the ground and wrapped it around June's shoulders. "Here. I really need to get some sleep, I have to work in the morning."

June closed her coat with one hand, and then she leaned over and gave Martin a light kiss on the cheek. "I'm sorry I bothered you."

Lilacs, thought Martin as he got a whiff of her perfume. He pulled away from her. "June, listen, they look great, okay. I just…I don't think you needed to do it, that's all."

June went to the front door and opened it. "Hey, I got a new car."

Martin looked past her, but it was too dark to see what kind of car she had. "What is it?"

"A Honda."

"Oh. What happened to the Porsche?"

"I got rid of it. The payments were too much and besides, it's so seventies, don't you think? Well, I better go. Maybe we'll go for a ride sometime," she said and then ran out to her new car and drove away.

———

Martin climbed into bed. He'd forgotten all about Vern and the crazy afternoon in his trailer. Seeing June again had thrown him into a weird state of mind. Had she really been there or was her appearance some bizarre apparition born out of his loneliness? He tried to remember back when the world—at least his world—didn't seem so insane, when reality had some kind of order, and seemed to make sense. He reached over and shut off the light. There was a time when a good night's sleep was all it took to make him feel refreshed. He wanted to feel that way again.

He closed his eyes; he was exhausted. There was no conscious thought of the vision, just an overwhelming desire for sleep, for a little peace. And then it was there—the shotgun—un-cocked, and then the hand reaching up to load it. Now the hand—his, he presumed—cocking the gun. Soon he would drift into sleep and the vision would vanish. But what was this other thing there in the distance, moving slowly toward the shotgun? It looked like a car. It was a car, a large black limo with little American flags attached to the fenders. It came to a stop and two men wearing dark glasses helped another man out of the back seat. The two men with glasses were faceless but the third one, the one in the middle, the one doing all the waving, was easily recognizable.

TWO

Chad and Karen Dalrymple pulled into the mall parking lot a little before eight o'clock. It was already eighty degrees outside and the idea of spending a couple of hours inside the air-conditioned stores sounded good to the wife, a cute twenty-eight year old blond who's ass had just in the last two years begun to expand, causing the husband to suggest she no longer wear her string bikini to the beach.

Chad was in the process of suggesting she join a gym when he spied an open parking spot way up at the front of the row, close to the mall entrance. He gunned his silver BMW down the isle and slid into the spot. Outside the Broadway, a small crowd had gathered, jockeying for position, waiting for the stores to open and the one-day sale to begin.

"You're not exactly Rambo, yourself," said Karen, slightly irritated.

Chad turned off the motor. "Don't get defensive. It's just, you used to have a really great body, and, you know, I just think you should get to work on it before it gets any worse."

"Maybe you should try having a baby, see what it does to you."

"You didn't have a baby. You had a miscarriage."

"Well, it still messes up your body. All those hormones."

He shut off the engine.

"Why are you parking here?"

"What's wrong with it? It's as close as we can get."

"But we're in the sun here. The car will be boiling by the time we get out. You should park in the structure."

Chad took a deep sigh. He didn't want to be here, sale or no sale (as far as he was concerned it was impossible to save money by spending it), and he didn't really care one way or another if the car got hot inside or even if the damn thing melted while they were shopping. What he wanted to do was push her out of the car and drive away, maybe play a round of golf or take a drive to the beach and go for a swim. But what he did was start the car, jam it into reverse, back it out and speed away, tires screeching. A shiny red Mercedes quickly filled up his space.

The BMW skidded around the corner and entered the parking structure. It was dark down there and Chad had to flip up his sunglasses to see where he was going, but it was definitely cooler under all that cement. He went about half way down the row and found a spot to park. The wife had sat there steaming throughout the little speed exhibition, but hadn't said a word. As soon as he turned off the engine, she got out of the car and slammed the door. Chad gave quick pursuit.

"So, are you gonna stayed pissed all day?"

"Fuck off."

"Oh, fuck off, huh. That's great language."

"Chad, you're a real jerk, you know that."

They came out from under the structure and Chad flipped his shades down for the short walk to the store. "If you're not going to talk to me, I'll just leave. It's not like this is fun for me, you know."

She turned and was about to speak, but before she could get a word out, they heard the explosion. It shook the ground beneath them and for an instant they thought perhaps it was an earthquake, but when Chad glanced over at the Mercedes—the one in their spot—he knew it was something else, something far more serious. A round object the size of volleyball splattered against the passenger door of the expensive car and actually became imbedded in it. But it wasn't a ball at all. It was somebody's head.

"My God," said Karen, "we could have been killed."

But Chad didn't bother to answer her. He had already begun running toward the Mercedes. He wanted a closer look.

Just three hours earlier, a newly hired janitor by the name of Raymond Dubois casually made his rounds at the Broadway. Raymond was a frail looking man in his thirties with pale, pot-marked skin, thinning brown hair, and wire rimmed glasses that tended to slide down the bridge of his nose. In his grey janitor outfit he looked more like a Bolshevik intellectual than one destined to sweep floors.

Upon reaching the lingerie department, Raymond took a small package out of his backpack, opened it and carefully placed the contents inside of a hollow box. Poised upon the box, her mongrel smile imbued with an eclectic blend of innocence and lust, was the top half of a female manikin, dressed only in a black push-up bra and a stringy red wig. Raymond was impressed with the attention paid to detail on the manikin's face, in particular her thick red lips. Negro lips, he thought. Very fashionable. He casually replaced the wrappings of his package into his backpack and continued on with his work.

The surprise that Raymond Dubois had taken from his backpack was a clever little device less than five inches tall, weighing about six and a half pounds. The official name was the OZM Series, Soviet-Made Bounding Antipersonnel Mine, but they had come to be known in the field as the Bouncing Betty, an ingenious weapon that fires a grenade waist high before exploding, has an effective radius of some eighty feet, and can quickly turn numerous human beings into spaghetti.

At precisely 7:58, Raymond took the escalator up to the second floor. From the landing he could see the entrance, the redheaded manikin, and the pretty young clerk who was about to unlock the doors to let the impatient crowd inside. He had seen the clerk before and had hoped today would be her day off; she was young and sweet looking and although Raymond was not fond of women in the biblical sense, he would just as soon spare this one the ugly destiny waiting under the manikin. But these were just thoughts and had no more impact on Raymond than his consideration of the manikin; just electrical impulses passing through a hunk of grey matter.

He reached into his backpack and removed a small transmitter. Down below, the young girl swung open the doors and fifteen sweaty, anxious shoppers flooded in. This was the moment Raymond had waiting for. He pushed his button, expecting to see the grenade pop through the top of the box like Jack, himself, but nothing happened.

Raymond shook the transmitter and pushed the button again. Still nothing. Once inside the door, the crowd quickly dispersed, the majority of them moving out of "Betty's" range. Raymond began to panic; this was his first solo mission for the People's Triumphant Army and he wanted to do well. Beads of warm sweat began to pour down his forehead and into his eyes. He removed his wire-rimmed glasses, wiped away the stinging perspiration with his sleeve, put the glasses back on and inspected the remote control. The Small plastic door to the battery compartment was gone and one of the batteries was missing. He began a frantic search of the bag, but there was so much junk in there he finally just dumped the contents onto the floor. There it was. Raymond quickly reinserted the battery into his transmitter. Without looking down to the first floor he gave a third push on the button and Bouncing Betty did exactly what she was designed to do.

By the time Tim Liddell got to the job site that morning, the place was swarming with picketers. Tim pulled his Ford pickup into the driveway and a plague of black faces swept in to fill the space between him and the gate. Tim rolled up his window, increased the volume on his radio and took a sip of coffee.

"Aa-boo-nye, folks. It's fresh-kill hour," came the voice over the radio. It was Russ Holloway. Russ had a three hour slot every morning from seven to ten, and at eight he liked to see just how far under the skin of animal rights activists he could get with his "fresh-kill" segment. He had other segments, too. At seven he did the homeless—he liked to start the day with them, get everyone driving to work all riled up—and at nine the illegal aliens. In between those slots was a potpourri of liberal bashing. No matter what the subject was or what the so-called experts had to say about it, Russ knew better. Was there a hole in the ozone layer? Absolutely not, just some crackpot environmental pseudo-scientists trying to pad their pockets with research money. Who caused the S & L disaster? Why, the liberals. Who else!

Yes, sir, Russ was an expert on everything from economics to inversion layers. Where did he get all this knowledge? Did he have a drawer full of post-graduate degrees at home? No, actually, Russ left school after the ninth grade. Or maybe he'd put in a lot of years working in different fields. After all, he was nearly forty; he'd had the time. Well, not exactly. Russ had been in a lot of different fields all right, but usually with a shovel in his hands. It wasn't that long ago when he'd called up a radio station to complain about the Berlin wall coming down—how the commies would infiltrate Western Europe and destroy the economy—that the station manager noticed Russ's smooth delivery and offered him an opportunity to come in and do a reading. Now here he was, probably the most recognizable voice on the radio, with over five hundred radio stations across the country carrying his show and, at last count, a devoted listening audience of close to ten million. Tim was one of the faithful.

"Time for all you intelligent Angelinos—and you know who you are—to call me up and share your most recent experience killing or maiming an animal. Now remember folks, there may be some of those weak-kneed, bleeding heart, so-called animal lovers out there, so make it gruesome."

Outside Tim's car, protesters pounded their fists on his

windshield and stuck their faces right up against the glass. Tim looked down at the radio and gave them the finger. Russ took a short dramatic pause from his delivery, then, lowering his voice and softening his tone, he continued.

"Now, remember good people, I'm not talking about people's pets; I'm a pet lover, too. Let's just get that clear right now. When I get the nasty letters and phone calls from the fanatics—and, I, will, get them, you can count on that—when the calls and letters come in about how I suggested we go out and kill Fido, those of us in the know will recognize them for what they are: lies and slander."

Russ returned to his normal boisterous tone. "But if you nailed a possum crossing the road or hammered a rat with a baseball bat, or even if you tasted a little dolphin in your tuna, I want to hear about it. So give me a call. The lines are open."

The angry protesters were starting to rock Tim's truck. Tim could tell because his coffee began spilling out over the rim. He glanced up at some of the faces and signs. The usual shit: Give African Americans jobs in their own community; Whitey go home; Our community, our jobs. God, he hated them. He wanted to put his foot to the floor and grind a few of them up against the chain-link fence—and maybe some day he would—but for now he simply eased out the clutch and applied a little pressure to the gas pedal and the black sea parted. For a moment Tim felt like Moses as he inched his way to the gate, where the nervous guards—two black men with rent-a-cop uniforms—slid it open just long enough for him to enter.

A caller had begun sharing his experience from earlier that morning on a fishing boat, how he had clubbed a baby seal to death that had gotten tangled in one of his nets. "Shoulda seen its eyes pop, Russ" Tim turned off the radio.

When Tim came in, Martin was sitting on a five gallon bucket of paint, nursing a red-hot cup of coffee, and watching Dudley Hammer trying his best to spit wads of tobacco juice into an empty paint can. Tim raised his left arm to look at his watch and kept the arm suspended as he looked toward the group. "Eight-fifteen. We start at eight, gentlemen." Tim checked his watch once more before dropping his arm to his side.

"Just waiting on you," said Hank Talbert. Hank was only fifty, but he had consumed so much scotch and inhaled so many paint fumes over the last thirty years, he looked closer to sixty-five—and a worn sixty-five at that. The skin on his face was tan, but very dry and taut like an old Apache. His hair was mostly grey and very fine, his hands coarse from years of cleaning them with solvents. But there was no denying Hank could paint. He worked his bristle brush like an artist, the enamel flowing out to a beautiful satin finish with just enough rope to distinguish it from the plastic look created by a sprayer. In fact, Hank absolutely refused to use a sprayer for finish work, even on commercial jobs. "Anybody can spray," he would say. "It takes a painter to use a brush."

"Been fighting those fucking niggers for the last fifteen minutes," said Tim.

"African Americans," said Martin. "I may be wrong, Liddell, but I think 'nigger' fell out of favor with them quite a few years ago."

Martin leaned back against the wall. He looked a mess, and he knew it. His clothes were wrinkled, he needed a shave and his hair—long for a man his age—was uncombed. He had a good build, five-ten, a hundred and seventy pounds, but in the last few months he'd noticed his stomach beginning to protrude over his pants. At first he was self-conscious about it and tried to suck in his gut, but lately he just let it go.

"Yeah, well I'm bringing it back. Where the fuck is Chang?"

"Hasn't shown up yet," said Hank.

"Fuck. Who the hell's gonna sand all these door jambs?"

Hank got up from the empty bucket he was sitting on and walked over to Tim. Hank was only six feet tall but he towered over the Five-three foreman. "Don't look at me, chief. I don't do prep."

"There's a couple hundred guys right outside that would be more than happy to come in here and sand for you, Tim," said Martin. "And I'm sure they'd love to hear your opinions regarding I.Q. being proportionate to the color of one's skin."

"Ain't no fucking spear chucker working on this crew, I don't care if I have to prep everything myself. You love them so much, why don't you get out there with them?"

"And miss all this. Tell me something, Tim, were you molested by a large black man when you were a small child, or what?"

"I've been molested by them all my life, in the welfare lines. Dudley, you start sanding jambs."

"Why do I gotta sand?" said Dudley. "That's nigger work."

Dudley reached back and scratched his skinny butt, spit a wad of tobacco juice down at Tim's feet and stuck some more chew into his mouth. He was the youngest guy on the crew, six-two, one hundred fifty pounds, an angular face with a hooked nose and a pair of window shutters for ears.

"Because I'm the foreman, Hank's a journeyman, Martin— I don't know what the fuck he is—but you, you are a fucking zero piece-of-shit apprentice, and that puts you just one rung up the ladder from those monkeys outside. Any questions?"

Dudley looked more perplexed than hurt. He didn't say a word.

"Good. Hank, you can follow Dudley around and put some finish on these jambs. You do paint door jambs, don't you?"

"Just like Picasso."

"Terrific. We got three weeks to get this fucking place finished, and get out of this hell-hole, so let's get with it."

―――――――――

Curtis Chang had every intention of getting to work on time. He'd gotten up at six, driven his oldest son, Hector, to his job in Santa Monica, stopped at Starbucks for some coffee and then doubled back across town on Jefferson to avoid the mess on the Ten. He made a right on Western but when he got down to Martin Luther King Blvd., the east-bound lanes were closed—some men in yellow hats were tearing up the street, and half a block away a large flatbed truck sat loaded down with huge sections of new sewer line. Curtis made a mental note of that; it was always good to know about any new construction going on in his turf.

So Curtis had to go up a couple of blocks to Vernon, instead. He was running late and in a hurry; the detour had cost him precious minutes. The last thing he needed today was to get on Liddell's bad side.

As was his ritual, Officer Wade Parker had pulled his Harley back into an empty lot where he could see the intersection at Vernon and Western without being spotted by his potential victims. He'd had an enormous amount of success in the previous six months and there was talk in the department about giving him a promotion. No one on the force wrote as many tickets as Parker, and many of the other officers joked that the real Parker Center was wherever Wade happened to be patrolling.

And of course, no one seemed to notice—or if they did, they didn't care—that over ninety-per-cent of his citations were written to minorities. If it were to ever come up, implying perhaps that Parker were prejudice, he would no doubt deny it whole-heartily. He did not actively seek out minorities to cite. He picked out the oldest, most beat up cars that came into his territory. Nine times out of ten he could find something wrong with the car and issue a fix-it ticket. If these junkers were usually driven by minorities, it was of no concern to him. The only color he was interested in was the blue ink he used to write his citations.

If anyone had dug even further into Parker's stats, they would also have noticed that over fifty per-cent of the tickets he issued were never paid, another little matter that meant nothing to Parker. That was a job for the courts to take care of; his was to keep the streets safe from bad drivers.

So it was only natural when he saw the rusted out '72 Chevy Van pass by that Wade Parker should give chase. He shoved the last section of a Snickers into his mouth, tossed aside the wrapper, swung his leg off the handlebars in a move as smooth as any cowboy about to round up steers, gave a quick start to his shiny bike and slid gracefully onto the road. How he loved this moment, the short pursuit, the roar of his bike's motor, the wind in his face, the fact that the next thirty minutes of his victim's life belonged entirely to officer Wade Parker.

He had his lights flashing and his siren blaring as he pursued the old van down Vernon. He was beginning to worry that he might have a runner on his hands—some guys liked the chase, but not Parker—when the brake lights came on and the driver pulled over to the curb and turned off the ignition. The old van shook violently for a minute and belched out a few clouds of thick, black smoke before finally sputtering to a halt.

Officer Parker sat on his bike trying desperately to snatch a breath of fresh air; the exhaust from the van was so thick it settled on the shiny motorcycle fender like a layer of coal dust. Parker took a hanky from his pocket and as he sat there waiting for a response from the dispatcher, he methodically wiped the fender clean. Finally the girl gave him the information he needed. The car was registered to a Juanita Chang; no outstanding warrants. That was good news; Parker hated fussing with arrests. He neatly folded the hanky and put it in his back pocket, unsnapped his helmet and casually walked up to the driver's window. This would be easy; the Chinese never gave him any problems. Someday he hoped to get a piece of Chinatown to patrol. Then he'd show some real production.

When he saw the driver, he nervously pulled back. "Put your hands outside the door."

"What's the problem, officer?"

"Just do as I say," said Parker, one hand resting on his pistol.

25

The driver stuck his hands out the window. "Let's see your driver's license."

"I don't have it with me, officer."

Parker had him get out of the car. Then he told him to turn around, face the van and place his hands up against it. The man quietly obeyed and Parker proceeded to frisk him. Parker figured he was in his late thirties but he was as lean and muscular as most eighteen-year-olds. His hair was clipped short like a marine. He wore a spaghetti t-shirt and white painter's pants and on his right shoulder there was a small birthmark the shape of a heart. One thing was certain: he was no more Chinese than Juan Valdez.

Satisfied that the driver wasn't carrying a weapon, Officer Parker told him he could let his arms down. "Turn around. What's your name?"

The man turned to face the police officer and spoke directly into the dark sunglasses. "Curtis Chang."

"You don't look like no Chang to me. Look more like a Rodriguez, or Martinez."

"Yes sir, I know," he said. Was that a smirk on his face? "Did I do something wrong?"

This was the question Parker was waiting for. It was the one he always waited for. The minute they asked that question, conveyed any doubt whatsoever regarding their innocence, they were his. "You mean you don't know?"

Curtis Chang paused for a minute as though he was searching his mind for the correct answer. Wade Parker loved this part. It was almost like he could see right inside their minds, watch them squirm, trying desperately to think of something, anything, to avoid the inevitable. God, he loved this job.

"Did I run the light?"

"How much have you had to drink?"

"Drink? It's eight o'clock in the morning."

"Well, the way you were driving…"

Chang lifted both his arms into the air and shrugged. "Look, officer, I just didn't see the light, that's all. I'm late for work."

"So you admit running the light?"

"Well, yeah, I suppose."

"Okay, Mr. Chang, tell you what, why don't you get back in your van while I write this up."

Parker wrote out two tickets and had Chang sign the back as a promise to appear.

"What's this one for?"

"That's for polluting the air. And messing up my bike. Better get this thing fixed."

Chang looked up at the grey-blue sky and then back at the ticket.

"Well, watch those red lights, Pedro," said Parker, and handed Chang a copy of the citations.

"Si, Senor," Chang said as Parker turned toward his bike.

Parker thought he heard him say something else, too—something in Spanish—but he couldn't quite make it out. He snapped his ticket book shut and got on his bike. He couldn't get over a Mexican named Chang. Only in L.A., he thought.

Chang waited for the cop to drive off, then he tore the two tickets in half and tossed them behind his seat. He started the van and turned on the radio, then nonchalantly pounded the dash with his fist to get it to work. Russ Holloway's voice blared forth from the speaker and Curtis quickly changed stations. "Fuck you, Russ," he said and sped away from the curb. It was now eight thirty and Liddell was going to be pissed off, but to hell with him. Curtis was just happy not to be on his way back to Mexico—again.

————

As was his routine, once he got everyone started at work, Tim Liddell made a run to the paint store for supplies. It was Tim's favorite part of the day and he always managed to stretch what should take twenty minutes into a good hour, hour and a half. When he returned to the job site, he was surprised to see the protestors had given up and left. It should have made

Tim happy (they usually stayed till noon) but as he pulled into the driveway and through the open gates, he couldn't help but notice a churning in his gut. Something had gone wrong.

That something greeted Tim as soon as he entered the building. He said his name was Spike, that Tim's boss, Clint Stoner, had hired him. Spike was very large, six-three, two hundred twenty pounds, and not an ounce of fat on him. But most importantly, Spike was black.

Tim was furious, but he didn't say a word. He just picked up the phone and dialed Clint's number. All he got was an answering machine. He slammed down the receiver. "Fucking asshole. Fucking! Ass-hole!"

It didn't seem to bother Tim that Spike was right there watching him throw a fit. The big man could easily crush him with one blow, and from the look on his face, Tim thought he might just try it. Still, Tim just couldn't help himself. He lit a cigarette, stood there quietly for a moment, staring at the large newcomer (who had now pulled up an empty five gallon bucket and taken a seat), then he picked up the receiver and dialed Clint's house again. This time he left a message. "If this is your idea of a fucking joke, it's not funny. You better get your ass off the fucking golf course and get down here and get this boo out of my face, before somebody gets killed."

Tim slammed the phone down, took a deep hit from his cigarette and walked over to Spike. "Well, he ain't home, and like I said, uh, he didn't say nothing to me about no new employee, so you might as well go on home." Liddell kept his head in motion as he spoke, his eyes never making contact with Spike for more than a split second.

The huge black man stood up and stared down at the little foreman. "The man told me to start today. I been here an hour, I expect to get paid for that hour and the rest of the day, whether I do any work or not."

"Well, that don't surprise me. Nevertheless, I got nothing for you to do."

Martin came down the stairs to where the two men stood facing one another. He had on a paper spray suit that protected everything but his head and feet, and on his head was a cloth spray sock with a circle cut out around his face. A respirator hung loosely around his neck. A fine mist of white paint encircled his eyes, giving him a racoonish appearance. Tim grabbed him by the arm and ushered him around the corner.

"That fucking spook don't get out of here I'm gonna fucking kill him."

"Clint hired him, Tim. I was right there. Why don't you just relax and let the guy work with me? Clint's gonna be pissed off if he shows up and finds out neither one of you have done any work."

"That fucking cocaine snorting son-of-a-bitch, Stoner. I can't believe he did this."

"Hey, you wanted to get rid of the protestors. Now they're gone." Martin smiled. "And remember, if it wasn't for Rodney King we wouldn't even be working here."

Liddell started in again but was quickly interrupted by the excited sounds of Dudley, who had run down the steps yelling to nobody in particular. Martin and Liddell ran around the corner.

"They blew up the mall! They fucking blew it up."

"What are you talking about? Who?"

"Some terrorists blew up the mall. Killed a bunch of people."

The news brought a smile to Spike's face. Tim poked Martin in the side. "You see that. He thinks it's funny. Fucking animals."Hey, Spike, better call all your friends, tell them to hurry over there, maybe they can get themselves a color TV."

By the time Spike reached Tim, the smile was gone. He grabbed the little man by the shirt and lifted him over his head, pinning him against the unpainted drywall. "Maybe I'll just have them come over here, take their anger out on you."

"What, and lose their place in the welfare line?"

Spike tightened his grip and brought his other fist up to Liddell's face. The vessels in Spike's neck looked like giant night crawlers. "Say one more word, cracker. Please."

Martin said, "Spike, when you're done there, can you help me on the third floor? Somebody knocked some holes in the drywall; they need to be patched. No big hurry. No need to drop what you're doing."

Spike held Tim up for a few seconds and then quickly released him, and the beaten foreman plopped down to the ground, landing hard on his butt.

"I'll deal with you later, little man."

"You won't be around long enough," said Tim.

Spike turned to Martin. "Show me what you want me to do," he said and then pushed his way past Martin and Dudley and started up the stairs.

Tim pulled himself up and brushed the dust from his clothes. He looked pathetic.

"You're not real good at picking your battles, are you Liddell?"

"I take them where I find them. You think I'm afraid of that gorilla?"

"I'm thinking you should be."

Martin turned and followed Spike up the steps. Dudley just stood there staring at Tim.

"The fuck you looking at?"

"Nothing."

"Get back to work. Show's over."

Dudley stuck his finger deep into one nostril and walked away. "Blew up the fucking mall," he said to no one in particular. "That's far out."

THREE

Actually, Raymond Dubois had not been quite as successful as he would have liked. By the time the bomb exploded, all but one of the customers had left the area of impact; an elderly woman with white hair and a ragged wool jacket, she kept busy rifling through a pile of assorted bras, placing them one by one against her chest in front of a wall mirror. The clerk assumed she was picking one out for someone else, for nothing—in her opinion—could hold up the two huge chunks of flesh that flopped about freely under the stained yellow blouse.

The lady had one (bra) in hand, and had turned toward the clerk—her first sale already—when Bouncing Betty lifted out of the box. The clerk, reaching down for a bag, caught sight of the object out of the corner of her eye, but before the customer could turn her head to see what was going on, it (her head) was being catapulted through the hole that just seconds before had held the front door, and into the side of her Mercedes, where it stayed until the fire department arrived ten minutes later and dislodged it.

The clerk, having bent down, was forced to the floor by the concussion from the explosion. She suffered some loss of hearing and received a few cuts from flying glass, but it was the psychological damage from having been plastered with gooey body parts that would eventually result in her receiving a two million dollar settlement from the department store.

Although the news story about the woman made for sensational spectacle, it did not particularly please Raymond's cohorts. The four of them were in the kitchen in his apartment. The leader, Wanda Blade, was pacing the room inhaling a liter of Pepsi Cola. In her other hand was a tightly clasped cigarette. Her t-shirt and jeans were a matching brown, not unlike the copper shade of Spike's skin. Her hair was cropped short around the ears, military style, betraying her soft delicate features, the very same features that only a few years earlier had earned her large sums of money modeling everything from lipstick to underwear.

"I can't believe you fucked this up, Raymond," said Wanda.

Raymond was sitting at the table meticulously cleaning his nails, his frail body dwarfed by the two large men on either side of him. His glasses kept sliding down the bridge of his nose, causing him to unconsciously push them back in place, a gesture that was beginning to irritate Spike, who would stop between bites of his sandwich to glare at the nervous bomber.

"We all agreed that I would be referred to by my new name: Cervante," said Raymond.

The other large man looked up from his comic book. He was equally as large as Spike, but where Spike was two hundred twenty pounds of rock-hard muscle, Jimmy (Two-ton) Perkins's muscle had long ago turned to flab, most of it now gathered in a series of soft sticky crevices, folding over one another like a pile of dirty sheets. "He's right about that, Wanda," said Jimmy.

"If you don't stop fucking with those glasses you're gonna be one dead no-name mother-fucking faggot," said Spike.

Raymond stopped his hand in mid-air. "I don't have to take this abuse," he said, glancing up at Wanda.

"Will you all just shut up! Raymond…Cervante, you were supposed to deliver a body count with that bomb and all you get is one old lady. People are watching and I don't think I need to remind you what's going to happen to us if we fuck this up."

Raymond dropped his nail file on the table and removed his glasses. He felt bad for having let his comrades down and yet he didn't feel it was entirely his fault. After all, Jimmy had prepared the bomb, had given him the remote and shown him how to use it. It wasn't his fault the battery fell out—it wasn't even his bag—so why were they trying to blame him. He was really trying to do his best. They should appreciate that. "I'm sorry, Wanda. I tried my best. Sometimes things happen…"

"I don't want to hear about the battery again, Raymond, okay. We've got two weeks to get it together before the President arrives. If you can't manage a simple assignment like today, how do you expect to assassinate the President of the United States?"

No one said a word. Only Spike was bold enough to look Wanda in the eye. He wasn't the least bit intimidated by her and she knew it. She was reluctant to bring him into the group to begin with; he was hotheaded and overly emotional, making him—in Wanda's mind—unpredictable. But Two-ton had vouched for him—Spike had spent a summer working at the Cowboy's training camp back before Two-ton's fall from grace—and they needed a fourth member, so she let him in. Still, she was keeping an eye on him, just in case.

"How's it coming at the Center? Are you going to get those keys?"

"Don't worry about the keys," said Spike as his eyes dropped to Wanda's breasts. "They're as good as in my hands."

"How do you know the President's even going near that building, Wanda?" asked Raymond.

"That's for me to worry about."

Wanda stared down at the three men. Six months of planning and this was what she had to work with. It had taken a brutal rape to make her discover her own strength, realize her own potential. Now that she had found herself she couldn't believe that she had ever been intimidated by such a lowly species as man.

Spike still had his eyes glued to Wanda's chest.

"You see something there you like?"

Spike looked up. He had a wicked smile on his face. "Maybe."

She moved right up into his face. "Better men have tried. Concentrate on your work."

———————

Martin managed to get away from the job early that Monday, so he stopped at Leroy's Shocks and Bar-B-Q to pick up some chicken. The proprietor, George, Leroy, Washington, had purchased the establishment a few years back with the money he had saved from years of pimping and drug dealing. A benevolent soul, Leroy never mistreated his girls and had dealt only in soft drugs, mostly marijuana. He had even established small retirement funds for his girls and encouraged them to get out of the business as early as possible. A couple of them had done just that, giving up the night life to come work at the barbeque stand, where they were able to use some of their well honed sales skills to help move Leroy's famous chicken. And of course, the high heels and hot pants didn't hurt business any, either.

Despite leaving the prostitution business, Leroy never completely lost his feel for the street life. So when an opportunity arose for him to purchase a truckload of hot shocks, he was quick to lay down the cash and change his sign from Leroy's Barbeque to the now infamous Shocks and Bar-B-Q. He took over the lease on the small building adjacent to his (a former mom and pop grocery store done in by a new Alpha Beta two blocks away), gutted the interior to make room for a couple of cars, stocked the walls with shock absorbers and bought a couple of used floor jacks.

Leroy smelled money. And why not? It seemed like the perfect compliment. Leroy promised his customers he could have a new set of shocks on their car by the time they finished eating their chicken, and all for the unheard of price of ten dollars a wheel. Any car! And, he figured the shock business would help the barbeque sells, too. If a customer came in asking for shocks,

Leroy would suggest they go next door and grab some chicken while they wait. He even gave out coupons.

But the rush never came. Now and then he'd manage to coerce some out-of-towner into a new set of gas shocks, but locally the word was out: Some of Leroy's shocks were defective. Somehow, they weren't retaining their gas, resulting in either a gradual loss of vibrancy or, in the worst cases, an abrupt collapse of one or more of the shocks.

Customers had come in screaming at Leroy about everything from punctured oil pans to busted axles. Leroy would stand there quietly listening to them rage on until they finally ran out of gas, then, without the slightest bit of anger or hostility in his voice, he'd offer up some perfectly logical (to him) explanation for their misfortune. "Musta been some kids playing a joke on you," he'd say. Or maybe he would pull the husband off to the side and whisper in his ear, "Sure your wife didn't run over a curb?"

In most cases the disgruntled customers would end up walking away, shaking their heads in disgust, wishing they had gone to Sears, and some actually paid for another set to replace the first one. But now and then a particularly stubborn customer would hang in there until Leroy just flat ran out of things to say and agreed to replace the shocks for free. But even then he would never admit the shocks were in any way defective. "I sell only the finest product," he'd say, "but they can only stand so much abuse. But I'd rather give away a few pair of shock absorbers than have folks badmouthing my good name. Now why don't you go next door and get yourself some barbeque while my boys get your car all fixed up?"

Martin was happy to find out Leroy had already left for the day; he just wanted to grab his chicken and get back on the freeway without hearing the shocks sales rap. He got half a dozen legs for himself and some breasts for Vern, hit the freeway around three-fifteen and pulled into the trailer park in Laguna at four-thirty.

It was a beautiful afternoon, the sun's rays, cooled by a stub-

35

born westerly wind, sparkled on the backs of the tiny waves beneath a sheet of pale blue sky. Martin stuck the chicken in his fridge, put on his swimsuit and headed down to the beach. He hadn't gone over the weekend (he couldn't stand the tourists) and was happy to see it pretty much deserted. He hit the water running and headed towards the buoy a couple hundred yards offshore. He liked it out there where the water was deep and cool and he could float along on his back and let the rhythm of the small southerly swells massage his tired back. There was too much cement in the world; too many hard surfaces.

It was during these moments that he felt as close to being free as one could possibly get. When out here he would not allow thoughts of work or controversy—poisonous thoughts— into his mind; although the scuffle between Liddell and the new guy did bring a smile to his face. He quickly dispelled that image and set about making his mind blank. He wanted only to feel; feel the water; feel the sun; taste the salt on his lips; hear the tiny splash—was that a gull diving for fish?

He closed his eyes. The sky was too full of images; images breed thoughts; thoughts seek order and structure. But he had to think that just to realize it. Not deep enough. All that train- ing, that personal history as a human being, keeps getting in the way. Then, nothing: No words, no sentences, no preconceived notions. He is a limp strand of seaweed coerced by a gentle ocean current. No fear, no apprehension; the self-dissolves into the giant body of liquid around it. He can't move his arms or legs because he has none—he needs none. And now he can see himself from above. Who is that creature, that thing, floating below him in the water?

And then far away, a sound, a deep hum moving closer, quickly, changing now to a harsher, crueler buzz. Suddenly, Martin is drawn back into his body. Images pass through his mind: a saw slicing through a huge redwood, an airplane speeding toward earth, inside the plane, women and children screaming. The noise louder now, piercing; a bee trapped in his ear tunneling its way through his brain to the other side. The sound unbearable, his eyes open, a wake slaps his face. He looks to the side and sees a jet ski zoom by, the pilot grinning over his shoulder at Martin. Just a practical joke. Martin imagines his shotgun.

Frank Noble's plane had to circle L.A.X. for half an hour waiting for an open runway. Of course, Frank had no idea what was going on. He had started drinking an hour before he got on the plane in D.C. and hadn't stopped until somewhere over Arizona. It wasn't a fondness for alcohol—Frank rarely drank—but rather a severe case of acrophobia that drove him to drink. And it wasn't only airplanes that bothered him. At work he had insisted on an office on the ground floor and on the rare occasion when he absolutely was forced to go higher in the building he would avoid the elevators; at least on a stairway, he would be the only thing in motion.

Of course his high-ranking position with the Secret Service did present a bit of a problem for Frank. He dreaded those trips on Airforce One. The President was kind enough to allow him a stiff sedative before take-off, but being a teetotaler himself, he could not allow any consumption of alcohol on board. Besides, he could just imagine the pictures in the paper of the drunken SS man stumbling down the plank ahead of the President.

But Frank had a problem with sedatives: They gave him nightmares, horrible visions from his years in Viet Nam. No, there would be no drugs for Frank. The only thing that worked for him was alcohol, and if he couldn't have that he'd just have to tough it out. On one flight to Europe, strapped in at the wrists and ankles, he had lost seven pounds of water from sweat and was shaking so badly when the plane arrived, he could not stand up and had to be carried off the plane.

So Frank felt fortunate that he had been sent ahead of the President to the West Coast office of The SS. He would have preferred the train but there just wasn't time. There were a lot of angry people in L.A. and the President's upcoming visit would require extensive planning.

When it came to his safety, the President felt most secure when Frank was around. There were other agents equally as intelligent as Frank and perhaps technically more adept, but Frank Noble had the instincts of a champion guard on a football team. He always seemed to know from what direction trouble would arrive, and he was more than willing to greet it. He had the bullet wounds to prove it.

The two men had met in Vietnam. The president was a congressman at the time and had come over to get a first hand look at the war that was tearing both countries apart. His group was visiting a small village that had been ransacked the day before by the Vietcong and the young congressman was both saddened by the devastation and impressed by the tenacity of the people. He was about to reach down and pick up a small child when a huge blond-headed marine threw a tackle into his side and sent him plummeting to the earth. There was a loud explosion and when the two men were pulled apart, the young soldier was bleeding from numerous parts of his body. He looked up at the congressman and asked if he was okay and the congressman shook his head, yes, not a scratch. The small child who had smiled and extended her arms to the young congressman was nowhere in sight. The young marine's name was Frank Noble.

Frank went directly to his hotel upon arrival, took a short nap and then caught a cab to the office. The six aspirin he had taken did nothing to soften the blows of the hammer within his head. When he checked in at the front desk, the secretary gave him his messages. There was one from the President, saying he hoped the trip wasn't too terrible. His mother had called to remind him he promised to come see her and meet her new husband while he was in L.A., and one other one that made Frank want to rush out and have another drink; it was regarding someone he hadn't seen in over twenty years. Someone he would never forget. The message read: Remember Jackie Davis?

He handed the paper to the secretary. "Was this the entire message?"

"Yes sir, that's all he said."

"He?"

"Yes, sir, a man."

Vern grabbed a breast off the plate, let out a loud belch, and ripped a hunk of the soft white meat from the bone. Martin opened a couple of beers.

"This fellow, Leroy, is a genius," said Vern. "Nobody makes barbeque sauce like this in L.A. He must be from the south."

"Says he was born in L.A., Vern. I've told you that a hundred times."

"Well, there's just no way."

Vern took a swig from his beer. He was on his fourth breast and still going strong. To watch him eat was almost an act of voyeurism, for Vern loved food like most men loved women. "Next time, get some ribs. I'm getting a little tired of chicken, good as it is."

"No ribs, Vern, I told you, he only does chicken, and shocks."

Vern took another bite and washed it down with more beer. "Shocks and barbeque. It's brilliant. If I were a traveling man, I would definitely want to bestow the grace of my presence upon such an establishment."

"It's not much to see."

"I don't care about seeing it. I would just want to observe Mr....what's his name?"

"Washington. Leroy George Washington. He added the Leroy part when he was pimping. Said it wasn't right for a pimp to be named George Washington."

"He imparted this to you?"

"Yeah."

"Is he still pimping?"

Martin couldn't help but note more than a look of curiosity in Vern's face. He had set his chicken down on the plate and had brought his beer bottle up just short of his mouth. "Why, Vern, you interested in a couple of young black girls?"

"I have no desire to indulge in any form or color of carnal pleasures. I was just curious." Vern quickly changed direction. "So, what's the story on this bomb that went off today?"

"You're the guy with the television. You tell me."

"It's pretty close to your job, isn't it? Any shot-guns involved?"

Martin shook his head. "Oh, I see. No, Vern, no shotguns, and the mall is probably ten miles away from where I work. That's a bit of a reach, don't you think?"

Vern switched gears without so much as a blink. "You know, this Leroy fellow might be able to help you acquire a rifle."

Martin shook his head. "You're incredible. What makes you think I'm getting a rifle?"

"You will. It's just a matter of time. Something's going on. You know it as well as I. People blowing up shopping centers. The President's coming to L.A."

"Los Angeles is a big place."

Vern leaned across the table toward Martin. "The vision's changed, hasn't it?"

"You never quit, do you?" Martin got up from the table, shuffled over to the kitchen window and opened the shade a few inches. He could see just a sliver of ocean from there. He wished he were back in it. He glanced down at the jar in the corner. There were three cockroaches climbing over one another trying to get out of their new prison.

"Getting kind of crowded."

"Your vision?"

"Your jar, the cockroaches."

"Oh, yes. You should see the one in the bathroom. If I put them all in a large container will you take them out and set them free?"

"Don't I always? Did I tell you we got a new guy on the crew, started today? A huge black guy, looks like a football player. You should have seen Liddell's face."

"Liddell, I take it, is not fond of our darker brethren?"

"Liddell hates blacks. He also hates Mexicans, Jews, Poles, and just about anybody else whose heritage doesn't trace back to the Rhineland. The thing about this black guy that's really going to drive him crazy, is, I think he's part white. And he has an attitude."

"Perhaps..."

"What?"

"I was just thinking of the robber fly," said Vern in a casual tone, as if everyone knew just exactly what they were. He took a long gulp from his beer.

"Well, I'm waiting," said Martin. "What's a robber fly?"

"Oh, well, they're very clever. They can mimic their prey and merge right into the colony, unmolested. Then, they pick them off, one at a time. Are you going to eat that leg?"

"Help yourself."

Vern snatched the leg from Martin's plate. "The down side is, they only have a life span of four to six weeks. Pity."

"You think this guy hates painters?"

"Oh, I don't know. I'm just ruminating out loud. Maybe he just hates white people. Or maybe he just needs employment."

Martin turned away from the window, bent over and picked up the jar with the roaches. One of them had just reached the top of the jar where the oil was spread and had plopped back down to the bottom, landing on its back. It wiggled and squirmed until it finally managed to flip itself over, then quickly proceeded up the side of the jar again.

"You better gather these up so I can release them on some unsuspecting homeowner. They're likely to develop some psychosis stuck in these jars."

"I'll make my count this evening and you can take them in the morning. You still haven't answered my question."

"About what?"

"The vision."

Martin set the jar back on the floor. The image of the President walking alongside the limo flashed in his head.

"No," he said. "Nothing's changed."

FOUR

Curtis Chang made three trips around the block before finally parking down the alley from his house, a small bungalow not far from the beach in Santa Monica. Rush hour had come and gone and things were pretty quiet in the neighborhood; it looked safe enough. He backed the van into an empty lot, grabbed his pistol from under the driver's seat, stuck it behind the small of his back, and then strolled casually up the alley and through the back yard to the house.

Something was cooking; it smelled like chicken. The aroma drifted through the open kitchen window and brought a smile to Curtis's face. He had his key in hand but when he reached for the door it was unlocked. He quietly opened the door, and moved slowly through the laundry room toward the kitchen, one hand resting on his pistol, still lodged in his jeans. Then he heard the humming—Juanita always sang when she cooked—and saw his wife cross the room to retrieve something from a cupboard. She was an attractive woman, half Apache, full-figured, thick black hair that hung straight to her shoulders.

"Hola, Juanita."

Juanita turned from the cupboard. "Curtis!" They met in the middle of the room and shared a long embrace. "Curtis, you shouldn't be here. That pendejo from La Migra has been here two times already this week."

"That son-of-a-bitch. I am going to have to kill him some-day, I think. What did he say?"

"Both times he came, I pretended I was not home. I am afraid he will come back; you should go."

"You should keep the door locked when I'm not here. But don't worry, if he shows up…" Curtis passed his hand in front of his neck to signify cutting a throat.

Juanita laughed. "You couldn't kill nobody. Better to let me do it. I am a descendent of Geronimo, you know."

Curtis began teasing her. "Oh, sure you are, and I am the grandson of Zapata."

"But it is true."

"I know my sweet. I am only playing with you." Curtis kissed her on the neck and put his hand on her breast.

"No, Curtis. Los muchachos estan en su cuarto."

"Good, I want to see them." He kissed her passionately on the lips and drew her even closer to him.

Juanita gently pushed him away. "I will call them." She went to the doorway and called out. "Carlos, Hector. Aqui esta su padre."

Curtis came up behind her and put his arm around her. "It smells good in here. What are you cooking?"

"Enchilada de pollo."

"You must have known I was coming. After dinner"—a slap on the butt—"maybe we have some desert, no?"

Hector and Carlos came into the kitchen. At sixteen, Hector was already taller than his father and outweighed him by a good twenty pounds. His cheeks were high and well defined—like his mother—his chin strong and proud. Carlos was thirteen and fair skinned like Curtis, reaffirming Curtis's belief that there was some gringo in his own blood.

"It's not safe here," said Hector. When he spoke to Curtis it was more like man to man than son to father. It warmed Curtis to see his son growing so strong.

"I have my two brave sons to protect me," said Curtis.

"Papa," said Carlos, but his mother shook her head no and Carlos stopped.

"What? Que pasa?"

"No es nada, Curtis."

"Is there a problem?"

"No, papa, it's nothing."

The family had a pleasant dinner together, despite the incessant fear of unwanted visitors arriving; with every closing of a car door, or any unfamiliar sound, the four of them would pause in silence momentarily until one of them would rise from the table and move casually to the window or door and check it out. It was handled nonchalantly, sort of an unspoken vow to one another not to allow the enemy to ruin these few precious moments together. There was talk of school and girls and, as usual, Curtis entertained his family with tall tales surrounding his profession as a coyote. The boys always knew when Curtis was embellishing but they never interrupted; they enjoyed the wild tales and the possibility that there was a little truth in them.

After dinner, Curtis pulled some money from his pocket and handed it to the boys. He suggested they go to a movie, which they quickly accepted. Juanita started to clean the kitchen but Curtis said no, leave it. They took a long bath together, and then Juanita lit some candles, broke out some tequila and beer, and the couple slow danced to the breathy tone of Ben Webster.

They were lying in bed; Juanita had her head on his chest. It was good to be there together like a normal man and wife, and it was times like these that made Curtis wonder if maybe he should give up the coyote business altogether. His family had always understood, and they were strong, but still it bothered him that they should suffer, especially now that Sukowski was putting so much pressure on them; he was an evil man and there was no telling what he might do. And it was hard on Curtis, too. Sometimes he wouldn't see them for a week at a time, a week of short naps on dirt floors, cold burritos and hot pursuits, and then they might get one or two days together before he'd have to disappear again. And of course, when he was home, he was working as a painter; it was something for the books, a way to look legitimate.

"So tell me," said Curtis, "what is wrong with Carlos?"

"I don't want to bother you."

"No tenga pena. Tell me what it is."

"Promise me you will not be angry."

Curtis pulled his wife on top of him and buried his head between her breasts. He loved the feel of her skin, the smell of her sweat. "You're the one with the Apache blood."

"Carlos says the boys make fun of his last name. They call him Chink."

Curtis pulled back. "Who does this?"

"Different boys. They call him laundry boy and rice head. They say Chang is not Mexican." She paused for a few seconds. "He wants his name to be Lopez, like my family."

"No! I am Chang, my sons are Chang or they are not my sons." Curtis rolled her off of him and jumped out of bed. He couldn't believe what he was hearing. All his life he had taken similar abuse, people asking him where to find a good Chinese restaurant, or how to make fortune cookies. All the time he held his head high, proud of his name and the father he had never known.

He grabbed his pants from the floor and started dressing. "And you, do you want to change your name, too?"

Juanita got out of bed and went to her husband. "I am your wife. I have been your wife almost twenty years. I have lived this life with you. How can you ask me such a thing?"

Curtis hugged his wife. "I'm sorry. I am very tired."

"Carlos is young. Please do not be angry with him."

"I have to go now, Juanita. Tomorrow night I am going to bring in a family from Chihuahua. They have two ninos and I am worried about the trip."

"Which way will you come?"

Curtis pulled on his socks, then his shoes. "Through Nogales."

46

"With Garcia?"

"Yes."

"You told me you did not trust him."

"I know, but I have no choice."

"But, Curtis..."

"Juanita, I have to go. Everything is set. Don't worry about me; I am smarter than Garcia. I will be fine. Tell Carlos I will speak with him when I get back." He pulled her to him and gave her a long kiss. "After this one, I am thinking maybe I will quit."

"But the pendejo from La Migra is not going to just let you walk away."

"I'll think of something. Maybe we can move." He grabbed his shirt from the bed. Juanita was standing there, completely naked, beautiful in the half-light of the candles; every sag, every wrinkle warmed his heart. "I have to go now. I love you."

When Wanda Moore found her apartment, it was pretty beat up. All three suites were occupied by renters, and the landlord, a retired pilot by the name of Pinleaf, now living in Tahoe, refused to put any money into repairs; the plumbing was bad, the roof needed replacing, paint peeled from every wall. But Wanda, who had just turned twenty-five, was making a lot of money modeling and she could see the possibilities in the old place. She bought the building way below market, gave the tenants thirty days to move out and set about remodeling the tri-plex into a modern duplex, complete with the finest furnishings. Wanda kept the larger of the two suites for herself, and rented the other to a writer who had just moved to L.A. from Berkeley to start his own magazine. The writer's name was Raymond Dubois.

For four years life was grand at Pinleaf Palace, as Raymond Dubois referred to it. Raymond's magazine, which had a gay slant and featured the works of local writers and artists, was doing well, bringing in a large amount of advertisement from gay businesses in the area. The magazine also provided Raymond the opportunity to get his own writings—from poetry to editorials— published, something he had been unable to accomplish on the outside. In addition to advertising money, Raymond also had a willing investor in Wanda, who was in it more for the money than the cause. Because she made such a large investment, Raymond insisted she be listed as publisher. Of course, it could only help, having a beautiful famous hetero-sexual model publishing an alternative lifestyle magazine, and Wanda, despite her fame and fortune, was still young and somewhat naive, and could not imagine any potential backlash from this seemingly low profile gesture.

Meanwhile, Wanda's career was skyrocketing. She had signed a three-year, five million dollar deal with Electra push-up bra, the only stipulation being that Wanda not be photo-graphed in any other manufacturer's bras. (Obviously, Wanda had a terrific looking chest.) There were negotiations under way for a movie deal, and Wanda had a new boyfriend.

So life was good at Pinleaf. Plenty of thrills in Hollywood. One afternoon as Raymond opened his mail he was pleased to discover a check for the sum of ten thousand dollars from a very famous actor, heretofore assumed to be heterosexual. A note was attached to the check, which read: 'Dear Mr. Dubois. Keep up the good work. Maybe one of these days we can all come out of the closet. Of course, your discretion is manda-tory. Sincerely, Perry Griffin.'

Now, Raymond had received donations before, many of them anonymous, but never had a famous "heterosexual" celebrity enclosed his identity and revealed his homosexuality. Raymond showed the letter to his editor Todd Bradley, and the two of them agreed: this story had to be told.

The headline they chose was very simple and straight for-ward, none of the usual flash associated with The Gay Parade. Just three simple words: Perry Griffin Gay. Photocopies of the check and the note were placed directly below the headline. (Raymond, not one to take chances, had made the photocopy then headed straight to Griffin's bank to cash the check.) It was shortly after that when the party ended.

Perry Griffin had spent five years doing small parts in B movies before finally getting a leading role in an independent film, one of those cop buddy movies so popular in the early eighties. The movie was a huge box office success and catapulted Perry into leading man territory. Over the next five years he made eight movies costarring with some of Hollywood's most beautiful leading ladies, and bringing in over five million dollars per picture. Rumors had circulated about Mr. Griffin's sexual leanings, rumors that he always steadfastly denied, not only for fear of losing his leading man status, but more importantly for his own ambiguity regarding his homosexuality. He wanted desperately to be straight, get married, have a family, but there was this other part of him—this desire that always left him full of self-loathing-that could not be denied. He had spent thousands in therapy trying to figure out if he were indeed gay and if so, why he couldn't accept it. The donation to the Gay Parade came about after one of his therapy sessions, one that had left him feeling a little better about himself than usual. Perhaps if he slowly emerged himself into the gay community he could eventually find the comfort he so desperately sought.

The first call that Sunday morning came from his manager, a forty-year-old mover and shaker who handled half a dozen top name actors.

"Are you out of your mind!"

"What are you talking about?"

"What am I talking about? I'm talking about the magazine, the donation."

"What...how did you know?"

"The whole world knows, Perry. It's on the front page of the Gay Parade!"

"That can't be," said Perry.

"It be, all right. Now listen. We've got to get hold of this and spin it around, and I mean today. You have to deny this whole thing. I want you on Oprah, Larry King…Jesus Christ, what were you thinking?"

Perry hung up the phone and ran out of his house. He jumped into his car and sped off before either of his bodyguards could join him. Two minutes later he was standing in front of a magazine stand with the new issue of the Gay Parade in his hands. He couldn't believe his eyes.

He dropped the magazine and returned to his car. He sat there in total despair, the motor running, tears flowing down his face, dark clouds circling his mind as he wondered what would happen next, until finally a sharp knock on his window snapped him out of his reverie. Perry lowered the window. A young man poked his head halfway inside.

"Hey, you Perry Griffin?"

"Yeah," said Perry, almost in a whisper.

"Yeah, I thought so. I've seen all your movies."

Perry felt his spirits begin to lift. Perhaps things weren't as terrible as he imagined. "Oh, good," he said. "I hope you liked them."

"Yeah, I always thought you were a faggot," he said, and then he punched Perry in the face. "That's for being a homo," he said, and then punched him again. "And that's for being a liar." Then he walked away. Perry sat silently for a moment, blood running down his face. He reached up to his rear view mirror and turned it toward himself. He was quite a mess. He could feel the anger moving from his stomach into his chest and then slowly taking over his entire body until finally he let out a primal scream as he ripped the mirror from the car.

Perry returned to his home, his shirt covered in blood. His bodyguards ran to his side but he quietly waved them off and went inside. Slowly, methodically, he washed his hands and face, scrubbing fiercely to remove every last drop of dried blood. He put on a clean shirt and then went into the bedroom and checked his answering machine.

One by one he went through the messages. His father's was only five words long. "This better not be true," it said. Not all the messages were negative. A couple of former costars had called offering their support, and of course numerous leaders of gay organizations had called to compliment him on his courage. By the time these last few messages were playing, Perry had already left his house again; he had one more action role to play.

Before he went to see Raymond, Perry Griffin stopped off at the office of The Gay Parade. It was Sunday and the office was closed but Perry easily gained entrance with the help of a thirty-two ounce Louisville Slugger. He then gathered up a large pile of papers and files into the middle of the room, doused them with gasoline and lit a match. The office was in an old wooden building causing the fire go grow very large, very fast. Satisfied with his diligence, and not being particularly interested in pyrotechnics, he did not bother to stay and watch it burn; he still had one more stop to make.

———

That night, Wanda was about to leave to meet her boyfriend at the Ahmanson. They had front row tickets and Wanda had bought a beautiful gown for the occasion; it was mint green silk and revealed an ample proportion of her rather generous bosom.

She stopped at Raymond's on her way out for one quick glass of wine. He was about to show her the headline of the new issue and share with her his new mission—to reveal the identity of famous gays still in the closet—when the doorbell rang. Wanda offered to get it but Raymond waved her off, making a joke about it probably being one of his many admirers.

"It's probably Two-ton," said Wanda. "He was supposed to be here by now."

Raymond was pretty excited to see Perry Griffin standing at his front door. Who would have thought he'd be getting visits from the Hollywood elite. Then he saw the baseball bat.

Things moved pretty quickly after that. Raymond turned to run as Perry came in swinging. He clipped him in the right shoulder, knocking Raymond against the wall. A second swing bounced off the wall and then made solid contact with Raymond's head, knocking him unconscious.

Raymond had managed to get out a yell after the first blow to his body, which brought Wanda running toward the door. When she saw Raymond hit a second time she ran for the phone. She managed to dial the first two numbers before Perry ripped the cord from the wall.

The two beautiful young celebrities stood facing one another. Both had risen so far so quickly and at such a young age. And now here they were at a crossroad, two people who had never even met, their lives about to change forever, one of which had no idea why all of this was taking place.

"What do you want?" said Wanda.

"Yesterday," said Perry.

Then the actor threw the gorgeous publisher onto the floor and set about proving to her and the world that he was heterosexual, after all. He did not hear her pleading with him to stop; nor did he hear her cries of anguish as he drove himself inside her. After brutally raping the beautiful young model, he carved an X across her chest with a knife, then slit his own wrists and wrote repeatedly on the walls, until he ran out of blood: NOT GAY, NOT GAY, NOT GAY.

The weeks that followed were not pleasant for either Raymond or Wanda. The single blow to the head had crushed part of Raymond's skull and had sent him into a coma that lasted three weeks. Wanda had to have extensive plastic surgery on her chest, and although they did quite a remarkable job, it was not good enough to satisfy Electra Push-up Bras, who quickly cancelled their contract, settling out of court with Wanda's attorneys for two million dollars. It was also not good enough for her boyfriend, who took one look at the bright pink scar across her chest and made the infamous trip to the liquor store for a pack of cigarettes.

As it turned out, both Raymond and Wanda were discharged

on the same day and each left the hospital with a reminder of their horrendous experience. Wanda had her scars and Raymond had a steel plate in his head, and a bald spot the size of a beanie on top of it. Shortly after her release, Wanda changed her last name to Blade. It would come to suit her well.

Cervante sat on the floor in his apartment, pecking away on the typewriter. The lavish furnishings were all gone now, sold by Wanda to help finance her new career as a terrorist. She still had half a million tucked away in a bank account, just in case things went sour, but the expensive trimmings could go; they would not exactly attract serious revolutionaries. Besides, it was painful enough just being in the apartment where the rape had occurred without having to sit on the same couch or feel the same expensive throw rugs that had served as a bed during those ten or so horrific minutes. (They had seemed like hours.)

Cervante was having trouble with the opening of the letter. He thought it should be sensational, a short catchy phrase, not unlike many of the old headlines from The Gay Parade. "We need to catch the reader's attention," he said.

Wanda was busy cleaning one of her guns, a Soviet made pistol called a Makarov. Wanda liked the fact that it was lightweight, but what she liked most about it was the feeling of authenticity it gave her. She had read all about the Baader-Meinhoff gang, and in particular, Gabrielle Krocher-Tiedemann, who had carried two Makarovs and had killed two men with them.

"How about something like this. NOW YOU FEEL OUR PAIN! All in caps."

Wanda set her pistol on the floor and took a sip from her rather large bottle of Pepsi. "Just state our position, Raymond. I really doubt the paper is going to reprint it in caps anyway. It's not like they want it to be successful. Probably won't print it at all."

Raymond was about to remind her of his new name, but

stopped short. He knew she hadn't forgot, that she was purposely calling him Raymond just to remind him that it (the rape) was essentially his fault, and that changing his name would not erase that from her mind. He could be Cervante in front of the others and to the world at large, but to Wanda he would always be Raymond Dubois.

"I guess I'm a little rusty," he said. "It's been a while since I've done any writing."

"Yeah, what a tragedy," said Wanda, almost in a whisper. Then she kicked up the volume. "It's not exactly the great American novel, Raymond." She pointed her empty pistol toward the window and pulled the trigger. "Just give them our position. Make it like an ultimatum."

Cervante struggled with the letter for most of the day, Wanda rejecting half a dozen attempts until he finally came up with one she felt they could live with. This is the letter that Cervante sent to the L.A. Times:

> Until the heterosexual purse holders start supplying the needed funds to fight Aids; until the male dominated business world ceases to manipulate women by repeatedly projecting them as sexual toys for the reckless abuse and abandonment by men\boys; until the white power structure recognizes the plight of humans of color and redistributes the wealth accordingly; until all these demands are met, you can count on the People's Triumphant Army to recreate yesterday's bedlam, ad extremum. Brothers and Sisters of America—join our cause!

Cervante had added the part about the people of color for Spike's benefit, but later that evening when he got around to showing it to him, Spike didn't even bother to read that far; he really didn't give a shit. He hadn't joined up for a revolution; he'd come for a killing.

FIVE

'I wanna go home. I wanna go home. Oh, how I wanna go home.' Martin recognized the tune, a Country Western hit from sometime in the sixties, maybe earlier, he wasn't sure. Russ Holloway was using it to introduce his homeless segment.

"Aa-boo-nye, Angelinos (those of you selfish enough to own a radio, and a home or car to listen to it in), it's nine o'clock in the morning, and we all know what that means: It's time for your hero (me) to expose some more of the liberal gibberish concerning the alleged unfortunate homeless, those regular working class folks who, through no fault of their own, have found themselves on the street. It's not because they're crazy, it's not because they're lazy, it's not because they're dazed from drugs. No. Whose fault is it? Who else: the Government."

Martin couldn't believe he was actually listening to Russ's show. It was one of the things he felt contributed to his and June's separation—June thought Russ was the funniest, most entertaining person on radio. Martin believed he was the closest thing yet to the anti-Christ. But here he was on his way to work, actually listening, searching for the irony, wondering if June were on to something that perhaps he had overlooked.

"Yesterday, folks, our illustrious mayor announced, in a glowing example of his profound wisdom, that some of the buildings—he wouldn't specify which ones (more on that later)—some of the buildings that were burned out in the riots last year will be turned into hostels for the homeless." Pause. "Hostels for the homeless. Why, it's almost poetic, folks." Russ cleared his throat. "He said, and this is a direct quote, 'people need an opportunity to pull themselves together, a place to shower and shave, get into some decent clothes and make themselves presentable for work.' And then he goes on to say, of course, that all of this will be paid for by, guess who; that's right Angelinos, you. Can you believe it? You're on your way to work right now, or maybe you're already there, making money the old fashioned way so that our mayor can give it to the 'less fortunate'—as he puts it—so that after they wake up with their hangovers, they'll be able to take a shower and get a shave. Ah, don't it make you proud?"

Martin could feel his anger growing. How could a radio station give a man like this an opportunity to preach such ridiculous nonsense? He twisted everything just enough, left out just the right amount of truth, to make his argument seem plausible. He was like one of those guys who call you on the phone and tell you you've won this fabulous prize and all you have to do is come down and visit the beautiful time-share—no strings attached, no high-pressure salesman—then they get you in and start passing you around from salesman to salesman, beating you up with guilt and humiliation: "Well, Mr. Jones, if you can't afford the beach front unit (not everyone can), then how about one facing the patio. It's *only* two hundred dollars a month. How can you say no to that?" And on, and on.

Martin turned off his radio and exited the freeway. He wanted to pull over and call Russ and tell him how he felt, but he was running late for work and besides, Russ Holloway was no dummy. The only people who got past his screeners were those who agreed with Russ, and there were plenty of those eager to get on the radio and hear themselves bitch. On the rare occasion when someone managed to sneak past the screeners, Russ would quickly squash them with a disparaging personal remark, then disconnect them.

Martin was so angry when he pulled up to the jobsite, he forgot all about the jar filled with cockroaches sitting on the dash. He had covered the top with tinfoil, poked some air holes with a pin and wrapped a rubber band around the foil to hold it on. He had planned on throwing them over the fence into the dumpster next door.

Liddell started right in on him when he came in. "You're over an hour late."

"So dock me."

"Look, you're in charge of the jungle bunny, so if you're late that means he's late, and that means…"

"Listen Liddell, I'm in no mood for your bullshit today, okay. Just tell me what you want us to do and leave out the boring clichés."

The one redeeming quality about spraying was that Martin could put on his respirator and his headphones, crank up the Walkman and tune everybody out. There was a certain Zen quality to painting in general, and spraying was perhaps the pinnacle in this aspect of the trade. It wasn't as good as floating in the ocean, but if he had to be at work, it would do.

Spike had gotten most of the windows in one room masked off while Martin boxed a couple of five gallon buckets of PVA together and got the airless ready to go.

"What's in the box?" asked Spike. He'd been working with Martin all week and hadn't uttered more than an "okay" yet.

"This? My tapes. Helps pass the time."

"Yeah, what do you have in there?"

"Old stuff, mostly. Let's see, I've got some John Coltrane, Boz Scaggs, Beattles, Louie Jordan. Ah, here's my favorite."

He handed a tape to Spike.

"You listen to James Brown?"

"I love James Brown. Great driving music. What's that one tune, *Talkin' loud and Sayin' Nothin*. That's some great shit; without a doubt the best groove I've ever heard. And good lyrics, too."

Martin started singing. "You can't tell me, how to run my life…"

"Yeah, I like that one," said Spike. "Only, he does it better than you."

"You think?"

"Let me ask you something. Why do you work for someone like Liddell?" said Spike.

"What can I tell you, Spike. I need money, just like you, so I try to ignore him. What people like Tim hate most is to be ignored. They're like little children, clamoring for attention."

"I'm not here for the money, and I'm about to pay Liddell a whole lot of attention."

"You just love to paint, huh?"

"I got my reasons."

"Well, I hope they're good ones. Just do me a favor: if you decide to pull a Nat Turner, do it on my day off."

"Who's Nat Turner?"

"Just a guy. Somebody who got tired of being pushed. I'm about ready to start, so you might want to put on your mask."

"I don't need a mask."

"Oh. How old are you?"

"Twenty-three."

"Twenty-three, huh. Well, let me tell you something, Spike. I realize that right now you probably think you're gonna live forever, but I can guarantee you, this stuff will kill you, and it won't be pleasant."

"I'm not gonna be around here that long. Besides, I ain't afraid to die."

"Well, great. I finally met one."

––––––––––

Chang usually picked up lunch for the crew but he didn't come in on Thursday, so Liddell gave Martin a twenty and sent him. "Take Kunta Kinte with you," he said.

It was close to ninety degrees outside and Martin's car was parked in the sun. Spike opened the passenger door and a rush of hot air smacked him in the face. The two of them fanned the doors for a minute before braving the oven-like interior of the old Vega. The seats were covered in cheap vinyl and burnt their asses when they sat down. Spike reached up and grabbed the jar off the dash.

"Hey, man, what is this?"

"Oh, shit." Martin grabbed the jar from Spike. Stacked up on the bottom, their bodies shriveled from the heat, were two dozen toasted cockroaches. Martin tipped the jar to its side and the few live roaches crawled out from under the pile. They moved in slow motion as if they were drunk.

"Do me a favor and toss this into the dumpster, will you?"

Spike took the jar from Martin and set it back on the dash. "I'll do it when we get back."

"They may not make it that long."

"Dead or alive, they'll do just fine."

"For what?"

"You'll see."

―――――

They got to Leroy's about a quarter till twelve so there wasn't much of a line. Leroy was out front of the garage talking to a customer. The man just kept shaking his head no, as if he were upset. When Leroy saw Martin, he just abandoned the other man and came right up to Martin, grabbed him by the arm and coerced him out of line.

"Leroy, I'm gonna lose my place."

"Who's the brother?" When Leroy spoke it was almost a whisper. His tone of voice made you feel like you were about to break the law, even if he were just trying to sell you some potato salad to go with your barbeque.

"He's the new guy at work. Just a minute." Martin returned to the line and gave Spike the twenty dollars, and then went back to talk to Leroy.

Leroy pointed at the large black man. "He got a car?"

"I don't know, Leroy. I don't think so."

"Listen, my man. Why don't you let me put some shocks on that fine looking mobile you driving? I'll make you a special deal. Have'm on before your chicken hits the grease."

"Not today, Leroy." Then Martin said something completely unexpected. "You know anybody that could get me a gun?" The words just spilled out of his mouth like shattered teeth.

Leroy pulled him farther away from the line. "Say man, why you wanna come around here saying things like that? You knows I only sell shocks and barbeque. I'm legit now."

Spike was almost up to the window, now. He called out to Martin. "What am I supposed to get?"

"Half breasts and half legs and some potato salad."

"I like wings."

"Get some wings then, Spike, whatever." He turned back to Leroy. "Yeah, I'm sorry, Leroy. I don't know…"

The man Leroy had been talking to earlier walked up and tapped him on the shoulder. "What about that refund, Mr. Washington?"

Leroy turned around, looked at his shoulder then glared at the man, a white businessman dressed in a five-hundred-dollar suit. "You don't wanna be doing that, Mr., poking at ol' Leroy and such. Just ain't smart."

"Well, I need some satisfaction, here. I've only had those shocks three weeks, and just look at my car."

Martin looked over at the car, a newer BMW. It was black and had tinted windows and was sitting about four inches off the ground. It looked like some gang-banger's car.

Leroy put his arm around Martin's shoulder. "You see this boy, here. He come in here three, four times a week, just to eat my chicken. He ain't got no fancy car or fine suit, but he don't never make no trouble, neither. You, I only seen in here one time and all you do is complain. 'That's too much money Mr. Washington, ain't enough meat on that breast, Mr. Washington.' Why I want to listen to you yakking all the time, when I can talk to him? Now, get out of my face until I finish with my business."

"Well, just don't think I'm going to let this go, because I'm not," said the man, who then turned and walked back to his shiny car, opened the passenger door and sat down.

"Now, where were we? Oh, yeah, you want me to get you a gun. What kinda gun you looking for?"

"I don't know, I don't even know why I said it. A rifle, I guess?"

"A rifle? You mean like a oozy, something like that?"

"Something more like a shotgun."

"Well, shit man, you can get that in a fucking store."

Spike paid for the chicken and walked over to the two men. "All set," he said.

"Say, brother, you got a car?"

"No," said Spike.

"You don't got a car? Boy, you can't live in L.A. without a car."

"I ain't gonna be here that long."

"We'll see you later," said Martin. "Just forget about that other thing. I was just curious."

———————

Leroy removed his Dodger cap and scratched his head. His short, curly hair was mostly white now and his hands shook a little as he replaced the hat. Here he was sitting on three thousand pairs of shock absorbers and this fool wants to buy a rifle. He watched as the Vega pulled onto the street. If ever there was a car needed shocks, that was one, and Leroy was determined to sell him some.

The man from the BMW was on the move again but Leroy just ignored him as a couple of motorcycle cops pulled in to the lot. Leroy was on them before they had time to remove their helmets. "What kinda shocks you officers use on them bikes?"

"The older of the two officers unzipped his leather jacket. "Leroy, why don't you stick to chicken and forget about these shock absorbers."

"I can make you a great deal. Why, I could take care of the whole police department."

"The city maintains our bikes, Leroy," said the other officer.

"Yeah, but you know, they's probably paying way too much, like them military bases paying seven hundred dollar for a hammer and such."

"I can guarantee you, the city of Los Angeles is not as frivolous with its money as the United States Government. And besides, what if they called you tomorrow and said they wanted you to replace the shocks on all the cop cars. How would you do it?"

Leroy scratched his scruffy chin. "Hmmm. That'd take some doing all right. I could hire me some boys from the neighborhood."

"Oh really, which ones, the Crypts or the Bloods?" All three men got a laugh out of that. The older officer slapped Leroy on the back. "President's coming to town next week, Leroy. Gonna be a big parade, lots of people. Probably sell a lot of chicken."

"President, huh?" Leroy rubbed his chin. They got those big limos."

"Yeah, Leroy, and I spoke to him just yesterday. Says he wants shocks for the whole fleet."

"Don't you go humoring me, boy, you can just march your lily white ass down to Taco Bell for lunch."

"Now, no need to get sore, Leroy. I'm just pulling your leg."

"You wanna pull on something, try grabbing that tiny thing you call a dick. I ain't here for your entertainment. And don't think you can do to me like you all did to Rodney King. I will kick your ass."

The cop turned red in the face and started to respond but Leroy looked over at his partner and winked. "He riles up pretty easy, don't he?" He turned back to the other cop and slapped him on the back. "I'm just fuckin with you son. Lunch is on me."

———

Martin tried to find some shade when he got back to the job, but no such luck. Spike opened up the jar with the roaches and pulled out a couple of dead ones. Then he opened one of the containers of potato salad and stirred the dead bugs into it until they were well camouflaged. An amused Martin watched with interest.

"Make sure Liddell gets this one," said Spike.

"Sure," Martin said as they got out of the car. He removed the lid from the jar then walked to the fence and tossed the rest of the bugs over into the dumpster. "But we don't want to hand it to him. Just leave it in the bag, let him grab it, himself."

"What's that fellows name, Nat something?"

"Turner."

"Is this something he would do?"

"I think you've captured the spirit."

They were up on the roof having lunch, the whole crew. Tim Liddell hadn't touched his potato salad yet and Martin and Spike kept looking at each other, then down at the container of salad. Liddell had set it right in the sun and Martin figured if he left it too long the cockroaches would be the least of his problems; which would not altogether be a bad thing.

Hank and Dudley were stretched out in the sun. Hank had fallen asleep and Dudley, his shirt removed, was already turning red. He had red hair, and skin like mayonnaise. Every once in a while, Spike would pick up a small rock and toss it onto his milky stomach. Dudley would just swat them away like flies, never once opening his eyes or voicing any complaint.

Clint Stoner showed up dressed in a pair of white shorts and a powder blue golf shirt; with his neatly trimmed mustache and tanning booth glow, he resembled a buffed out Errol Flynn. He had his estimate book in hand; he always carried it when he showed up at the job so the rest of the guys would think he was working. Everybody knew he was either on his way to or from the golf course.

"How's it going today?"

"Fuck, Clint, it's a fucking furnace in there, man," said Liddell.

"They were supposed to have the air in by now," said Clint.

"Yeah, well, that don't do us much good, does it?"

"Where's Chang?"

Liddell pulled another piece of chicken from the bag. "Hell, who the fuck knows. Probably home fucking his old lady so he can get another kid on the welfare payroll."

"Chang called me this morning," said Martin. "Said his kid had an appendicitis, had to take him to the hospital." Martin was making this all up, anything to thwart Tim.

"Oh, wow, I hope he's okay," said Clint.

"Hey, Clint, want some chicken?" said Liddell.

"You got any white meat left?"

Liddell scrounged through the bag. "Just a couple of legs."

"That's okay. What's that?" He was pointing at Liddell's salad.

"Potato salad. You want it?"

Martin and Spike looked at each other with concern. "I got some left, Clint. You can have it," said Martin.

But Liddell had already reached over and grabbed the plastic cup. "Here." He reached into a bag and pulled out a plastic fork. "Here's a fork."

Clint grabbed an empty bucket and pulled it into the shade next to Martin. He removed the lid from the potato salad and stuck the fork in.

"You guys know the President's going to be touring this area?"

Hank let out a loud belch and Dudley wiped another rock from his belly. Martin kept his eye on the fork.

"What for?" asked Liddell.

"He wants to see the progress since the riots." Clint dug a forkful of salad out of the container and stuck it into his mouth. Martin grimaced and looked over at Spike who had a big smile on his face.

"Anyway," he continued, his mouth full of potatoes, "we have to do a real good job, just in case he comes to this building. Be good publicity for us."

"What's this we and us stuff?" Hank said, sitting up from his nap. "Is this the People's Painting Company?"

"Just trying to keep us all working," said Clint.

"Why don't you keep us working in Orange County?" asked Martin. "This drive's killing me."

"Have to go where the work is, Martin. He took another bite of his potato salad. "This stuff tastes pretty good, but I don't like the texture; too crunchy. Feel like I'm eating a snail or something."

Six

They showed up at noon the very next day. It was Friday, hot and smoggy, the air so calm even smoke wouldn't drift. The leader, Marvin Sukowski, liked conducting his raids at the end of the week for two reasons: First, he figured most guys show up for work on Friday so they can get paid, giving him a better chance for a large roundup. Second, anyone he did bust would end up spending a weekend in jail before going before a judge and eventually finding themselves in a truck headed back to Mexico. Marvin Sukowski hoped their unpleasant experience with the law would dissuade them from returning. It rarely did.

When they first entered the building it looked deserted. Perhaps someone had blown the whistle; it wouldn't be the first time. He and his men methodically checked each floor, room to room, working their way toward the roof. Sukowski was disappointed to see the job so far along; the drywall was finished and the painting seemed well under way. Now and then he'd catch an illegal working as a painter but usually they were either hanging drywall or cleaning up. He had no idea why that was so, nor did he care.

Each floor seemed ten degrees hotter than the one below it and on the fourth floor the heat was compounded by the fresh paint fumes; a couple of the walls were still wet. Where the hell was everybody?

The door to the roof burst open and the three men in dark suits stepped into the bright sun. "Marvin Sukowsi, Immigration," said the leader. Hank pulled his cap down over his face; Dudley brushed a rock from his belly.

"Looks like they got you, Martin," said Liddell.

Sukowski walked up to Martin and flashed his I.D. One of his men stood guard by the door, as if he were expecting someone to make a break, while the other proceeded to search what few nooks and crannies existed on the roof.

"Marvin Sukowski, INS. You got a green card?"

Martin looked up at the chubby officer. His suit was cheap, the jacket barely reaching around his belly, and sweat oozed from around the yellowed neck of his white shirt. The afternoon sun bore down on his bare head and forced his tiny eyes to retreat behind the fatty lids. He reached into his jacket pocket and pulled out a pair of black sunglasses.

"No, do you?" Martin's mother was Sicilian and Martin had inherited her dark eyes and olive complexion, causing others on occasion to mistake him for a Mexican. When he was ten years old, a crosswalk guard had asked him if he spoke Spanish at home and Martin—confused by the question—answered innocently, "No, do you?"

"What are you, a wise-guy?"

"He no speaka da English," said Liddell.

"Okay, get up."

"Hey, I'm trying to eat my lunch, okay. Do I sound Mexican to you?"

Sukowski turned his attention to the five men as a group and went into his speech. "Anybody caught hiring an illegal is subject to criminal prosecution. Now I'm looking for a particular Mex today by the name of Chang. Any of you know him?"

Martin glanced over to Liddell who tore into another piece of chicken.

"I have information he's been working as a painter in one of the buildings in this area. Any of you have any information about him I'd suggest you share it with me."

Hank pulled his cap away from his face. "Whoever heard of

a Mexican with a name like Chang?"

"Sounds Polish to me," said Martin.

"What's so special about this Chang?" said Liddell.

"And who are you?"

"I'm the foreman on this job."

Martin got to his feet. He glanced over at Hank who just shrugged his shoulders and pulled his cap back over his eyes. Tim was champing away at his piece of meat, you could hear him smacking all the way across the roof. Martin moved toward him. He wasn't sure what he would do if Tim started in about Curtis, but he wasn't about to sit there and let him give him up.

"Well, I'll tell you. Mr. Chang is what we refer to as a coyote. He takes large sums of money from innocent people, poor people, and promises to get them into this country. Most of them never make it past San Diego. I've been after his greasy ass a long time and when I catch him…well, let's just say he'll wish he was still making tacos down in Tijuana."

"Poor people with large sums of money, huh?" said Martin. He was standing right next to Liddell, now. "Sounds like an oxymoron to me."

"You trying to be a smart ass?" said Sukowski.

"He doesn't need to try," said Liddell. He stuck his fork in his potato salad, scooped some into his mouth and then wiped his mustache with his sleeve. "Is there a reward for this Chang?"

"Yeah, there's a reward. You get to protect your job from cheap labor. If you know something, better spit it out now."

Dudley sat up from his nap. Spike, who had sat quietly up till now, removed his dark glasses, got to his feet, his arms folded across his massive chest, and stared over at Liddell. Tim glanced up at the big man and then to Martin who simply raised his eyebrows and smirked with delight at the scene.

"No, I don't know him. If I did I wouldn't hesitate turning him over to you. Fucking wetbacks are screwing everything up."

By now, the sweat was beginning to drip from the fat officer's face. He lifted his glasses and wiped his eyes with the sleeve of his jacket. He turned to Spike and for a second it looked like he was going to say something to him, but something, maybe a tinge of common sense, changed his mind. He turned instead to Martin. "I'll be back, smart ass. You know more than your saying."

"Well, I know more than you're saying, anyway."

The three agents retreated through the doorway and disappeared into the building. Spike was still staring over at Liddell.

"You got something to say?" said Liddell

Martin interrupted. "Why didn't you tell them, Tim? Could it be you've got a conscience, after all?" A glance toward Spike. "Or was it something much simpler, like fear?"

Liddell pulled a cigarette from his shirt pocket, lit it, and took a deep hit. Then he folded his arms in a mocking gesture of the larger man, and stared up at him. "I ain't afraid of nobody, least of all him. I'm just looking out for my job. If I turn Chang in, then Stoner gets busted, and if that happens we're all out of work; which I'm sure wouldn't bother Mandela, over there. I'll tell you this much, though. If that taco-bender does show up, he's fired."

"We'll see about that," said Spike.

Jimmy (two-ton) Perkins pulled his brand new Oldsmobile into the carport behind Wanda Blade's apartment, turned off the motor, got out of the car and stepped into the alley to make sure no one was around. He was trying his best to look casual but he was such a conspicuous sight that if anyone were to spot him they would never forget it.

Two-ton was wearing a golf shirt with blue, red and white horizontal stripes, causing his immense middle to appear even larger. His pants were a khaki colored polyester and his hair (what there was of it) was clipped short around the ears. From a distance one might have mistaken him for a huge beach ball waiting on a breeze.

Hard to believe that just a few years earlier Two-ton had

been a two hundred twenty-five pound wall of muscle firmly ensconced as a first-string linebacker for the Dallas Cowboys. A drug habit and an inability to clean up his act had lead to numerous short-term suspensions until finally he was ousted for two years. He did manage to get off the drugs but over the two years he had put on another hundred pounds, rendering his career virtually over.

Like many former athletes Two-ton turned to bodyguard work. He wasn't that quick on his feet anymore, but he still presented a serious physical deterrent for any fan who wanted to get a little too close to Two-ton's clients. Had he been on time that fateful night at Wanda's apartment, things might now be a lot different. Two-ton was acutely aware of this fact and although he felt awful about what had happened, there was no guilt associated with it. He felt a genuine affection for Wanda, and it was this, and this alone, that kept him from ever questioning his decision to stay by her side after the events of that evening. He was, if nothing else, loyal.

He opened the trunk of the car and removed a large cardboard box, rested it on the rim of the trunk, then squatted down and grabbed it, his fingertips barely reaching the outer edges. The package secured against his gut, he managed to let go of one hand long enough to close the trunk, and then proceeded cautiously to Cervante's front door.

Cervante wasn't sure who it was behind the box until he looked down at the ground at the fat, bunion-riddled feet exploding out of the leather sandals. He opened the door wide and Two-ton navigated his way through and into the kitchen.

"Where's the table?" He was breathing hard. "Where's the table," he repeated, a bit of panic in his voice.

"Just keep coming, straight ahead, couple more feet."

Two-ton pushed forward. It had been a long time since he'd done any physical labor and this trek from the car to the apartment was pushing his limit.

"Okay, hold it, it's right in front of you."

He set the box on the table. Perspiration ran down his cheeks and neck. He was panting pretty hard. "Boy. Give me a glass of water, will you."

"I only have Avion, that okay?"

"Anything. I'm dying here."

Cervante retrieved the water from the refrigerator. "So, what did you get?"

Two-ton downed half the bottle of water. "Where's Wanda?"

"I don't know. Is her car gone?"

"I didn't see it." Two-ton chugged the second half of the bottle of water. "I'm out of shape."

Cervante started digging through the box, pulling out different sized metal containers. "Oh, my, this one looks impressive."

"TM-46," said Two-ton, still trying to catch his breath. "Soviet Antitank Mine."

"It's heavy."

"Well what do you expect, Cervante? It blows up tanks."

"Oh, now this is cute. What are all these straws?"

Two-ton wiped his brow with his shirtsleeve and picked up the empty bottle of water, then set it back down again. His heart was pounding like a bass drum at halftime. "That's a Valsella Valmara 69—Italian made. When it explodes, it sends hundreds of these little metal splinters flying, and, it's waterproof. I got three of those, two more "Betties" and two TM-46s."

"I can't wait to try one of these Italian jobs out," said Cervante.

"They're a nasty piece of work, alright. Bring one in the living room and I'll show you how to rig it up. Man, I gotta go on a diet. You got any chips or something?"

———

If you live in Orange County and you work in L.A., you have to get on the freeway before three o'clock to head home, or forget it. And of course, even if you do get out early, there's always a chance an accident has occurred up ahead. Now, if it's Friday and you've gotten out late, and there's been an accident, you would really be better off going to a movie or having dinner, because there's no way you're going to make it home before seven o'clock and you'll be hating life all the way there.

Which is exactly what Martin was doing that Friday afternoon. He'd been on the road for half an hour and hadn't gotten two miles on the Harbor Freeway. The cigalert said there was an accident just prior to the interchange, backing up the 110 all the way to the 405. Martin had considered getting off the freeway and cutting across to the 405 on surface streets, but previous attempts under similar conditions had proven fruitless.

It was ninety degrees out, hotter yet on the freeway, and Martin could tell which cars had air conditioning by looking to see which ones had their windows rolled up. His was down.

He'd made that drive many times, but today he had plenty of opportunity to really check out the scenery. That stretch of the 110 cuts right through South Central L.A., from Martin Luther King Boulevard to Florence Avenue, with mile after mile of graffiti-covered walls, iron-clad windows, barren lots serving as graveyards to burned-out cars and the skeletal remains of useless furniture, some of it remnants of the riots, most just life as usual.

The smog was especially thick that day, the air still and hot and you could taste the chemicals. Martin watched two young girls playing jump rope on a side street, amazed that they could even breath in this weather, then he quickly bolted back in fear as a souped up Camaro swerved around a corner and headed right for them. But the girls, reacting almost instinctively (or so it seemed to Martin), jumped back up onto the curb until the car disappeared, then they quickly returned to their game.

It seemed like some sort of ride in an amusement park to Martin and he imagined Disneyland or some other park setting one up just like this in the future, a place for White America to experience the thrills and excitement of ghetto life—watch out!

there's a Blood with an automatic weapon; don't forget to wear your oxygen mask; rats!

It was seven-thirty before Martin got home and there was nothing waiting for him but bad news. He had applied for a grant from the NEA and had finally gotten his reply. The letter said that although his idea for the novel sounded good and his sample chapters looked promising, there just wasn't enough money to go around this year. The NEA had been under a lot of pressure the last two years and on the verge of losing it's funding from the feds.

Martin tossed the letter on the kitchen table. It had been six months since he'd sent in his application; he'd almost forgotten about it. Now, it only served to remind him of his situation. Those three chapters had come so easily, so quick, and then he'd gone blank, almost overnight. He'd had such high hopes. It had taken him two years since he'd finished his previous novel to even get up the nerve to start another. Was it the rejections that had shut him down, or had he just run out of things to say? He was beginning to think he might never write again. After eight years and four novels without so much as a bite from a publisher, he was giving up, and he knew it, yet he seemed powerless to do anything about it. All the jokes he had made about the rejection slips, all the pep talks he had given himself, all the stories he'd read about other writers, (better writers than he) who'd gone through similar experiences, did nothing for him now; he was running out of tricks. There was a tightness in his chest, an inability to breath deeply, a slight stoop now in his gait, and worst of all, an unrelenting self-doubt constantly gnawing at his mind like a rodent on a piece of cheese.

That night he sat on the beach with a fresh bottle of bourbon, watching the waves crash in on the shore. A new moon hung low in the sky and cast a band of silver across the glassy ocean surface. There was perfection out here, perfection one could only grasp for a second before it fell out of focus. If you could just stay in that place, that instant when you realize the awesome beauty before you, if you could somehow bottle that feeling—was it happiness?—and carry it with you all the time, if you could do that, then perhaps everything else would just wash away like small pebbles in a receding tide.

He flashed back to the two girls playing jump rope. There they were playing games in the middle of what looked like a living hell, and here he was sitting on the beach feeling sorry for himself. It seemed ridiculous yet justifiable at the same time.

He was getting pretty drunk now—the bottle was half finished— and he began taking off his clothes. It took him awhile to remove his shoes but once he got past those he was able to strip naked rather quickly, and managed to stumble down to the water's edge; the wet sand massaged his tired feet. It was late and not a sound emanated from any of the waterfront trailers, but he really didn't care if anyone saw him or not. He needed soothing, and being as how he didn't have a woman, the ocean would have to do. He knew he was too drunk to swim, but he could at least jump in, immerse himself in the warm salt water—it always made him feel better—and he was about to do just that, when he heard a voice, a familiar voice, call out.

"Martin. That you?"

Martin was not a religious person, but his first glance was toward the heavens. Then he heard the voice again and as he looked to his side he saw something, (someone?) approaching. He tried to focus on the figure but everything was a blur. "Who is it?" he mumbled.

"It's me, Curtis."

"Curtis?"

"Chang, man, from work. I'm glad I found you, man; I need your help."

"I don't, need...any help."

"No man, I need yours. Are you okay?"

Martin felt a hand on his shoulder, and all of a sudden standing wasn't so difficult. "Of course," he said, and as he finally managed to focus in on the small dark man before him, he proceeded to throw up all over him.

———————

Curtis got Martin back to the trailer and helped him into bed. By now, Martin was mumbling incoherently and Curtis realized his problem would have to wait until morning. He pulled a blanket over his naked friend and turned off the bedroom light. He made up another bed on the couch then went out to his van and retrieved two small children. They were both sound asleep so he had to carry them in one at a time, placing them gently on Martin's couch. Then he threw a pillow on the floor, turned out the living room light and laid down for some well-deserved rest. Tomorrow, he thought, things will be better. Tomorrow.

SEVEN

On August 2, 1969, his eighteenth birthday, just two months before he was supposed to report for duty in the Marines, Frank Noble borrowed his father's brand new red convertible Cadillac and headed for the south end of town for a little fun and relaxation. There was a club called Candy's, where for twenty-five dollars, a white boy might treat himself to the pleasures of any of a number of attractive young black girls, most of whom were still children themselves, many already raising families.

Frank had friends who went there regularly but he had always demurred, fearful of crossing the color line so vividly painted by his father. But with a pint of scotch under his belt and the birthday party given by his folks winding down, Frank discovered a surge of courage and a desire for adventure. As soon as the lights went out, he climbed out his window, pushed the Cadillac out the driveway and down the street before starting it, and headed south.

It was a clear, warm night and a million stars winked at Frank as he drove along in his father's new car, his heart pounding in anticipation of some great, unknown carnal adventure. Every young man imagines what his first time will be like; he considers the movies he has seen, the stories relayed to him by his friends—most of them lies—and his own conjured images he's carried with him since puberty. The question was, would it all live up to his expectations. Would he?

———

Fifteen-year-old Jackie Davis was without a doubt the most

beautiful girl in Shelby County, black or white. Her father's skin had been black as pitch, her mother's—whose parents were Cherokee and Mexican—a golden brown. Their three children were varied in shades of brown with Jackie ending up the color of milk chocolate, her skin soft and tender like a baby's, long after the baby fat had given way to firm solid muscle. From her mother she had inherited the high Cherokee cheekbones and dark straight hair; from her father the tall athletic build and eyes like coal.

The Klan hanged her father when Jackie was five years old. No one knew why it had happened. He wasn't a politically active man, just another poor farmer who kept to himself and stayed out of the white man's path. But then again, it wasn't like there had to be a reason. His death left Jackie's mother alone to care for her three small children. By the time she was eleven, Jackie had taken over the care of her two younger brothers—her mother had taken to the bottle—and on her fourteenth birthday she found a note from her mother saying she'd left for California with an insurance salesman. The kids were up to Jackie.

Under different circumstances, Jackie might have gotten off to a better start in life, she might have become a teacher or even a doctor or lawyer—she definitely had the brains—but with the two small boys to look after, there wasn't time to concentrate on school; she needed money, and there was never enough of it around. She had done all kinds of work. She took in laundry from some well-to-do families in town, tutored a few grade school children in math, cleaned houses—the list was long. Then a girl friend told her about Candy's and how a girl could earn as much as fifty dollars a night just for having some fun with a white boy. At first Jackie was appalled at the idea—she was a good girl; she had morals—but as the weeks and months passed after her mother left and Jackie found herself too tired from work to study for school, saw her slender fingers swell up and toughen from scrubbing floors and washing clothes, saw the tender skin around her eyes begin to sag and wrinkle, she decided to give it a try. She had to do something.

When Frank saw Jackie that night he was immediately struck by her beauty. He bought her a drink and told her it was his birthday, even showed her the gold watch his father had gotten him. He didn't quite know how to pose the proposition of sex for money—this was all new to him—and nobody had given Jackie the specifics either, and so the two of them sat there at the bar trying to find a way to bring up the subject when Frank finally mentioned that he had come there specifically to treat himself on his birthday, to which Jackie replied she knew a place where they might go and celebrate together, but they— she emphasized (they) would need fifty dollars.

Frank said he couldn't think of any better way to spend fifty dollars and the two of them slipped off in his daddy's car and headed out to Realfoot Lake. They drove along the empty country road, sipping on a pint of twelve-year-old Scotch whiskey, Jackie snuggled up close to Frank, neither of them saying a word, both slightly apprehensive yet excited over the possibilities awaiting them. And it wasn't just the idea of trading sex for money that had them aroused—they needed no such aphrodisiac—it was the soft touch of Jackie's hand on Frank's leg, the purr of the Cadillac's huge engine, the sweet smell of the hot leather seats, the thought (the fear?) of leaving their innocence, their virginity, behind.

There by the water's edge, Frank wasted no time getting the slim, brown girl undressed. He was awestruck by her beauty; she looked beautiful in the bar but out under the stars she resembled a goddess. If only she were white, he thought, he could parade her in front of his friends, bring her home to his family.

Frank thought of his father—what would he say if he knew?—but the fear quickly passed as Frank lay Jackie down on the moist bank, pulled her firm little ass up and drove himself inside her. She was small and tight and Jackie winced with pain, but in Frank's state of arousal, it didn't last long.

During the following weeks, Frank made numerous trips to Candy's. Each time he would meet Jackie out in front—neither of them cared much for the bar—and they'd head for the lake where they would wrestle naked on the soft bank at the water's edge, beneath a blanket of shimmering stars. At the end of each night Frank would drop her off in front of the club and gently place a small stack of bills in her hand, more like a gift than a payment. Though they met at the club for convenience, Jackie never went inside, never went with other men. She had fallen hard for Frank; being with another man now was out of the question.

Two months quickly passed and before either of them could prepare themselves, their final evening together had arrived. Frank was to leave the following morning for the service. He had spent the day in dread of what was to come, for he knew their parting would be hard on Jackie. For Frank, his inability to break from tradition and his father's grasp precluded any idea of him and Jackie continuing on together—if anything, the Marines offered him an easy excuse—but he did care for her and did not want to see her hurt.

Jackie stood out front of Candy's waiting for the familiar headlights to come up the street. The months had passed like minutes. Those nights together with Frank had been the only light in her young life since the day her mother left. Her heart was very heavy and when at last the Cadillac arrived, she feared she might soon break into tears.

She climbed into the big car and shut the door.

This time she did not greet him with the usual smile and long embrace but merely stared straight ahead, not so much as a hello.

"Are you okay?"

"Just drive, Frank."

They made the twenty-minute drive to the lake in total silence. It was a little cool out as fall had begun to insinuate itself, and Frank had raised the convertible top. Jackie gripped her sweater tightly just below the neckline as she gazed out the window at the passing scene. By now she knew every curve in the road, every tree whose thick canopy would blot out the stars during those hot summer nights. Now the leaves were gone, the branches bare. Driving under these bare limbs with all the stars now constantly revealed, Jackie felt exposed. She pulled her sweater even tighter but there was no getting warm. She wondered if she would ever feel warm again.

Out by the lake, Frank tried to kiss her but she pulled away. He tried again and she began to cry.

"What's the matter, Jackie?"

"I didn't get my period yet?"

"What do you mean, you didn't get it?"

"I mean, I'm late Frank, and I've been sick the last few days. I'm pregnant."

"Pregnant? No, you probably just got the flu or something."

"Frank, it ain't the flu. I'm pregnant."

Jackie watched his eyes and waited for his response. She had been praying about this moment for the last three days, but she knew already in his hesitation, in his inability to look her in the eye, her prayers had gone unanswered.

"What are we gonna do, Jackie?"

"We're gonna have a baby."

"We can't do that. I'm leaving tomorrow and besides…"

"What?"

"Well, you know, it just wouldn't work out. I've got some money. We'll get it taken care of."

"I ain't having no abortion, Frank."

"We don't have any choice. Don't you see?"

Jackie broke down and began to cry. Frank tried to hold her but she ran up to the car and got inside. She didn't say a word all the way back to Candy's, just stared out the window, wondering where her mother was now and just what it was she had done to deserve this life she'd been living. She could hear Frank's voice but it seemed a million miles away.

When they pulled up in front of Candy's, Jackie hopped out of the car and shut the door. Frank called out to her but she just kept walking until she heard the car pull away. Then she turned and watched it go until the tiny red taillights were swallowed up by the night. She felt something heavy in her sweater pocket. She reached in and pulled out a small leather pouch. Inside the pouch was a bundle of twenty-dollar-bills and Frank's gold watch. He must have put it there while they were driving.

The door to Candy's swung open and a young man held it ajar for her to enter. "Going in, miss?"

Jackie looked down at her stomach. "No, no, I'm not."

When Frank Noble read the PTA letter in the Times, his first instinct was to call Washington and try to persuade the President to cancel his trip. No actual threat had been made against his life but Frank didn't feel it was his place to make life any easier for the terrorists. He put in a call to the White House, and another to the local office of the FBI to see what he could find out about the PTA. He was not pleased with either return call.

The President called back first, saying he was not about to let a bunch of lunatics get in the way of his mission in Los Angeles. "The whole country is watching L.A., Frank. I can't ignore what's going on out there."

"I understand, sir, it's just that, maybe if you rescheduled your visit for a month or two from now, we'd have time to clear up this mess. It could be very dangerous, right now."

"Frank, that's why I want you to work closely with the FBI and the Police Department. Find out who these fanatics are and stop them. You've got two weeks. I know I can count on you."

"Yes sir. I'll do my best."

The second call was worse than the first. The FBI had absolutely nothing on the PTA. They were obviously a new group. The boys in the lab were busy checking out what little physical evidence they had gathered after the explosion, but there wasn't a lot to go on; the letter sent to the Times was a photocopy of the original, making it exceptionally difficult to trace the typewriter. And the bomb, a Bouncing Betty, was about as generic as you could get, easy to find, easy to use. But not to worry, they said, something would turn up.

Frank hung up the phone, poured himself a glass of water and popped a couple of pain pills. His back had never been right ever since he threw a block into a protestor who had gotten a little too close to the President at a fund raiser.

Frank dialed the phone again. "Yeah, this is Frank Noble, Secret Service. I want to speak to the detective investigating the shopping mall bombing."

"You mean bombings, sir."

"What are you talking about?"

"As of fifteen minutes ago, there are two, and detective Mallory is on the way to the scene, right now."

Frank got directions to the mall, called the car pool and took another pill. The day was not off to a good start.

―――――――

The lingerie department of Robinson's was a smattering of shattered glass and metal fragments enmeshed in a net of shredded undergarments. The soft jazz piped into the department mingled with the moans of the wounded shoppers so that a passerby might think they were overhearing the religious service of some new-age cult. On the floor, ghost-like chalky renderings of the dead quivered beneath the sterile florescent lights.

Detective Kate Mallory was busy picking through the rubble, searching for clues. She was in her early thirties, slim, straight brown hair pulled back in a ponytail. She had on a pair of old Levis, a lightweight tan jacket that was unbuttoned, and a plain white t-shirt. She carried her gun in a shoulder holster beneath her left arm.

Kate felt a hand on her shoulder.

"Excuse me, sweetheart, I'm looking for Detective Mallory."

Kate had a large piece of shrapnel in her hand. It was still warm, so she kept juggling it like a potato as she stood up to face the arrogant man. She found him rather attractive, but managed to keep a smirk on her face as she spoke. "Oh, good. You must be from cleanup. We'll be done here in a few minutes." She turned to walk away from the handsome stranger but he reached out and gently grabbed her shoulder. "No, you don't understand. I'm with Secret Service." He pulled out his ID.

"You're a long way from home, aren't you?"

"Well, the President's due to arrive here in two weeks."

Kate called out to another officer. "Baker, can you bag this for me?" Officer Baker took the piece from Kate Mallory and dropped it into a bag. Kate turned her attention back to the Secret Service man. "I'm Kate Mallory."

The agent went flush in the face. "Oh, I'm sorry, I didn't realize…"

"What can I do for you, Mr., I'm sorry I didn't catch the name."

"Noble. Frank Noble. What have you got so far?"

Kate picked a bra up from the floor. "Well, I don't think these are the same people who were burning their bras back in your day."

"You think this has something to do with brassieres?"

"We've got two department stores hit in one week, both of them in the lingerie department, both with explosives. I can't say for sure but I would guess this is another Bouncing Betty."

Frank Noble reached down and picked up a severed manikin head and removed a couple of metal fragments. Then he glanced around the room. The damage covered a good eighty feet in diameter. "It's bigger than that. My guess is Italian, maybe a Valmara. How many bodies?"

"Four dead. A dozen injured. Bomb went off shortly after the doors opened. Probably hidden under another manikin."

"More likely a trip wire?"

"Why is that?"

"There's only two ways to detonate these. One requires pressure on one of the fuse prongs, the other's by a trip. Waiting for someone to step on it's a little risky, could be spotted. My guess is our bad guy strung a wire across an isle. Check the bottoms of all the racks, start with those by the entry, you'll probably find a small section of wire still attached."

"Well, you certainly know your bombs."

"Yeah," said Frank, disgusted by the carnage before him, "lucky me. Listen, I'm sorry about the sweetheart thing. It's just kind of a habit."

"Right. One of those southern things. Let me guess. Mississippi."

"Not quite that deep. Tennessee. Memphis, to be exact."

"Well, I think the accent's cute, but just so we understand one another, I'm not your buttercup, your honey child, your chickabiddy or any of the other sobriquets currently in fashion in Memphis." She laid on a thick accent with the word "Memphis."

"I read you, loud and clear. How about we start over?"

"We already have."

"Good. I was thinking maybe we could get some lunch, and you could fill me in on the details. Dutch treat, of course."

"Sure, why not. I know a place. You like barbequed chicken?"

"I'm from Tennessee. We invented chickens."

"Great. You can buy me lunch and tell me all about it."

––––––––––

Martin could hear music coming from his living room but it sounded strange, almost surreal. When he lifted his head to check the time it felt as though a huge weight were shifting inside from ear to ear. It was twelve o'clock. Fragments of the previous evening were beginning to come back to him. He had drank a lot of booze, that much he knew for sure, and he recalled wanting to go for a swim but he couldn't remember actually going in the water; but then why was there so much sand in his bed? And he was naked; he never slept naked. Had someone helped him back to the house? Now there were voices in the other room, they seemed to blend harmoniously with the sounds emanating from the radio.

Martin slid into a pair of jeans and ambled cautiously into the living room. The song on the radio became more distinct now. It had a cheerful, celebratory tone to it and was in another language: Spanish. Two children, a boy and girl, attempted to sing along with the song on the radio. Martin put one hand to his head as if to control some object that continued to shift its weight. "Hello?" His voice was weak and inquisitive.

The boy, the older of the children, stopped singing and called out. "Curtis, el hombre esta despertado."

Martin's legs began to give out from under him and he quickly sought refuge on the couch, plunging both elbows into his legs and supporting his head in his hands. When he looked up, Curtis was setting a cup of coffee on the table before him. "Here, amigo. Drink this. I'll fill in the missing parts."

Curtis explained how he had found Martin on the beach, that he was pretty drunk and had to be carried to his coach. He was kind enough to leave out the part about Martin throwing up all over him.

Martin was trying his best to concentrate on Curtis's story, but the music in the background was beginning to unnerve him. "Can we turn off the music?"

"Juan," said Curtis, "pon la musica."

"What I don't understand, Curtis, is how you happened to be here in the first place."

"That is what I want to talk to you about, my friend." He turned to the children who, having lost their entertainment, now concentrated on the two adults. "Jueguense a fuera. Cerca de la casa."

The two children were quick to obey, neither uttering a word of complaint as they exited the trailer.

"Where are they going?"

"Just outside to play. I need to ask of you a very big favor, amigo. As you know, from time to time I have helped a few people come into this country."

Martin chuckled. "From time to time?"

"Well, okay, quite often. But I don't do this for the money. I want to help my people."

Martin took a drink of his coffee. "You're a good man, Curtis, you don't have to explain anything to me. So, what is the favor?"

"Last night I brought these two ninos and their mother across."

"Where is the mother?"

"I am coming to that. We were supposed to meet the father in Nogales."

"Mexico?"

"Arizona. We waited for three hours but he did not show. There was a large group of us, another family and two other men. We decided to split up but before we could, the border patrol arrived and arrested most of the others, including the mother of these two ninos. I think someone turned us in, but that's not important, right now. We were fortunate enough to escape."

The fog was beginning to lift from Martin and he began to sense where Curtis was heading. "Curtis, are you about to ask me what I think you're about to ask me?"

"I need a place for the children. Just for awhile, until I can find out where the mother is and where she wants me to take them."

"But why me? I mean, don't you have any friends, you know...I don't even speak Spanish."

"There is no one I can take them to and be certain they will be safe. The mother will be questioned by immigration. They will frighten her and maybe she will tell them who I am. I cannot go home and I cannot go to my friends. They may be watching them."

"You had a visitor at the job yesterday. A Kuwoski or something like that."

"Ah, that pendejo, Sukowski. He is a bad man. He takes much pleasure in hurting my people. Someday I will cut off his huevos. But he is stupido; he will not catch me."

"Well, I should tell you, he seemed to think I knew you. Maybe he'll be watching me."

"I have to take that chance. Can you help me?"

"I don't know, Curtis, I'm not exactly set up for children here. I mean, you saw me last night." Martin got up from the couch and went to the window. He watched as the girl pulled a hunk of grass from the earth and tossed it into the air, then delighted in it's slow decent to the ground. He envied their resilience, their ability to rebound. "How old are they?"

"Juan is eight and the little one, Maria, is five. Their father has been in this country for a year. He has his papers now and wants his family with him. I know this is asking a lot...we don't really know each other that well..."

"They can stay," said Martin as he turned away from the window. "For a little while."

"Muchas gracias, amigo. I promise you, it will not be for long and the children will be no trouble."

Curtis went outside and talked to the two children, grabbed what belongings they had from the van and returned to the house.

"Martin, this is Juan and this little angel is Maria." He spoke again to the children. "Este hombre se llama Martin y el va a cuidarles. El es un gringo pero es un buen hombre. Hagan todo lo que el dice."

The children smiled at Martin. "What did you tell them, Curtis?"

"I said you were not a bad person, for a gringo, and that they should obey you."

"Gee, maybe you should talk to my ex."

Curtis kissed the two children goodbye then he took Martin aside. "Here, keep this with you, too," he said as he opened a long box and took out an item wrapped in cloth.

Martin reached down and pulled back the cloth. It was a double-barrel shotgun. "Whoa, Curtis. What am I going to do with that?"

"You must protect the children."

"Yeah, I know, but..."

"Take it, just in case."

Martin took the shotgun and a box of shells and stuck them in his room. His stomach was unsettled and it was more than just the booze. He hadn't had the vision last night, what with the all the booze, but he was sure that when he went to bed tonight, it would be there. And it would be different; he knew that too.

EIGHT

"Whose crib is it?" said Cervante.

Two-ton scooped the cards up from the table and started to shuffle. "It's mine. You had six points in your crib. See, right there's where you pegged them."

Cervante rubbed his chin. He was meticulous about shaving and was constantly checking for stubble. "Are you sure? I don't remember dealing."

"Well, you did," said Two-ton. Cervante was way ahead thanks to a triple three-card run and the six point crib the hand before. Two-ton had just set the deck on the table for Cervante to cut when the front door flew open and Wanda Blade burst in. She had a newspaper in her hand, rolled up like a club. Cervante had looked up at her and then back toward the cards to cut them when he was promptly greeted by a whack across his head, and then another.

"You fucking idiot! Who told you to set that bomb?"

She hit him again with the paper.

"Hey, knock it off. I was just trying to make up for the other day. What's the problem?"

Wanda tossed the paper onto the table, scattering the rest of the deck of cards. She grabbed the front of Cervante's shirt and leaned down to him, putting her face right up to his. "The problem, you little faggot, is, I'm the one calling the shots around here, not you."

"I thought you'd be pleased."

"You thought I'd be pleased!" Wanda grabbed the paper from the table and wound up to smack Cervante again. He threw his hands up to block the shot but she just tossed the paper down onto the table, then looked over angrily toward Two-ton, who quickly diverted his eyes from hers.

"Don't look at me, Wanda. You told me to get more mines. All I did was show him how to use it. If you don't mind me saying, though, everything went okay, so what's the big deal?"

Wanda studied the two men. Two-ton was trying to put the cards back in order. Cervante sat quietly rubbing his wounds, his head bowed down at the ground like a rejected puppy. "You realize you just narrowed their potential suspects, don't you? Every time you establish some kind of pattern, you make their job easier."

Cervante continued to stare at the ground. "Look at me when I'm talking to you Raymond," Wanda said, and Cervante slowly raised his head.

"I don't appreciate you calling me a faggot," he said, sounding more hurt than angry.

"Then quit acting like one. The idea of being locked in a cell the rest of your life may sound appetizing to you, but it's not at all what I have in mind."

"What pattern?" Two-ton asked.

"What pattern. Last week he blows up the Broadway. Now he walks down to the other end of the same shopping center and hits Robinsons."

"Didn't they merge with May Company?" asked Two-ton.

Wanda glared at Two-ton for a few seconds, her mouth pried open as though a word had gotten stuck in her teeth.

"Unbelievable," she said and returned her attention to Cervante. "Just how many people do you suppose have access to both of those stores when they're closed?"

The two men looked at each other inquisitively.

"Okay, let me explain it to you. When it was just the Broadway, it could have been any one of hundreds of employees. Now, it has to be someone with keys to both stores." She leaned down so that her face was just inches from Cervante's.

"Someone like a custodian, maybe."

Cervante turned his head away from Wanda and rolled his eyes. "Anyone could have stolen the keys, Wanda."

She pulled back. "Sure, but first they're going to check the obvious, and that means you." Wanda looked around the room. "Where's Spike?"

"He went to pick up some lunch," said Two-ton.

"Did he get those keys yet?"

"We're gonna get them tonight."

"Well, make sure you do. And get everything out of this apartment that can possibly tie you to the bombings. Take it upstairs to my place, or better yet, take it all out to Malibu. And no more striking out on your own, Raymond. Got it?"

"Yeah, sure," said Raymond, still upset.

Wanda pulled a pack of camels from her shirt pocket, removed one and lit it, inhaled deeply and then released a stream of smoke from her nose down onto the top of Raymond's head.

"I wish you wouldn't smoke in here, Wanda," said Cervante.

"Boy, that's rich," said Wanda, the cigarette dangling from her mouth. She went to Cervante's refrigerator and helped herself to a Coke. Two-ton and Cervante sat quietly staring across the table at one another, both afraid to start back into their cribbage game lest Wanda think they weren't taking her seriously.

Cervante glanced up as Wanda took a long swig of soda, smoke from her cigarette easing out from around the top of the can like some fire breathing dragon. How she had changed since the days of the Parade. They used to shop together for her clothes—Wanda thought Raymond had terrific taste—and stay up all night sharing stories about each other's lovers, or talk about the future, how Raymond would someday reign over a chain of gay newspapers and Wanda, well Wanda was obviously destined for stardom. She was the only person who ever caused him to regret his homosexuality. Had he been born straight, who knows, they might have been another Sonny and Cher.

"I'm sorry about the faggot thing, Raymond," said Wanda, staring into the refrigerator as though she were searching for some long lost item. She dropped her half-spent butt into the can of coke and closed the door. "You just really pissed me off."

Cervante perked up with Wanda's apology. "Well, there's no need to be calling names. You never used to be that way."

Wanda turned to face the two men again. "Yeah, well, I never used to do a lot of things. Anyway, I said I'm sorry, okay?"

"Sure," he said and grabbed the cards from the table to deal. "My crib," he said to Two-ton, who nodded and reached for his beer.

―――――――

Vern Melnick poured himself a shot of bourbon and offered one to Martin, who declined. "I gotta take care of those kids, Vern, I probably shouldn't be drinking."

"One drink doesn't exactly constitute drinking."

"It's not one drink I'm concerned about."

Vern downed his shot and poured another. "Oh, I see, you have a drinking problem, maybe? You want I should call Betty Ford for you?"

"No Vern, I just want to keep a clear head, okay."

"Fine with me." Vern was sitting at the kitchen table, viewing some slides under his microscope. "You want to take a look at this?"

"What is it?"

"Trichogramma eggs. Wasps."

"Sounds charming, but I think I'll pass."

"You really need to take more interest in the world around you, Martin. The trichogramma lays its eggs on the eggs of other insects. When the larvae emerges, it feeds on the host eggs."

"Sounds yummy."

"Well, I'm sure the trichogramma enjoys it, and, they provide a service by ridding the gardener of unwanted pests."

"Oh, I get it." Martin grabbed the bourbon and poured himself a drink. "Well, I'm not a wasp, Vern, and I'm not using the shotgun on the President or anybody else."

"My, you writers. Everything is all symbolism and metaphor with you guys. I'm just trying to have a conversation about a very intriguing subject. You must admit, though, this does change things. The shotgun, I mean."

Vern set the microscope aside and glanced toward the kitchen window. "You expecting company?"

"What do you mean?"

Vern motioned toward the open shade and Martin got up from his chair to take a look. Two men in dark suits got out of their car and approached Martin's trailer. One of the men started pounding on the front door while the other tried peeking through a window. Martin couldn't make out their faces but there was something familiar about their suits."

"Oh, shit. I think it's those INS guys. I better get over there before they wake up the kids. Martin started for the front door, but Vern grabbed hold of his arm.

"Go out the back and circle around. Act like you're just coming up from a walk on the beach. Take off your shoes, and dampen your feet so you'll pick up some dirt and sand. And Martin, if they don't have a warrant, don't let them in your house. Understand?"

"Why all the cloak and dagger, Vern?"

"If you were hiding a couple of illegals, you probably wouldn't leave them there while you went for a casual stroll on the beach."

"You watch too much TV, Vern."

"Hand me the shotgun."

"Jesus Christ, they're the law."

"And this is private property. Don't worry about it. Just a little insurance. Now go on."

"Maybe they'll just go away."

"What they'll do is make enough noise until they wake up

those two kids and then your ass is grass, if I may digress into the vernacular. Now go."

Martin quickly removed his shoes and socks, splashed some water from the kitchen faucet on his feet, then slipped out the back door and moved swiftly behind the row of coaches toward the end of the street.

It was a beautiful afternoon, the morning overcast had burned off and a strong wind out of the north had left the sky a sparkling cobalt blue. The whole scene reminded him of a painting—he couldn't remember the artist—of a small village in Mexico (or maybe it was Greece, he wasn't sure). In the picture, a young couple is walking down a dirt road behind a series of adobe houses. The lovers are barefoot and dressed in brightly colored shirts, the man has his arm around the girl's shoulder and hers is wrapped around his waste; the roofs are red tile—Mexico, it must be Mexico—and the sky is a brilliant, deep blue. The couple appears to be walking into the sky and though their faces are not shown, there can be no doubt they are smiling. Martin wished he were there now.

As he cut through between two coaches, he came upon a narrow bed of sand. He rolled up his pant cuffs and walked through the sand then emerged onto the street just above the coast highway.

As he approached his place he recognized the man at the door making all the noise. "You're not exactly dressed for the beach, Brukowski."

Sukowski let go of the screen door and it slammed shut. His partner, who had been peeking through the window, had evidently given up, for he was now leaning against their car. Sukowski removed his sunglasses and moved away from the door. "Well, look what we have here, it's Moondoggie, himself."

Martin glanced up at Sukowski's balding head. "You really shouldn't come out in this sun without a hat, officer. You could have another debilitating stroke."

94

Sukowski's partner started to crack a smile but quickly reined it in.

"I'm looking for your little wet-back hombre. I know he came into Laguna and I'm sure it wasn't to visit his masseuse."

"Have you tried the Taco-Bell? You know how they love their rice and beans."

"Suppose we take a look inside your bungalow, Frankie."

"Suppose you show me a warrant, Lennie."

Martin knew the first time he met Sukowski that he was a man easily provoked, but he just couldn't help himself, now. It didn't take much to imagine the terror the agent had instilled in the immigrants he confronted and Martin felt somehow obliged to irritate him as much as possible.

Sukowski walked slowly past Martin as if he were going to give up the search and drive away, but as soon as he got behind him, Martin felt his hair being yanked back, followed by the cold steal of a pistol being poked in his ear.

"Now you listen to me, Kookie. You're not talking to some queer Laguna Beach cop, now, so you can take that warrant crap and shove it up your tender little ass. Now you and me and my friend Mr. Bradley over there are going to take a look inside of your house." Sukowski started pushing Martin toward the door. "Of course, being as how we don't have a warrant, we'll need you to invite us in." He gave a yank on Martin's hair. "Please invite us in."

Then Martin heard a most familiar sound. He had been hearing it every night for the past eight months, though not quite as distinctly as now. He liked this version much better than the one in his dream.

"I got an invitation for you gentlemen."

Sukowski spun Martin around, the gun still in his ear, and faced Vern, who had evidently attached his prosthesis, for there he was standing on two legs, his crutch jammed into his armpit for support. He was wearing a pair of dark shades and a Dodger baseball cap and he had the shotgun cocked and pointed at

Bradley's head. "How would you like a close-up of hell?"

Bradley stood up straight from the car. "You're asking for a lot of trouble, mister. This is INS business. Now just drop the shotgun and get back in your house."

Vern adjusted his aim. "You gentlemen got thirty seconds to clear off this property before this fellow gets himself a face lift."

Sukowski cocked his gun. "I'll blow his fucking brains out."

"Well, that's alright. He uses them too much, anyway. You're down to twenty seconds."

Bradley started to shake. He didn't even notice the piss running down his leg. "Marv. Let's go."

Martin could feel the gun barrel tight against his head, as if it were about to be screwed in, then he heard the hammer being released and felt his head jerk back as Sukowski gave a final tug on his hair before letting him go. "You're a dead man," he said and then headed for his car. "I'll be seeing you again, too, old man," he yelled to Vern.

"Bring some balls with you next time," said Vern and the two agents got in their car and drove away.

Vern hobbled over to Martin. "He's got a lot of nerve, calling me 'old man.' I'm no older than him."

Martin bent over and turned away from Vern and began to vomit.

"What's wrong with you?"

Martin spit out the last remnant of his lunch. "You almost got us all killed."

"I don't think there was much chance of that. Did you notice the plates on his car?"

"The plates on his car? No, Vern, actually I was busy reviewing the last forty years of my life."

"They're not government plates. I think our friend is doing some free-lancing."

Martin wiped his chin with his sleeve. "He's just the type." He glanced at Vern's fake leg. "I like the two legs thing."

"Seemed like a nice day for a stroll."

"I better check on the kids. You coming in or are you off to the beach?"

"Don't make me regret coming out here."

Martin unlocked the front door and stepped into the trailer. A beacon of light shot across the room through the open door, illuminating a small section of wall papered with rejection slips. Martin stood transfixed in silence as a million tiny particles of dust danced before his eyes. He felt like a stranger in his own house, like he was seeing it for the first time, but really seeing it, without any misconceptions. Was this his life? His reverie was broken by a poke in the back with Vern's crutch.

"You're blocking traffic."

Martin's voice cracked as he called out to the children. No response. He made his way through the small trailer softly calling their names. "It's Martin. It's okay, you can come out."

He heard a noise coming from the bedroom closet. It sounded like a small whimpering dog. He slowly opened the door. There was a large pile of clothing in one corner. Martin got down on his haunches and called the boy's name then gently removed some of the items from the pile. The two small children were huddled together, the girl weeping quietly in her brother's arms, the boy brandishing a small knife in his right hand, his eyes aglow with a burning determination, causing Martin to hesitate. "It's okay, Juan. They're gone. It's alright now."

Vern limped into the room. He spoke in Spanish. "The bad men have left. You can come out now."

The children slowly abandoned their sanctuary and Juan surrendered Maria to Martin's outstretched arms. He turned to Vern. "I didn't know you spoke Spanish."

"Actually, I speak seven languages. There are certain advantages to being confined in your home. But, enough of that. You better get some things together and get these kids out of here in case those two decide to come back."

"What about you?"

"I'll be fine. It's not me they're after." Vern turned to leave, then hesitated. "I'm curious about the guy with the gun."

"What do you mean?"

"I just wonder how he lost his leg."

"What are you talking about, he had two legs."

"One of them isn't real, Martin, it's a prosthesis."

"How can you tell?"

Vern tapped on his own prosthesis with the shotgun. "Trust me. Oh, by the way, before you go, I've got some more cockroaches for you to take."

"Cockroaches? Jesus, Vern, I've got this maniac after me, and these kids to take care of. Can't you just kill this bunch?"

"If it's too much trouble…"

"No, fine, I'll take them." Martin set Maria down. "Listen, Vern, there's something I need to tell you."

"Yes, I know, I love you, too."

"Seriously, it's about the vision. I lied to you before. It has changed. I was on top of a building, with the gun, and the President was getting out of his car."

"Well, that's quite a development."

"There's more. The gun definitely gets fired."

"At the President?"

"I don't know. I see him, and I see my finger on the trigger, and I feel the gun kick, and that's it. I don't know what happens after that."

"Well, don't lose hope. Maybe you hit him."

"You really find this funny, don't you?"

"Well, Martin, it is entertaining. And so far, nobody's been hurt, so I think it's fair to keep to the sunny side of things. But, that's just me. Mr. Sunshine."

Martin stared down at the two small children who seemed to be mesmerized by Vern. "They don't understand a word you're saying and they still know you're full of shit."

NINE

Martin got off to a late start Monday morning and was paying for it now as he crept along in the fast lane of the 405 at ten miles an hour, thousands of cars stretched out in all four lanes like multi-colored links of sausage.

It didn't seem that long ago when there was no 405. Martin had come to California with his parents in '59, right behind the Dodgers, and there was only the Santa Ana Freeway then, connecting the distant smog shrouded L.A. with the soft rural fields of Orange County.

His father had taken a job in a packing plant in Orange and every Friday he'd bring home a crate of oranges along with his paycheck. Martin still had some of the labels off the crates, pastoral scenes of fields of orange trees pregnant with fruit, young girls in soft flowing dresses gathering up the bounty in bushel baskets, and in the distance, the majestic snow capped mountains poking their tips into a pristine pale blue sky. But all that was gone now. Oh, the mountains were still there, you just couldn't see them anymore. The orange groves? California's oranges came from Florida now.

Traffic seemed to open up a bit and Martin picked up speed to about twenty-five. When he was back in his trailer in Laguna he was able to blot out the blight that had become California, but on these journeys to L.A. he just couldn't help but look back. He was not a nostalgic person in general, and he had already done his mourning for the state back in the sixties and seventies when all the ruination had taken place, but he was so bombarded with images and ugliness it was impossible to shut them out: tracts of houses nestled under the shadow of the freeway seemed to droop in despair, their paint chipping away, weeds overrunning the yards; smokestacks spit their waste into a grey sky (scientists claimed the smog levels had improved since the sixties but Martin didn't believe it); and everywhere, on the overpasses, across the face of billboards (ugly in their own right), on the fences, the houses, the industrial buildings, everywhere, there was graffiti.

He felt it was ironic how the community had become so enraged over the scribbling of inner city youth. After all, were they really any different than the ads for Coppertone or Winston or Black Velvet? Weren't they just staking out their territory, flying their flag, laying claim to a community that, from the looks of it, nobody really cared about anyway? He felt a sadness come over him as though he had lost someone close. Were all the people in all these cars feeling it too, or was he alone out here on this urban cattle drive? He needed a drink, or some drugs, something to take his mind off things, to help him escape. But just the fact that he was thinking of alcohol at seven-thirty in the morning just added to his depression. God, he felt awful.

It was eight thirty when he finally arrived at work. He was surprised to see Hank and Dudley sitting on the hood of Hank's truck, drinking coffee. As Martin's car approached, the two men got down off the truck and walked over to the gate at the entrance to the property. Martin stopped his car in front of the gate and got out.

"What's going on?"

"The gate's locked," said Hank.

"Where's Liddell?"

"Haven't seen him. We were hoping you knew."

"How we gonna work if we can't get in?" said Dudley.

"We'll just have to wait for Tim to get here. Where's Spike?"

"He was here. I think he went for some coffee," said Hank. "I'm not sticking around here all day waiting for Liddell."

"So why tell me?" Martin said. The drive had not left him in the best mood. "I'm not your boss. He probably got stuck in traffic. Just relax and drink your coffee. I'll go call Clint."

Clint was surprised—and not very happy—to find out about Liddell. The two men had been together drinking the night before and Tim hadn't said anything about not coming to work. The last thing Clint wanted to do was drive to L.A. He had a ten o'clock appointment at the tanning booth and was supposed to play tennis at noon. He suggested maybe everyone could just take the day off and Martin said that would be fine with him and he was sure the rest of the guys would be perfectly content with four hours show up pay, which hurled Clint into a minor stammering fit about costs and loyalty and job security. Martin let him go on for a good three or four minutes before interrupting. "Clint, if I can use one of your phrases, we are all 'on the clock' as of eight this morning. Are you coming up, or not?"

Clint agreed to head up there to unlock the place but said that if Liddell showed up in the meantime, Martin should call Clint on his car phone.

By the time Martin got back to the job, Spike had returned. He was sitting on the ground with his back against the chainlink fence. He had a huge cup of coffee in one hand and a cinnamon roll in the other.

"You haven't heard from Liddell, have you Spike?"

Spike took a sip of his coffee and looked up at Martin. There was something in his eyes, something that made Martin feel uneasy. He hadn't noticed it before today and couldn't help but wonder if it wasn't merely a reflection of his own anxiety over the previous day's events. "We don't exactly hang out together," said Spike.

"So whadda we do now?" Dudley asked. He was busy trying to dislodge his underwear from the crack in his butt.

"Clint's on his way with the keys. We're all on the clock so just relax and enjoy your free time."

Frank Noble was busy trying to make Leroy understand he had no interest in shock absorbers, that the car he was driving was government issued and he had no idea who made those types of purchases. This was Frank's second trip to Leroy's place. The first time was with Kate Mallory. They had come for lunch the day of the second bombing, and had decided to work closely together on the case. She suggested Frank return to Leroy's and see if he couldn't get some information from him. He had helped her with cases in the past and seemed to know just about everybody in that part of town. Kate was going to continue checking out the employees from the mall.

The two men sat at one of the small metal tables in front of the barbeque stand. Leroy was chewing on a sandwich that looked like a half-inch slab of lard and a handful of sprouts, while Frank sipped a diet soda. It was hot and smoggy and the tattered umbrella did little to protect them from the blazing sun.

"Listen, Leroy, Detective Mallory tells me you might be able to help us locate these terrorists."

"She the white girl with the pony-tail? Fine looking woman; I sold her a full set of shocks. Yeah, she got one of those Japan-ese cars."

"What we're looking for is anyone who might have tried to purchase some weapons."

"What you talking about? That got nothing to do with me. I sell chicken and shocks, just like the sign says. Or didn't they teach you how to read at them fancy colleges."

"I know. Listen, Leroy, nobody's pointing the finger at you. It's just…"

"Everybody seems to think just cause I used to handle a few ladies, that makes me some kinda large criminal type."

Frank wiped the sweat from his brow. It was just too damn hot, and it was no wonder the wind wasn't blowing. How could it ever cut through all this smog? "I understand, Leroy. Kate, Detective Mallory, seemed to think if someone were looking for weapons, they might come to you."

Leroy took a bite of his sandwich.

"Do you mind me asking just what that is you're eating?"

"Tofu."

"Tofu?"

"Yeah, man, tofu, soybeans. Something wrong with that?"

"No, no, I just assumed, being as you have this place, you'd be eating chicken."

Leroy laughed. "Not anymore. I ate so much chicken I was beginning to shit eggs. I'm strictly vegetarian, now. What kinda weapons we talking about?"

"Big stuff, mostly. Land mines, hand grenades. That kind of thing."

Leroy set the sandwich down on his plate. A couple of young black men, teenagers, had gotten in line to order some food and appeared to be harassing the girl in front of them. Leroy got up from the table. "I got to talk to these boys for a minute."

Frank watched as the older man approached the two boys. He was not a large man but he appeared to be in good shape. His moves, as he walked across the cement toward the line of people, were graceful and light, like a boxer. Frank saw him dig a hand into each of the boys' shoulders, and he could tell by the look on their faces when they turned to face the older man, that it hurt. A few words were exchanged, and then Leroy gave them each a gentle pat on the back and walked away. The two boys did not bother the girl anymore.

"Nobody's asked me 'bout no weapons, except some white boy comes in here wanted to get a shotgun. I don't think he's any kinda terrorist, though."

"Well, you never know. Who is this guy?"

"Don't know his name. He comes in here a lot, though. He's a painter."

"What, like an artist, you mean?"

Leroy cracked a smile. "No, man. A painter, you know, like houses. So, let me ask you something. You and this detective Mallory, you getting hooked up?"

"I hadn't really thought about that…"

Leroy let out a laugh. "The hell you ain't, boy. That's the first thing every man thinks about. Less of course, you be walking on the other side of the street. Which is fine by me; we all gots to have our thing. But she's a mighty fine looking woman."

"Yes she is, Leroy, and, yes, I do like women."

"Can't be sure these days."

"So, this painter who wanted the shotgun; you have a name?"

Leroy shook his head. "I'm good with faces. Names I don't bother with so much. Even when I had my girls I never bothered with any of my regulars' names. Folks in that situation tend toward dishonesty, anyway. So I don't bother."

Frank took a card out of his jacket pocket and handed it to Leroy. His face was burning up and he could feel the sweat running down his neck and onto his shirt. He loosened his tie and undid the top button of his white shirt. "If he comes back in, or if you hear of anything that might be of help, you call me right away."

Leroy took the card and kept it in his hand until after Frank had gotten into his car and pulled away, then he tore it in half and put it and the trash from his lunch into the can by the side of the building. He wasn't about to hand over a good paying customer to Frank Noble—not in the middle of a recession.

———

The only person Martin could think to turn to the previous night was June. He stopped at a phone booth and called her to make sure she was alone, then he zigzagged through the neighborhood in case he was being followed, and shortly after dark, made his appearance. She sounded anxious to see him, but then, he hadn't told her about the kids.

When she opened the door, he thought perhaps he had come to the wrong building. Her hair was dark brown and cut to her chin. She had on a crisp white blouse and a pair of dress slacks, and looked like a paralegal for some Newport Beach law firm. He pushed his way through the doorway, still somewhat shocked by her look, and closed the door behind him.

Maria was asleep in his arms and Juan was so tired he could hardly stand. Martin went into June's bedroom and put Maria into bed. Juan climbed in next to her.

"Would it be too much to ask you to remove their shoes?" June was standing in the bedroom doorway. Martin took off their shoes and pulled a blanket over the two children. Then he and June went back into her living room.

"Martin, who are those children? I hope you're not going to tell me some story about a double life you've been living."

"Do you have any booze?

"They're Mexicans, aren't they?"

"What the hell did you do to your hair?"

"What's wrong with it?"

"Can I have a drink? Nothing. It just...you look like a real estate agent. What do you mean, 'They're Mexicans?'"

June got Martin a glass of white wine. Everything about her seemed different than the woman he had lived with. June had always drunk bourbon and never wore this much clothing at home. What she did wear was usually revealing and had a tendency to keep Martin sexually aroused. And there was something else: She wasn't smoking.

Martin plopped down on the couch and June sat across the room on an overstuffed chair. He had never seen the chair before today. In fact, most of the furniture was new to him, more elegant. June had always gone for the earthy look, an eclectic, post-hippie accumulation of wood and overstuffed chairs that said, I'm hip, but I also have some money. But this stuff, it almost screamed, *don't sit on me.*

June took a small sip from her wine and set it on a silver coaster atop the small table by her chair. "Now, are you going to tell me who those two children are?"

"Yeah, in a minute, June. But first, you tell me. What the hell's going on with you? Where are your cigarettes?"

"I quit smoking. I went to a hypnotherapist. I'm making some changes in my life, Martin. I'm tired of the old me. I want people to take me serious."

"About what! What was wrong with the old you?"

"If you're going to yell at me, I'll have to ask you to leave. My therapist says…"

"Your therapist? Oh, God."

Martin slowly fell over so that he was now spread across the entire couch.

"Please keep your feet off the couch. Now, who are the children?"

He pulled himself upright again and told June a story about the two kids, how their mother was a neighbor of his whose husband had been arrested for child abuse but had recently escaped prison and she was afraid he would come and try to steal the kids from her. They just needed someplace to keep them for a few days until the cops could find this guy.

"But, Martin, what am I going to do with them? Do they speak English?"

"Oh, yeah, well, you know, enough to get by. You won't have any problem with that. Maybe you could take them to Disneyland or something."

June stared a hole right through him. "Disneyland, huh."

"You always wanted to go there. Mickey Mouse, Fantasia…"

"Don't they have any relatives, or friends…?"

"There's nobody else, June. Believe me, I wouldn't be here if there were."

June shook her head. She looked slightly disgusted. "Okay. I don't know why, but okay. I'll give you two days, and that's it. I want you to pick them up Tuesday evening. I have a date that night, so be here by six o'clock."

"Let me guess. Phantom of the Opera, La Traviata?"

"You're never going to grow up, are you, Martin?" June got up from her seat, went to the front door and opened it. "I'd like to go to bed now."

Martin pulled himself off the couch, then mockingly smoothed out the wrinkles in the cushion with his hands, and shuffled over to the front door. He felt the slightest stirring of sentimentality as he brushed past the brunette but he quickly buried it. "I suppose it's inevitable."

June looked puzzled.

"The growing up part. Thanks for your help, June, really. It means a lot."

Clint unlocked the building and let the crew in. He was in a hurry to get to the tanning salon and was pissed off about Liddell not showing up. He gave Martin a set of keys, made a quick survey of the progress of the job, then hopped in his van and left. As he reached the end of the block, Curtis Chang's van turned the corner, headed toward the job site. Clint waved at him and considered returning to the job to inquire into Curtis's sick relative, but it was already ten o'clock and his tan was fading fast. Actually, he would probably have saved a little time if he had gone back, compared to the fifteen minutes he was about to spend with officer Wade Parker. And then of course there would be the seventy-five dollar fine for speeding.

Martin had already gotten into his spray suit and was about to start putting a coat of finish on the drywall when Curtis came in. He was working on the second floor, which was just one large room earmarked for meetings and parties. Spike had boxed twenty gallons together and then gone up to the third floor to help Dudley sand doors.

"Ola, amigo."

Martin was surprised to see Curtis, but he was too tired to show any emotion. He loosened his respirator and let it hang freely around his neck. "I don't think it's very wise for you to be here, Curtis. Your friend, Sukowski came to my house yesterday."

"What about the children?" Curtis seemed ready to panic.

"They're okay. They're with a friend. But this guy is serious. He pulled a gun on me."

Curtis's fear quickly turned to rage. "That pendejo! I am sorry my friend to have caused you this trouble."

Martin went to the front window to keep a lookout. "What's going on between you two, Curtis? He seems to be taking this a little too personal."

"He is angry because I took away his leg."

"You took his leg." Martin checked the window again.

"Before he got his job with INS, this man, Sukowski, he used to be with the Border Patrol in Nogales. All my people know about Senior Sukowski. Sometimes when he catches someone he beats him up. Some of the women say he has made them to make love with him. He is a very bad man.

One time, a few years ago, I am bringing a man and his wife across and he catches us. It is very late and no one else is around and I recognize his face. I can tell by the way he looks at the young woman that there is going to be very much trouble. I tell the young husband that we must jump this man, but the husband, he is very much afraid. The gringo, Sukowski, holds a gun on us and tells the wife to tie us up. She is very frightened and begins to cry. He pushes the husband and me to our knees and points his gun at the husband's head. The young woman pleads with him not to hurt her husband. She throws herself at his feet and wraps her arms around his legs. When he tries to push her away I am able to reach over and grab his arm that holds the gun and then the husband also grabs him so we are all four of us wrestling together and then the gun goes off and the gringo screams, and I can see he has a very big hole in his knee. Then I shot the tires on his truck and we ran away."

"Back to Mexico?"

"It was not safe to stay in Texas."

"But how did he know it was you?"

Curtis smiled. "My name is very well known. I have brought

many people to this country. It would not have been hard for him to find out."

"All this time you've been bringing people across, you've never been caught?"

"Oh, no, I have been caught many times. But I always say my name is Rodriguez or Gonzales and I no habla inglés, senior. They think we are all very stupid, you know, and only smart people lie. Then they put me in the truck and take me to the border and drop me off."

"So what about the children, Curtis. Did you find the mother?"

"Not yet. I need for you to keep them a little longer. Can you do this for me?"

Martin tried to imagine June in her new yuppie image dragging the wrinkled pair of orphans from thrill to thrill down the gay streets of Disneyland. "Of course," he said. "Don't worry, they're safe." He reached inside his spray suit and took his wallet out of his pants pocket. "Clint gave me your pay to give you."

"No, you keep the money. The children will need food."

"Don't worry about it, Curtis. Here take it."

Curtis ignored the money. "I must go now. I will contact you in a few days. You are a good friend."

"Take the money, Curtis." But Curtis was already on his way out the door.

TEN

Frank Noble got a call first thing Tuesday morning from Kate Mallory. A body had been found stuffed in the trunk of a seventy-two Cadillac, tucked back in the corner of a junkyard in Long Beach. "So what's the connection?"

"I think you should see the body, Frank. It has some unusual markings."

Frank checked a car out from the motor pool, had one of his staff write him directions to Long Beach and he was quickly on his way. He had told Kate not to let anyone touch anything until he got there, which only served to piss her off. She reminded Frank that she was a detective, that she had a master's degree in police science and that he was the guest in her city, not vice-versa. Frank apologized (he hadn't meant to insult her) and then reminded her he was in charge of the safety of the President of the United States and if that meant occasionally stepping on a few toes, so be it.

So he was a little worked up as he pulled onto the freeway, a sugar donut in his lap and a cooling cup of coffee in his hand. The cluster of cars reminded Frank of a giant Rubik's cube as he attempted to manipulate the tiny red Ford Escort across the lanes. He couldn't get used to the traffic in L.A. and couldn't understand how any intelligent person would want to live here. He rolled up his window to shut out the noise and the stench, and turned on the radio. Frank wasn't sure if it was bad reception or a cracked speaker but something was causing the sound to break up so he turned down the volume and cut back on the bass. He had to strain to hear what was being said.

"And already, folks, our good mayor, what's-his-name, is questioning the President's motives for visiting our—and these are his words—'great city.' Can you believe it? My question to the mayor is: Why should he come at all? Why should the President of the United States take the time to visit South Central Los Angeles, when the people who live there would just as soon burn it down? And in fact, they already have; or at least a good portion of it."

The man on the radio paused and took a deep sigh. Frank reached over and turned up the volume.

"It boggles the mind. Do you remember the Watt's Riots in the sixties—or whenever it was—how the media went on and on about how it was bound to happen, what with the poverty and the lack of jobs—you know, the usual liberal gibberish—so the United States Government poured millions of dollars—your tax dollars—into the area for new schools and roads, loans for small businesses. Do you remember? So what happened? I'll tell you. The good citizens went right back to their old life style, painting graffiti on the walls, dealing drugs on the corner, prostitution. Now, there are people out there who are going to start screaming and pulling their curly hair and accuse me of being a racist, when nothing could be further from the truth. The fact of the matter is, there is a strong criminal element out there—and yes, folks, let me be clear on this, I'm including Rodney King—a strong criminal element, the offspring of a welfare system run amuck; and to treat these people as anything other than what they are—criminals—is unthinkable. Preposterous!"

Frank turned off the radio. It seemed to him that the speaker was simplifying the problem, and there was something about his voice, an edge of self-righteousness that was grating on Frank's nerves.

It took him half an hour to get from Santa Monica to the Long Beach Freeway, only to miss his off-ramp, causing him to curse out loud and spill his coffee in his lap in the process—at least it was no longer hot. No wonder people rioted here, he thought. I would too.

The trunk of the Cadillac was large enough to accommodate the small man, with his legs bent slightly at the knees. Kate Mallory had one of the uniform cops pull the lid down to try and stifle some of the stink while she finished her breakfast, an Egg Mcmuffin one of the other officers had been kind enough to pick up for her. A half a dozen uniformed cops searched the area for clues while two other detectives dusted for prints. One of the uniformed cops had taken a break and was leaning on the car next to the Cadillac when Frank arrived. Frank went directly to him.

"You like your job?"

The officer had no idea who Frank was, and was a bit put off by his tone of voice. "Yeah, I like it fine."

"Then get the fuck away from that car, while you still have one."

Before he could say a word, Kate Mallory interjected and sent the officer away.

"I thought you were going to keep the area clean," said Frank.

"What's the problem?"

"Well if I had just lifted a body into the trunk of a car, I might be a little tired and lean on something for a moment, like the fender of that car, or that one over there."

"Well, that's very possible. And if you were the first detective on the scene, you would probably dust those cars for prints, like I did an hour ago while you were busy..." Kate glanced down at the wet stain on Frank's pants. "...wetting your pants?"

Frank looked down at the stain from the coffee and took a deep breath. "It's coffee. These freeways out here are insane. I'm surprised a lot more people don't end up dead in somebody's trunk."

"Okay," Kate said, "are you ready to see the body?"

"Sure. By the way, you look real nice today."

Kate was wearing a royal blue jacket, black slacks and a black silk blouse. With her dark glasses on, she could easily pass as an actress. "That some kind of an apology?"

"Just an observation."

The detective lifted the trunk lid and a rush of putrid air hit Frank in the face. He pulled back. "Boy, how long has he been in there?"

"We figure day and a half, two days, and in this heat that puts him at about medium rare." Kate took a bite off her sandwich.

The victim was dressed in a cheap pair of beige slacks and a dark blue turtleneck long sleeve t-shirt. There was blood all over the shirt and some on the pants. He had on one shoe, a new brown leather Topsider, and no socks. His feet looked to be large for his height; Frank guessed size ten. The man's face had been badly beaten, especially around the mouth, and there was a huge gash in the back of his head, his hair matted with dry blood. His fingertips had been burned and one of his feet was badly bruised. But what stood out the most, were the three initials carved into his forehead: PTA.

"Where's his other shoe?"

"It's not in the car." She pointed at the bruised foot. "From the looks of that foot I'd say it most likely fell off during the fight. The shoe, that is."

Frank smiled. "Thanks for clearing that up." He reached into the trunk and pulled back the dead man's upper lip. "Jesus. Look at this." The teeth were completely destroyed. "Somebody doesn't want us to know our vic."

"That does seem a bit strange, doesn't it?"

"What's that?"

"Well, they kill the guy, leave their calling card, and then hide him away in this junk yard with his teeth smashed in and his fingertips burned. Doesn't make sense."

"Were dealing with terrorists, Kate; everything and nothing makes sense. But this guy here, this is their mistake. He's going to lead us to them. I want his body gone over with a fine-toothed comb. I want tests on every speck of dirt. Find out who manufactures these shoes and who carries them. And let's find the one that's missing."

"Sure, Frank, we'll just check every alley between here and Ventura. That shouldn't take more than one, maybe two years."

"Both bombings were in West L.A. Start there. Check any homeless shelters, places like that, see if anyone's wearing one new shoe. I'm no detective, but it seems to me, if we find the shoe, we'll find the scene of the crime. Or, is that the proper terminology?"

"You know, I think I liked you better when you were calling me sweetheart."

Frank softened his tone a bit. "Find these people for me, Kate. He gave the body a final look then turned away from the car. "Let's get this poor son-of-a-bitch out of here."

With her hair dyed brown and her deep tan, June almost looked like she was related to Juan and Maria as the three of them strolled down Main Street, Disneyland, hand in hand. She had been trying all morning to communicate with the children but the only English words that had made any impression were Mickey Mouse and Donald Duck. She had finally stopped on the way to the park and picked up a translating dictionary and had managed to put together a few key sentences: stay close to me; don't talk to strangers; do you have to go to the bathroom?

Their first ride was the Pirates of the Caribbean. Maria sat on June's lap, confused and somewhat frightened by the distorted figures. Juan, however, kept reaching out trying to touch one, and repeatedly yelled out to them: "Los malos pirates deben morir!" June noticed a few people watching her and she tried to quiet the young boy, but to no avail.

By twelve o'clock, they had been on half-a-dozen rides, including one on which Maria, perhaps fearing she was actually shrinking, let out a horrendous scream at the sight of the giant snowflakes, forcing Juan to cup her mouth with his hand. Then the eyeball appeared, looking like a Cyclops with a hangover, and Juan let go of Maria's mouth and both he and June joined in the howling, triggering sympathetic wails in adjacent cars, the cries building to a crescendo that echoed through the small tunnel like a chorus of wounded banshees.

The two children had tears in their eyes as they left the ride and June figured it was a good time for a break. She stopped at one of the concessionaires and bought the kids hot dogs and Pepsis, then found a table in the shade and sat down. She got out her dictionary and tried piecing together a few sentences. "Es usted temor, Maria?"

Maria wiped her eyes and shook her head no.

"Are you ready to go? Listo salir?"

Maria was getting tired and nodded yes, but Juan, who had recovered quickly from the scare, and in fact seemed to draw energy from it, was adamant about staying. He kept pointing toward the Matterhorn, shouting "Vamos en la montaña!"

Once again, June paged through her book, managing at last to tell Juan the line was too long and Maria was tired. But Juan, who was mesmerized by the bullet shaped cars darting in and out of the side of the mountain, would not relent. He pleaded desperately, trying his best to explain to June that he would go on the ride alone, and she and Maria could wait for him. He finally edited his request down to four words, "I go, you wait," animating his plan while he spoke.

"Oh," said June, "no, no bueno."

"Por favor, senora, por favor."

June did not have to look this up. Some expressions can cross any language barrier and a child's plea is high on that list. June gazed up at the fake mountain before her. As a child, she had wanted desperately to take that ride, but could never muster the courage, and sitting there that day her fear of heights was just as strong as ever. And here was an eight-year-old boy, his life in disarray, prepared to go it alone. How could she say no? "Okay, you can go. But be careful," she said.

––––––––––

Juan could tell by her tone of voice that he had won and was about to take off, but June grabbed his sleeve and opened her book. She managed to make clear to him to return to their table. He started to leave but June grabbed him and gave him a hug. "Be careful," she said, and then sent him on his way.

Juan stood in line for forty-five minutes. As he approached the boarding area his heart began to pound with excitement at the thought of the adventure before him. People around him were staring at him and seemed to be talking about him, but he had no idea what they were saying. At long last he reached the front of the line. He darted toward one of the cars but the attendant grabbed hold of him and pulled him away.

The man said something, it sounded like a question. Juan stared up at him. "La montaña," he said and tried to free himself.

The man spoke again. Juan looked up at the mountain. He could hear the other children's screams as they passed by overhead. He wanted on that ride. "La montaña," he repeated.

The man asked another question. This time Juan recognized the word 'english' and started to respond but then remembered June's warning about speaking to strangers. Perhaps the man was just curious, he thought. If I just tell him I can't speak English, maybe he'll let me on the ride.

A mother with two children got into one of the cars and another attendant sent them on their way. Juan watched them go with envy. "No inglés," he said. "La montaña."

The man took a black box from a holster on his belt and spoke into it. Juan listened with curiosity as the nonsense spilled from the gringo's mouth. Families and other young children poured onto the ride, laughing and cheering. Juan looked back toward the table, hoping to spot June, but the large crowd blocked his view.

It didn't take long for the two people in uniforms to arrive. They looked like police. One was a clean-cut man around Martin's age and the other a woman with hair the color of Juan's. She knelt down to the boy. "Como te llamas?"

Juan looked into the woman's face. She was pretty and spoke his language very fluently. Juan thought of his mother. "Juan Arnoldo Gutierez."

"Juan, donde está tu madre?"

Juan had been anxious to get in the small tube and speed through the mountain. He had been confused and then angry when the attendant had stopped him. But up until this instant there had been no fear. The mention of his mother brought the picture of that evening into mind, he and his sister hiding in the bushes with Curtis while his mother was loaded into the van by the two gringos in uniforms, and taken away. He looked at the badge sewn onto the sleeve of the pretty woman. The two men that night had also worn badges on their sleeves.

"Juan, donde está tu madre?" she repeated.

A crowd of people had gathered to watch the incident and as Juan stared past the young woman questioning him he could see the crowd beginning to part and then the familiar face of June with Maria in hand. "Mama! Mama!" he shouted and ran to June. The guards were quick to follow.

"Es usted la madre de este chico?" the woman asked, somewhat puzzled at June's Anglo features.

"I'm sorry," June said. "I don't speak very much Spanish."

"This boy says he is your son. Is that true?"

June looked down into Juan's pleading eyes. "Well, I'm not his natural mother," she said. The officers and the gathered crowd waited for an explanation. "Actually, it's a very long story. Basically, the children recently lost both their parents— June had no idea how true this was—and I've taken them in temporarily."

"So you're their foster parent."

"Right," said June. "I'm their foster parent."

"But you don't speak Spanish."

"Well, I do speak a little, and I have this book." June dug into her purse and brought out her dictionary.

The male guard wanted to take them all to the office and run some checks on June's I.D., call the Foster home, but the lady said it was obvious the children knew her—Juan had even referred to her as 'mother'—and so it was decided to let them go, but not before June was given a stern lecture on keeping her children close at hand.

When the guards left, June took Juan's hand and started to walk away but Juan turned back toward the Matterhorn and started pleading with her. "La montaña, señora, por favor."

June looked to the attendant. "He can come to the front of the line, but you'll have to ride with him."

June gazed up at the mountain. The screams emanating from far above her filled her with dread. With her heart pounding and her hands sweating she ducked under the rope with the two children and boarded the next available car. Juan jumped into the front seat and June sat behind him, Maria in her lap. As the car slowly pulled away from the boarding area, Juan turned to June, placed a hand on her chin and smiled. "No worry, señora, no is danger"

———

Martin arrived at June's apartment a little before six. There was no answer so he let himself in. He was surprised to find his key still fit and he wondered why June had never bothered to change the lock or at least ask for her key back. He rummaged through the refrigerator—it was pretty slim pickings—settling on a stalk of celery with some peanut butter and a diet Coke.

June and the kids showed up about ten minutes later. Maria was fast asleep in June's arms and Juan was carrying a stuffed Mickey Mouse that was bigger than him. Martin was stretched out on the couch watching TV.

"How'd you get in?"

"I still have my key. Hello, Juan. Hello Mickey."

Juan just rubbed his tired eyes then followed June into the bedroom. When she returned she went straight to the remote and shut off the TV. "This isn't a hotel, you know."

"What's bugging you? You said to be here at six o'clock. Here I am. I thought you had a date tonight."

"I cancelled it. I'm too tired. You better not get any peanut butter on my new couch. And I want my key back."

Martin slid off the couch and onto the floor. "How's that?"

"Look, I'm sorry, Martin, it's just, I've had a very long day and I'm really tired."

If he had had a drink or two under his belt he would have suggested a back rub, and one thing might have led to another. He guessed she would always have that effect on him, but he managed to control himself. June poured herself a glass of wine and told him about their adventures that day and suggested the two children spend the night with her.

"Actually, June, that would be great. Things are still kind of up in the air with their parents. In fact I was wondering if they could stay a couple more days."

"They can stay, Martin, but no more lies, okay."

"What do you mean?"

"I mean, I know you think I'm stupid, but give me a little credit, okay. Did you really think I would be with these kids for two days and we wouldn't talk? I know about their mother and I know about this guy, Chang, so please, no more bullshit."

Martin got up off the floor. June seemed somehow infused with an aura of calmness and surety that he had rarely noticed during their years together. Could it be the boob job? Had he underestimated the value of plastic surgery? He also couldn't help noticing the sheen in her hair; he rather liked it dark. "Exactly, how did you manage to get all this information from them?"

"You forget, I lived with you for three years. I'm used to foreign languages."

"That's funny, June, it really is." He meant it. "And how about Mickey Mouse? You win him at the shooting gallery? You some kind of a marksman? Or is it markswoman?"

June laughed. "I'm not that horrible, am I? The truth is, I spent twenty dollars trying to win him, but I couldn't hit a thing. I finally just gave up and bought the damn thing. The kids love him, though."

From where he was standing, Martin could see into the bedroom. The kids were fast asleep with Mickey stretched out between them. He looked back at June. A wave of sadness and regret washed over him as he imagined another life they might have had together.

"They're really great kids," said June, as though she were reading Martin's mind. He moved close to her and put his hand up to her chin. There were tears starting to form in her eyes. "I just hope…"

"Hey," said Martin. "They'll be fine. Don't worry."

"I'm sorry…"

"Don't be silly. Why should you be sorry?"

"No, I mean about us. I'm sorry it didn't work out. Sorry I quit on you"

"I didn't really leave you much choice, did I?"

"There's always a choice."

"Well, you made the right one, June. Trust me on that." He leaned in and kissed her gently on the lips. "I better go."

"Do you have to?"

"Listen, June. I'm still that same guy."

"That guy wasn't all bad. And I don't want to be alone tonight."

"You make it difficult to say no."

"Then don't," said June. "Don't say anything."

ELEVEN

The first time Curtis Chang crossed the border between the U.S. and Mexico was in nineteen fifty-seven. His name at that time was Richard Garcia, he was six months old, and he was headed south.

Richard's father, Miguel Garcia, was born in Brownsville Texas, as was his father before him. Miguel owned a small farm where he and his wife, a Texan whose family had migrated from Oklahoma in the thirties, lived with their three children. Richard was the newest arrival and the couple's first son, and it made Miguel proud to show the young boy off to all his neighbors and friends.

Richard was a handsome child; he had fair skin like his mother but his eyes and his hair were dark, like Miguel's. And like his father, Richard also carried on his shoulder a small birthmark in the shape of a heart. Miguel liked to joke with his wife that there could be no doubt as to who the father was.

Richard would grow up and help run the farm, and someday it would be his. Even more importantly, he would carry on the family name. At least, that was the plan.

On a cool Friday morning in March, Helen, Richard's mother, wrapped the young boy in a blanket, kissed her husband goodbye and headed off to town for supplies, as was her custom. As she drove along in the truck, Helen sang a soft tune to the baby lying beside her on the seat. Helen loved all her children equally but she was especially happy that she'd had a boy; she knew how much it meant to Miguel. And Richard had been the easiest of her three children, or maybe she had just gotten used to the rigors of motherhood, she wasn't sure, but he certainly seemed to be a good baby, rarely fussy, slept through the night, ate like a horse (so his father claimed).

Her first stop that morning was at the bank. Miguel had hired two men to help with the planting, neither of which had bank accounts, and so on Fridays Helen always made a point to get cash to pay them. The clerks were cool to her as usual when she entered the bank. The idea of an attractive white woman settling down with a Mexican had never taken hold in town and the clerks could still, after all these years, not help whispering among themselves whenever she arrived. Miguel had wanted to search for a bank run by Mexicans but Helen insisted they stay where they were—the closest such bank was forty miles away—and in fact she rather enjoyed watching them squirm every Friday morning when she arrived.

She quickly took care of her business at the bank and then proceeded to the feed store for supplies for the animals. The owner, Mr. Hunt, an octogenarian whose Grandfather supposedly died at the Alamo, was very fond of the Garcias and looked forward to Helen's visits. She gave Mr. Hunt a slip of paper with the list of items she needed and the old man slowly, methodically, gathered them up and loaded them into her truck, then lingered for a moment chatting with the attractive young mother before returning to his store.

Helen set Richard on the seat, placed a bottle in his mouth and was about to start the truck when Mr. Hunt rushed out to tell her Miguel was on the phone. Helen left Richard lying there on the seat and ran into the store to take the call. Mr. Hunt stayed by the truck and entertained Richard for a minute and then returned to his store to take care of another customer.

Helen was only on the phone for two minutes. Miguel had called to remind her to pick up his good shoes at the shoe repair. She asked why he didn't just tell Mr. Hunt to give her the message and he said he had no idea she was already in the truck. "Besides," he said, "you know I love to hear your voice."

She hung up the phone, thanked Mr. Hunt again and left the store. Clouds had begun drifting in from the south and she wondered if it would rain later. Then she had the oddest feeling, as though something were terribly wrong. She was right; Richard was on his way to Mexico.

The two men who stole Richard Garcia were very clever, but then, they had a lot of experience. For three years they had been kidnapping young children on both sides of the border and selling them on the opposite side.

Richard had been picked for an older couple that had been unable to have any children of their own. They were very wealthy landowners, both pure Spanish, and had stipulated they wanted a fair skinned child. It was going to cost them five thousand dollars, which they readily agreed to pay, no questions asked.

Now, the two men who took Richard had a house in Texas and another one in Mexico, sort of halfway houses where they could keep the children while they negotiated their deals. Nobody had a clue where the house in Texas was but the authorities in Mexico had gotten a tip and were about to close in on the one in their country. The two men had two other children in the Mexico house besides Richard, a set of twins destined for Guatemala.

Neither of the two men was especially fond of children or knew the first thing about their needs so they had hired a Chinese fellow named Chang to see to it the children were fed and changed and entertained while they were out taking care of business. Chang was a gentle man who loved children and was under the impression the young orphans had been abandoned and that the men were performing a service to the community in finding them decent homes.

Chang was very fond of the new arrival—the men had named him Curtis—and he found himself wishing for the first time in his life that he had a wife so that they might raise this beautiful little boy as their own. How could any parent have deserted such a priceless treasure?

The morning the police arrived, Chang had gotten up early, as was his routine, to do the shopping. He changed the twins' diapers, dressed them in matching sleepers, prepared their bottles for the last time and said farewell; they were to leave that morning for their new home in Guatemala. Then he bundled Curtis up and placed him in a stroller and headed out for his short walk to the market.

He hadn't gone more than a block before he heard the sirens and then watched in awe as the procession of police cars sped past him and screeched to a halt right in front of his house. At first Chang thought there had been an accident of some sort, maybe he had forgotten to turn off the stove. The children!

He started back toward the house in a panic, then stopped abruptly as the police began pouring out of their cars, guns drawn. Two of them kicked in the front door and the whole swarm of officers filed through behind them. Chang stood frozen in his tracks. When a moment later two of the officers came back out pushing the two kidnappers in front of them, their hands cuffed behind their backs, followed close behind by two female officers holding the twins, he quickly put two and two together, spun the buggy around and fled.

The police officers had no idea there was a third child and had considered their raid a complete success. Of course, had Chang not left for the market that morning, Curtis (Richard) might have been reunited with his family that very evening. So far in his young life, Curtis's shopping experiences were, to say the least, extraordinary.

Chang was no dummy. He was not about to walk up to a dozen Mexican police and hand over this kidnapped child. Even if they could understand Chinese, they would never believe he knew nothing about the kidnapping, and he was not at all interested in experiencing Mexican justice. In fact, Chang was growing weary of Mexico, in general. He couldn't speak the language, he didn't like the food—there were never enough fresh vegetables to suit him—and he missed being around his own kind. It occurred to Chang that if he were to hurry, he could slip easily into the United States and make his way to Los Angeles or San Francisco, where he'd heard there was a large population of Chinese, where someone like himself could easily disappear, where he'd never have to eat another refried bean. But first, he had to get rid of Curtis.

In the six months he had been in Mexico, Chang had become very familiar with his surroundings. An inquisitive man by nature, he spent all his free time wandering the streets of the village and the surrounding countryside. He found the people to be friendly and humble, and very religious. Chang was a Buddhist, and had hoped beyond hope that he might locate a temple where he could worship, but was quick to realize the futility of this desire.

His need for the spiritual life was such that on occasion he would visit some of the Catholic churches in the area. He liked the smell of the burning incense, and though the peasants seemed a bit solemn on their knees, the women always in black with their veils and rosaries, the experience was for the most part quite comforting.

He was thinking of one of these churches now as he hurried down the narrow street with the stolen infant. It was a small building with a second, even smaller, building next to it, and a yard often populated with numerous young children. He had often stopped there to watch them play. It seemed like a happy place, a place where Curtis might find a home.

Chang arrived at the churchyard just after nine in the morning. He had intended on leaving Curtis on the doorstep but the door was open and the small building empty, so they went inside. The main room was clean and simple, a dozen or so beds lined up against two walls, a solid wood floor, well swept, plenty of windows and what appeared to be two smaller bedrooms at the far end.

Chang placed Curtis on one of the beds. Then he took a piece of paper and pencil from his pocket and began working on a note. Though he could speak a few words of Spanish he had no idea whatsoever how to write it, so naturally he wrote it in Chinese, pinned it to the child's clothing, kissed him goodbye, and bolted teary eyed out the door in search of a bus headed north.

Sister Angelica returned from mass a little after ten, along with the small group of orphans who lived at the compound. The children were happy to be done with the service and have the rest of the day free to play and most were being loud and rowdy, as one might expect after a morning of church.

Two of the children had begun tossing a small ball around the room and Sister Angelica told them to take it outside, but of course the boys couldn't help but toss it one more time. It was this final toss, passing over the intended receiver's head, that landed on the bed and brought forth a cry, one very distinct and all too familiar to Sister Angelica, who quickly discovered the infant with the note attached and sent one of the boys to fetch Father Carlos.

The nun rocked the baby gently in her arms while she waited for the priest to arrive, and he soon stopped crying.

Neither the nun nor the priest could make any sense of the note. And why should they? It was written in Chinese. If they could have read it, this is what they would have seen.

'I believe this baby was kidnapped a week ago, but I don't know from where. Perhaps the police can help you find his parents.' Then there was one more line, this one in English. This the priest could understand. It read: 'You take care Curtis.' And then immediately after, Chang signed his name in English so that the note appeared to read 'You take care Curtis Chang.'

The priest and nun studied the baby closely.

"Perhaps the little one is half Chinese," said the nun in Spanish, "and half gringo"

126

This made perfect sense to the priest. After all, the child's first name sounded like a gringo name and his skin was very fair, and Chang, well there was no denying its origin. The priest pointed to Curtis's eyes, and noted their slight slant. Yes, he was definitely half Chinese. They would save the note and show it to the next Chinese person who entered their small village. Perhaps then they would learn more about the young child. But for now, he would join the orphanage and they would love him like the rest of their flock.

His name would be Curtis Chang.

———

Frank Noble had hoped to take care of business in L.A. and get away without having to meet his new stepfather, but his mother was unrelenting. She had called four times since his arrival, each message a little more insistent than the previous one. Having spent most of the day dealing with the short corpse stuffed in the back of the Cadillac, Frank figured this would be as good a time as any to get the visit over with, so he called his mother and told her he'd be over for dinner around six.

Bunny Skinner lived in Newport Beach on a glorified sandbar known as Shark Island. Located in the middle of the bay, and accessed from Balboa Peninsula by a two-lane bridge, the island is one of the premier chunks of real estate in Southern California. Bunny and her new husband lived in a six thousand square foot home right on the water, with a ninety foot yacht parked right out front at their own private dock. Bunny, at 63, was still radiant, her blonde hair and shapely physique turned the eye of many men ten years her junior, including her new husband Gerald Skinner, who had just turned fifty a week before their wedding.

It was Gerald who answered the door when Frank finally arrived around seven-thirty. Gerald was a big man—Bunny liked them that way—six-two, two hundred forty pounds with an unforgettable face of lumpy mash potatoes. He had on an orange golf shirt, bright green slacks and a pair of beat up brown Topsiders. Frank instantly flashed back to the corpse they'd found in the Cadillac; he couldn't understand the attraction to these ridiculous shoes.

"Well, good, you made it."

"Sorry I'm late."

"Your mother was getting worried, but I told her he's a man full grown, no need worrying about him. I'm Jerry Skinner." He extended his hand.

Frank was still standing outside. He had been fixated on the bad wig atop Jerry's head.

"Well, come on in, son."

Frank extended his hand to Jerry and stepped into the house. "I'm Frank."

"Well, of course you are," said Jerry and slapped him on the back. "Bet you hit some traffic."

"Yeah, it took me almost two hours to get here."

"Well, L.A.'s hell. That's why we live down here in Newport. Salt water, fresh air, and a better quality people, if you follow my drift."

"There's my baby!" Bunny Skinner seemed to glide across the floor toward her son. She had on a short leather skirt and a pink silk blouse. She was in her stocking feet. When she reached Frank she lifted off the marble floor, throwing herself into his arms, and he quickly did his part and cradled her like a child. "Didn't I tell you he was gorgeous, Jerry?"

Frank blushed and tried to set her down, but she wrapped her arms tightly around his neck and kissed him hard on the lips. "Bunny…"

"Oh, now, don't you worry your little head, Frank, I'm not going to embarrass you. Can't a mother give her only son a kiss?" Where Frank had worked hard at trying to lessen his accent it seemed as though Bunny had gone to equal extent to exaggerate hers. Her head even seemed to move in congruence with her lips, like a marionette, only perfectly synchronized, even graceful.

"How about I fix us all a drink?" asked Jerry.

"Not for Frank. He don't drink."

"I'll have scotch," said Frank. "Straight up."

Frank finally managed to unload Bunny and the three of them went into a large den. The house was opulent throughout but Frank was not at all surprised. His father had been dead for over ten years, and during that time Bunny had been through two husbands, both of which had money, a good portion of which Bunny took with her when she moved on. Frank figured when Bunny left Jerry—and it was just a question of when, not if—she'd take a good share of his too. He felt somewhat sorry for Jerry, but considering the wig and the awful way he dressed it was probably only fair he should pay to spend time with a woman as beautiful as Bunny.

"Frank, I'm making you the whitest, sweetest looking piece of veal you ever saw." She turned to Jerry. "When he was a boy he used to eat veal at least three times a week. All his friends wanted hamburger, but my Frank had to have his veal. Veal parmesan, veal picata, veal this, veal that, I swear that boy's probably eaten a whole herd of baby cows by now."

Frank sat at the table poking at his veal with the tip of his fork. He hadn't eaten any veal in over five years, not since he'd busted a meth lab that was set up on a farm and seen the way the calves had been hemmed into cages and kept in the dark. One look into their eyes had cured him of that taste for life.

"What's the matter, honey, you're not hungry?"

"I guess I'm just not feeling very well."

"Ooh, and I went to so much trouble. But never you mind. If you don't feel well, you don't feel well."

"If you're not gonna finish that meat, hand it over to me Frank," said Jerry. "I'll be more than glad to help you out."

Frank slid his plate across the table. Why had he come? What did he expect to find? Bunny was never going to be the woman he grew up with, he should know that by now, and yet he kept showing up for more. He couldn't stand being in the same room with her and he wasn't even sure why. She'd never been mean to him and as far as he could remember, she was a good wife to his father.

So what was it? Did he expect her to stop living after his father died, to just lock herself indoors and grieve? Frank's father had been a solemn man, deeply religious and not one bit fond of flamboyant behavior. Was Bunny's life with him a false one or was this new life phony? Was his anger at her some sort of ridiculous loyalty to his dead father? Or was it her ability to move on in life, to accept change, was that it? And when exactly had he started calling her Bunny? It wasn't even her real name.

"So, what kinda gun you carry, Frank?" asked Jerry.

Frank took a swig of scotch. "It's a forty-five."

"Mind if I take a look?"

"Jerry," said Bunny. "We're having dinner."

"I just want to look at the man's gun, honey Bunny."

"Well, you can just wait until after we eat."

"Actually, I'm not allowed to let anyone handle my gun."

"Well, surely that don't count with family," said Bunny, rising to her husband's defense.

Frank took another drink; he was down to the ice now. "Well, maybe, after dinner."

"Sure, after dinner is fine," said Jerry. "And I can show you my collection."

"Oh, you like guns?"

"Honey, he's got a room upstairs full of every kinda gun you could imagine. I always said I feel sorry for the burglar that breaks into this house."

Jerry wiped his face and dropped his napkin onto his plate. "Honey, why don't you get us some coffee and I'll take Frank upstairs to look at my collection."

"Maybe you could just bring a few down here," said Frank.

"Oh, that's right. Frank don't like heights, Jerry. Been that way since he was a wee little thing. Why, I'll never forget the time, Frank was only seven or eight years old, and we went to New York on a vacation—Frank's father was still alive then, rest his soul—anyway, we took Frank on the elevator in the Empire State Building."

"Bunny." Frank thought "mother" but it still came out "Bunny."

Bunny waived Frank off. "Well, the elevator was packed, I tell you and Frank just vomited all over…"

"Bunny, please."

"Well, it's nothing to be ashamed of."

"Is this true, Frank. You can't even go up a flight of stairs?" There was a sparkle in Jerry's eyes as he asked Frank the question, as if he had just tapped into a vein of pure gold.

Frank stared across the table at Bunny. He was both angered and embarrassed.

Then Bunny lit up with excitement. "Oh, my, I never thought…"

"I think I can help you, Frank," said Jerry.

"With what?"

Jerry stood up. "Come on in my office, I'll show you. Don't worry, it's on the ground floor."

Frank hesitated.

"Go on, honey. Didn't I tell you? Jerry's a hypnotherapist. He helps people with all kinds of problems."

Frank got up from his chair and glanced over at his mother. This is the last time, he thought, the last time I appease her. He pushed the chair away and slowly followed Jerry toward his office. It wasn't a hypnotherapist he needed—he was sure of that—it was a new life. A brand new life.

TWELVE

Clint Stoner had been calling Tim Liddell's apartment for two days, each time with the same result: Tim's offensive message. This is what it said: 'If you're that big of a loser you gotta talk to a machine, be my guest.' Clint left about six messages, and then he gave up on the idea of reaching him by phone and drove over to his place Wednesday morning.

Tim lived in a small apartment complex in a seedy area of Santa Monica. His manager, an overweight, stringy-haired divorcee in her late forties named Darla, thought the world of Tim. He would often bring her part of his catch after a weekend of deep-sea fishing and, depending on what he brought, she'd either smoke it or throw it on the barbeque, and the two of them would engage in an orgy of fish, bourbon and potbellied sex. There were never any tender kisses goodbye, no mention of love, just pure lustful fun, no strings attached.

Clint told her he had been unable to reach Tim, and she mentioned that she too had been worried; Tim's rent had been due two days ago and it was not like him to be late. She handed Clint the key and told him to lock up when he left.

Once inside the apartment, Clint wasn't exactly sure what to look for, some sign that Tim had been there, perhaps; and of course his biggest fear was stumbling onto a corpse—the way Tim drank and ate he was a strong candidate for a heart attack.

He started in the bedroom. Tim's bed was unmade and his painting clothes were piled in a heap at the foot of the bed. There were other clothes scattered across the floor too, but that was perfectly normal; Tim was not big on housekeeping.

Clint moved cautiously toward the bathroom. That's where it always happens, he thought. Guy like Tim has a few too many, wanders naked into the shower, turns on the cold water full blast and grabs his heart; happens every day. But not this day, not to Tim.

Relieved at the sight of the empty bathroom, Clint went into the kitchen. It was a mess, as usual, dirty dishes in the sink, the food on them all dried up like it had been sitting there for a while. He checked the fridge; there were a few beers and half a carton of sour milk. Everything looked normal. Then he spotted a Domino's Pizza box on the kitchen table. He opened it up. There was grey mold sprouting from the pepperoni. Tim loved his pizza, practically lived on it; he would never let it go to waste.

Feeling quite proud of his astute detective work, Clint decided to call the police. He knew it would piss Tim off, but he had this gut feeling that something was wrong and he was getting a little bit tired of not knowing what it was. And he had to get that damn job done. If Tim had left town somebody else was going to have to run the crew. God, he might even have to go to work, himself. He grabbed a photo of Tim and some fishing buddies from the coffee table and left the apartment. He figured if he hurried he could make the report and still have time to squeeze in a round of golf.

The autopsy report on the short man found in the trunk of the Cadillac showed the cause of death to be the blow to the back of the head. The medical examiner couldn't say for sure what it was, but the victim had been hit with a large blunt object—something like a brick or a frying pan—so that rather than leaving a small deep gash like one would expect from a hammer or an axe, the weapon had created a much larger, flatter wound about the size of a compact disc, and had completely crushed a four inch section of the skull.

There were numerous bruises all over his body, suggesting a prolonged struggle with his assailant—or assailants—and there were pieces of skin under his fingernails, most likely taken from his attacker during the struggle, and more skin and hair in his mouth, suggesting the victim had bitten his attacker. There was also quite a bit of hard white residue beneath his nails, which was scraped out and sent to the lab for analysis.

As soon as he got the results back from the lab, Mr. Fuji, the examiner, put a call in to Kate Mallory, who was not surprised with the findings; she had figured the cause of death herself. What did interest her was the residue under the nails.

"So are you telling me our vic is a painter?"

"Well, if it was just the paint under his nails, I would say it could be a homeowner but I also found spots on his legs and arms."

"Wouldn't a homeowner also get paint on himself?"

"Oh, yes, this is very true, however, most of this paint had been on your victim for at least three days before time of death. Most people would clean the paint off their body at the end of the day. At least, I would. Someone who paints all the time, especially someone with poor hygiene habits, might not be so diligent. I'm pretty sure victim is painter."

"I see. But how do you know how long the paint was on him? Maybe he hadn't had time to clean up."

Mr. Fuji laughed. "Oh, that part is very easy. The paint is an oil-base enamel. It takes at least six or seven days for it to cure and it was completely cured, which means the paint had been there for at least four days before the murder. I'm going to check his lungs; probably nice shiny semi-gloss." Fuji laughed again. "Yes, I'd say odds are your victim is a painter…and a messy one at that. "

Kate hung up and tried to reach Frank to let him in on their break but he was out of the office. Then she sat down at her computer and went through all the missing persons' reports filed in the past three days. Somebody out there must be wondering why his painter hadn't shown up for work. She had obviously never hired one, herself.

134

Cervante was enjoying an afternoon of solitude in his apartment. He had picked up a copy of the *Anarchist Cookbook* and was hoping he could make some homemade bombs so as to both save money for the group and impress Wanda with his assiduity. He was so deeply engrossed in his studies he didn't hear the doorbell until the third ring. He set the book aside and stepped quietly to the front door, then checked the peephole. He didn't recognize the large blonde man but his initial reaction was one of fear.

He pulled back from the door. The bell rang again and once again Cervante peeked through the hole. The man had blue eyes and a nice complexion. Cervante particularly liked the shape of his lips; they were thin and the top one seemed to turn up just a little. German, he thought. He knew it would be best to keep quiet and let the man leave but his curiosity was getting the best of him. He opened the door just as the large blonde turned to walk away. "Yes?"

The man turned around. "Are you Raymond Dubois?"

Raymond took a deep breath. He wanted so badly to lose that name and he made up his mind right then and there that when this was all over he was going to go to court and make it all legal. "Yes, I'm afraid so."

The man pulled out his I.D. and showed it to Cervante. "Frank Noble, Secret Service. Mind if I come in?"

"Well, I should say not." Cervante gave Frank the once over then pulled back and opened up the door. As Frank squeezed through the narrow opening he brushed up against Cervante, who felt an instant rush of goose pimples.

"I was just doing some reading. Come on in the kitchen and sit down. Can I get you anything? Coffee, tea, me?"

Frank let out a patronizing laugh. "No, well, maybe some water. What happened to your head?" He was referring to the large bandage on the back of Cervante's head.

"Oh, just a stupid accident," Cervante called out from the kitchen. "Nothing serious." He grabbed a bottle of soda water from the fridge and two glasses. He set the glasses on the table and handed the bottle to Frank. "This one hasn't been cracked yet. Would you mind?"

Frank took the bottle and twisted off the lid and a rush of water spit out the top.

"Oh, my," said Cervante. He grabbed a dishtowel and reached for Frank's shirt. Frank intercepted and took the towel away from him.

"I can get it," he said. "I'd like to ask you a few questions about your job at the shopping center."

Cervante stared past the agent. "I was just doing some reading."

"Yes, so you mentioned. About the shopping center…"

Cervante sat down. "Oh, I'll bet you're here about those awful bombings. Those poor people. And in the lingerie department of all places."

Frank set the cloth on the table and poured himself a glass of water. He seemed distracted by something in the living room. Cervante turned around and looked. There were quite a few framed photos on the wall, mostly black and whites of two or more men in various forms of embrace. In one of the pictures three naked men were down on all fours, each one mounted by the one behind him. A fourth man was on his knees facing the man in front of the pack, his penis partially erect and inches away from the man's mouth. Frank leaned forward in his chair and squinted, then quickly pulled back.

"That's me in the middle," Cervante said. "I'm not afraid to admit I'm gay. I came out a long time ago. A very famous photographer shot all of those pictures. And don't worry, we're just posing."

"Sure," said Frank. He took a drink of water. "Now, according to your time card, you worked the graveyard shift on both nights the bombings took place." Frank glanced into the living room again then quickly back to Cervante.

"I prefer graveyard. During the day you've got all those

lonely housewives with their unruly brats running all over the place spilling their cokes and wiping mustard from their hot dogs on the mirrors."

"What I need to know is, did you see any odd looking characters hanging around? Maybe somebody fooling around in the lingerie department."

Cervante folded his arms and brought one hand up to his chin as though he were deep in concentration. Then he glanced down at the chair next to him and noticed the book he had been reading, sitting open. The picture on that page was of a homemade bomb. "Well, you know, I get off work at seven o'clock. I did see one person as I was leaving, I think he was Mexican but I can't say for sure."

"Was he in lingerie?"

"I wish!"

"No, I mean..."

Cervante waved his arm. "Just kidding. I think it was in lingerie; that's my favorite department and I always clean it last."

"Why is that?"

"What?"

"Why do you clean it last?"

"What's that?"

"The lingerie department. You said you like to clean it last."

Cervante didn't remember having said that. "Oh, well I, I just like to look at things. Women get to wear the best clothes, don't you think?"

Cervante looked down at the book again. It was making him nervous and yet he couldn't very well reach over and move it without Frank seeing him; still, he knew he had to do something before the agent spotted it. "Have some more water," he said and as he reached over the table to grab the bottle he knocked Frank's glass over onto his lap. Frank jumped up from the table to get out of the way and as he did, Cervante pushed the chair with the book under the table, grabbed the towel he'd given to Frank earlier and started wiping up the water. "God,

I'm so clumsy. Did I get any on you?"

"No, no, I'm fine. Listen, I'll let you go. I may need to come back again and we may ask you to take a polygraph. Do you have any problem with that?"

"Polygraph? Oh, you mean a lie detector? No, why would I object? You don't think I blew the place up do you? If I were going to blow something up, it wouldn't be ladies lingerie, I can tell you that; it's my favorite department."

Frank took one last look at the picture in the living room. "No…I guess not," he said, almost in a whisper.

"You can take a closer look if you want," said Cervante. "Nobody's going to reach out and grab you." His tone of voice had changed dramatically, from the light hearted gay, to the hard edge militant, and he knew it, but he didn't care. This guy was just too square. Cute, but square.

Frank's face was turning red. He'd already gotten much too close for comfort. He quickly changed the subject. "You know, you ought to have that looked at. Head wounds can be very dangerous. How did you say it happened?"

Cervante searched his mind. How had it happened? "Uh, garage door," he said. "Busted spring."

––––––––––

When he got back to his car, Frank took a moment to compose himself and then put in a call to Kate Mallory's office. She had good news.

"Our vic's a painter, Frank."

"What do you mean, an artist?"

"No, a house painter. He had enamel all over him, and Fuji said his lungs were coated, probably from years of fumes; and I thought my job was dangerous. Anyway, I've been checking missing persons to see if anyone's missing their painter. Any luck with any of the employees?"

Frank pulled away from the curb. The image of the four men in the picture filled his head. "Just talked to this queer, Dubois; he's one of the custodians. I think he's clean."

"It's gay, Frank."

"What's that?"

"The term *queer*, it's not exactly politically correct; at least not out here."

"Oh, well then, I apologize to Mr. Dubois in absentia."

"Dubois?"

"Yeah, Raymond Dubois. I checked his rap sheet, clean as a whistle.

"Raymond Dubois," said Kate, quietly. "That name sounds familiar. Well, anyway, we'll find out who this painter is, and maybe that'll lead us to our terrorists."

Frank was silent.

"Are you still there?"

"Yeah, sure," said Frank.

"Is there something else?"

"No, no, just, it's been a strange day."

"You're in L.A., now, Frank, every day is strange."

Vern Melnick had everything ready to go. The birdhouse he was making just needed a roof. He had cut all the pieces with his table saw in the spare bedroom and had left the shavings there on the floor along with the small scraps of wood. When they came for him the evidence would make everything perfectly clear. The old man had been building a birdhouse and then, wham, he makes a mistake and there goes a finger. Poor old fool.

Vern put his finger up to the blade; it was as sharp as a razor but at a sixteenth of an inch thick it could take your hand off in a split second. He pushed the starter button and the saw roared to life. He shut if off. It was time to make the call. This was the most important step. The call had to be made before the accident or he would run the risk of going into shock before he could get to the phone, and wind up bleeding to death. Wouldn't that be something? He could just see the headlines: Crippled Vet Bleeds To Death For Birds. He lifted the phone off the receiver and then he remembered the blood. Anybody who had just cut off a finger would certainly get blood on their phone when they called for help.

He hung up the receiver, and then wheeled himself back to the table, pulled a razor blade from a drawer and sliced the little finger on his left hand till he got a good flow of blood from it. Now he was ready. He wheeled himself back to the phone, grabbed the receiver with his bloody hand and dialed.

The operator answered. "Nine-one-one."

"I just cut off my finger."

"You just cut off your finger?"

"I believe that's what I said."

"Well, you sound awfully calm. Do you know if you place a fraudulent call to nine-one-one, you can be arrested?"

Blood was dripping down Vern's arm now and onto the floor.

"I'm not lying lady, I cut off my finger."

"Which finger is it?"

"Which finger? What difference does it make? Let's call him Reginald."

"Reginald? You have names for your fingers? How did you do this?"

Vern was beginning to get a little upset. "Look, lady, I'm standing here bleeding to death. I bit it off, okay. I was having lunch, a Waldorf salad, to be exact—and you know how crunchy those walnuts are—and before I knew what I had in my mouth, I bit the damn thing off."

"Now I know you're lying. You can't bite your own finger off."

"Oh, really. Suppose you come over to my house and I'll show you just how quick I can take a bite out of your ass!"

She hung up. Vern was furious. He hadn't been this angry since the day he came to in Vietnam and saw his leg laying on the table adjacent to his bed. He picked up the phone and dialed again. This time he got a man.

"Nine-one-one."

Vern screamed into the phone. "Oh, God, I just cut my finger off. Please help me."

"Okay, try and stay calm, sir. Is there anyone there with you?"

"My finger's gone," said Vern. He was really hamming it up.

He finally gave the operator the information he had requested and then hung up the phone. Then he wheeled himself back to the saw and placed his hand flat on the table right up against the sharp edge of the blade. He was not afraid of the impending pain, nor did he have any second thoughts about sacrificing his finger. He just didn't want to make any mistakes. If he cut it off too soon and the ambulance got lost, or somehow delayed, he could bleed to death. He would wait until he heard the siren up close; it shouldn't be too long. But what he heard next was the sound of his back door shutting and then Martin's voice calling out.

"Vern, you in here?"

"Jesus Christ," said Vern, and he rolled toward the bedroom door. "Go away, I'm busy."

Martin came into the room and saw the blood all over Vern's arm. "Vern, what happened?"

Vern bent his little finger back. "I cut off my finger. It's okay, the ambulance is on the way. You can go."

"I'll stay with you until they get here. We should try and stop the bleeding."

In the distance, Vern could hear the faint sound of a siren. "No, you can't. You have to get out of here."

"Vern, don't be ridiculous. Let me see your hand."

Martin reached down and grabbed Vern's hand and the little finger popped up. "I found your missing digit. What's going on here, Vern? Are you drunk?"

The siren was getting louder now. Vern grabbed Martin by the shirt and pulled him close. "Are you my friend?"

"Of course…"

"If you want to stay my friend, turn around and get out of the house. And don't ask any more questions."

Martin looked around the room. There was blood on the phone and on the table where the saw was, and next to that sat the vacant birdhouse. "Vern..."

"Go, now, please."

Martin backed out of the room and left the coach. He stood outside the door for a minute trying to understand the scenario he had just left, then slowly crossed the road toward his trailer. An ambulance entered the park and sped down Martin's street, siren blaring. Then there was another sound, a high pitch whine coming from Vern's trailer, followed by a short muffled scream. Martin froze in the middle of the street as the ambulance screeched to a halt right out front of Vern's weather beaten trailer.

The siren stopped and the two paramedics jumped out of the ambulance and ran inside Vern's house. Martin was close behind.

THIRTEEN

The night that Tim Liddell disappeared he had gone to the Straight Up, a small bar not far from his apartment in Santa Monica. Tim generally stopped there for a quick one on his way home from work during the week and spent most of his Saturday nights seated on his favorite stool throwing back shots of Jim Beam and munching on tiny fish-shaped crackers right up until closing time when Helen, the bartender, would snatch the bowl of crackers away and point Tim to the front door and the waiting taxi driver.

Sundays were a bit tamer. Tim would take a cab to the bar to collect his truck from the previous night, then he'd drift quietly inside for a couple of quick ones before heading home. That Sunday, Clint Stoner met him at the Straight Up around eight o'clock. Tim was still pissed at Clint for hiring Spike, and Clint was busy trying to explain why he had done it.

"Christ, Clint, you know how I feel about those fucking spear-chuckers and then you go and drop one on me like that."

Clint looked around the room. Not many blacks frequented the Straight Up, and Clint didn't see any now, but it still made him uncomfortable when Tim talked like that. "I didn't have any choice. You know how these people are; they were going to shut me down. Besides, Martin says he's doing a good job. Why can't you just flow with it?"

"Martin. Hah! If it was up to him he'd give the whole damn country back to the niggers and Indians, and me and you'd be on welfare."

Clint shot another uncomfortable glance around the room.

"Do you have to use that word?"

"What's wrong with 'Indian?'"

"Very funny. And what's wrong with Martin? I thought you liked him."

"Hey, you know, he's a good worker but he reads too many of those fucking liberal books and shit. I'll tell you what, though. All that would have to happen is for one of those brillo-heads to go after his sister and he'd change his mind real quick. Guaranfuckintee it."

"I don't think he has a sister."

"Well, if he had one; that's not the point." Tim rattled his ice at Helen and she quickly poured the two men another round.

Clint looked around the room again. There were two men sitting at a table in the far corner that kept looking over at them. He couldn't help but notice what an odd couple they were. One of them was a huge, flabby sort, with a balding head, and the other was very slight and tidy looking. "I think those two guys are watching us."

Tim sucked the ice clean of what little Jim Beam was left in his old drink, then picked up the new one. "What are you talking about?"

"They're back in the corner. Just kinda casually look over my shoulder."

Tim glanced over at the men. "Those two? Couple of faggots. What are you worried about?" He took a large swig off his drink and set it on the bar.

"God, keep it down, will you? They keep staring at us. Maybe they're from the INS. This thing with Chang's got me nervous. I can't afford to lose my license."

"Just make sure you keep that wet-back off the job and you won't have to worry about it."

"I didn't know Curtis was illegal. It's not fair."

"Hey, Clint, you don't gotta convince me. Far as I'm concerned though, they're all fucking illegal. It's just a bunch of bullshit. We whipped their asses a hundred years ago at the

144

Alamo, now they're taking over the fucking state. We whipped the Japs and they're taking over the whole fucking country. Bunch of shit."

"We lost at the Alamo, Tim."

"Shit. Now you sound like Martin."

Clint stayed long enough to have one more drink and then got up to leave, but not before he asked Tim to keep an eye on the two guys in the corner, in case they followed him out. Tim said he would but as soon as Clint got out the door he returned his attention to his drinking. All that talk about foreigners had pissed him off and he was going to need a few more shots to calm down. He didn't even notice the two men had left when he finally stumbled out the door around eleven o'clock.

Tim's truck was parked in the far corner of the lot behind the Straight Up. Helen had told him she didn't mind him leaving it overnight just as long as it was back out of sight; she considered it a bit of an eyesore, what with the rust and dents—as if any of her patrons cared.

Tim dug his keys out of his pants pocket and was about to unlock his pickup when he felt someone grab him by the shoulder, spin him around and punch him in the chin. Tim hit the ground hard and lay there unconscious.

Two-ton grabbed Tim's keys and started going through them, trying to figure out which ones fit the building where Tim worked.

"What are you doing?" Cervante asked. He was bouncing nervously, his head constantly in motion surveying the area.

"I'm looking for the key."

"Just take the whole fucking thing. Let's get out of here. And get his wallet. We need that card."

Then Two-ton felt a sharp pain in the fatty flesh of his right calf. He screamed and looked down to see Tim, his teeth dug into Two-ton's leg, shaking it like a dog with a rag doll. "Son-of-a-bitch! Get him off me."

Cervante grabbed Tim by the shoulders and tried to pull him from Two-ton's leg, but Tim managed to give him a good kick to the groin and Cervante went down. Now Tim reached one hand up and grabbed Two-ton by the balls, his other arm still wrapped around the giant's leg. Two-ton lifted his free leg and tried to kick Tim, but the instant his leg left the ground, Tim grabbed it and upended the big man, dropping him hard on his back, then—his right hand still squeezing Two-ton's balls—pulled himself on top of him and began pummeling his face.

"Fucking assholes!" said Liddell as he landed a blow to Two-ton's nose.

Cervante, who had been rolling in agony, clutching his groin, had finally managed to get to his feet. Liddell had slid all the way up to Two-ton's neck, pinning his arms in the process. The only consolation for Two-ton was that Tim had now released his balls and was using both fists on his face. Cervante watched in horror as the fat man squirmed and kicked his legs into space in a desperate effort to throw the smaller man off him.

"Don't just stand there, do something!"

Cervante wrapped his arms around Tim's neck and tried to pull him off Two-ton, but Tim gave him a stiff elbow to the solar plexus and once again Cervante went down, hitting his head in the process, and almost knocking himself unconscious. It was what he hit his head on that would soon change the course of the fight.

Somebody had left a couple of dented metal wheels next to the trash bin and when Cervante hit his head, the wheel he hit fell over with a loud clang. The blow had drawn blood and had narrowly missed the steel plate in Cervante's head, and it had really pissed him off. He grabbed one of the wheels with both hands, got to his feet, did a full spin like a shot putter, then another so that his arms were fully extended from his body, the weight and momentum of the wheel now pulling him forward, until finally, half way through his third spin, the wheel thumped into the back of Tim's head.

Cervante had hit Tim so hard the impact forced the wheel from his hands and sent Cervante crashing into the side of Tim's truck. The wheel, after crushing Tim's skull, fell onto Two-ton's hand, breaking three of his fingers in the process. Tim, his brains mashed, the life gone out of his eyes, remained upright for two or three seconds, then fell forward so that his groin was now on Two-ton's face, and compared to his bony fists, Tim's warm piss almost felt soothing on Two-ton's battered cheeks.

"I thought you said nobody would find the body?" Wanda threw the evening copy of the Times onto the kitchen table, and grabbed another slice of pizza from the box. Tim's death hadn't made the headlines but it did rate the front page, not because of the brutality involved—that was commonplace in L.A.—but rather the initials on his forehead; they added a grotesque element that tended to spark one's curiosity.

Two-ton picked up the paper and started into the article. His face was still swollen and his left hand was covered with bandages. "Says here they still don't know his identity."

"They have ways to find that stuff out," said Wanda, her mouth full of hot pizza.

"We smashed his teeth and burned his fingertips, Wanda. There's no way they're going to identify him," said Cervante.

"Says here they think he might be a house painter and if anybody is missing one they should call the police."

"You guys are a joke," said Spike.

"Nobody's going to miss a house painter," said Cervante.

"Oh, really," said Spike. "I worked with the motherfucker, remember? I know his boss. Believe me, he'll miss him."

"Maybe we should take care of his boss," said Cervante.

"Nobody's taking care of anybody unless I say so," said

Wanda. "If one guy disappears from a job site it doesn't necessarily mean anything, but if two do...cops aren't that stupid you know."

"I had a visitor today," said Cervante.

"That's nice Raymond, but we have work to do," said Wanda. I got the plans for the sewer system." She took a gulp from her Pepsi.

"It was a guy from Secret Service."

"Secret Service!"

"Says here he only had one shoe on," said Two-ton. "I don't remember that."

Wanda snatched the newspaper from Two-ton's hand and threw it on the table. "Do you mind?" She looked to Cervante. "What guy from the secret service?"

"Some big guy, good looking blonde."

Spike shook his head in disgust.

"Well, what did he want?"

"He just wanted to ask me some questions. About the bombing. Don't worry, I handled it. The guy's a moron."

"What's his name?"

"I don't know. Hogle, I think, something like that."

"Noble," said Spike.

"Yeah, that's it, Noble. I remember now. Like the bookstore."

"Isn't that spelled N-o-b-e-l?" asked Two-ton?"

"I don't think so," said Cervante."

"Who gives a fuck how's it's spelled!" said Wanda. She turned her attention to Spike. "And just how do you know this guy?"

"I seen him on TV. He's the President's main guy."

"You know, it's funny, Spike," said Cervante, "he looks a little like you. In a white way."

Spike jumped up from the table, reached across and grabbed Cervante by the shirt. "I'll rip your fucking heart out you little fudge packing piece of shit."

Wanda pulled her pistol and stuck it in Spike's temple. "Sit down, and cut the shit."

148

Spike gave Cervante a shove and the smaller man fell back in his chair and slammed his head up against the wall. Trying his best to maintain his dignity, Cervante casually pulled his chair back up to the table, as though he hadn't been ruffled at all, adjusted his glasses and began toying with the half-eaten slice of pizza on his plate; a narrow vein of blood trickled down his bald spot above the steel plate and disappeared into his hair.

Spike turned and stared right into the barrel of Wanda's pistol. "You gonna use that?"

"Don't press your luck," she said, then she set her pistol down on the table and opened up the plans to the sewer system. "Raymond, Two-ton. Pay attention, because I'm only going to go over this once. This is the area, right here. I want every manhole on this page mined." She looked at Cervante. "You think you and Tiny Tim here can manage that?" Then she grabbed another piece of pizza. "You're bleeding, Raymond."

Cervante just stared into the map, as though he were already down inside the sewers. "It's Noble," he said. "N-o-b-l-e."

Martin had been in the waiting room three hours before they finally wheeled Vern out of the operating room. He was still groggy from the drugs but the doctor said it was okay for him to go home. He gave Martin some pain pills and asked him to stay the night with Vern, and make sure he didn't open his stitches.

They wheeled him out to the Vega and unloaded him into the front seat. Martin was having a hard time getting the seat belt around the huge man and he was already mad at him so he just said "fuck it" and sped off from the parking lot. "Maybe if we're lucky, Vern, we'll get in an accident and you'll be catapulted through the windshield. That should yield a few bucks."

Vern muttered something incoherent and then closed his eyes and fell asleep.

"Just tell me why, Vern. I have a right to know."

They were sitting in Vern's kitchen. Martin was having a drink and Vern was fooling with the bandage on his hand, what was left of it. "Look around the room, tell me what you see."

"What?"

"It's a simple question."

"You know what I see, Vern. Is this some sort of game?"

Vern sat patiently waiting for Martin's accounting of his kitchen.

"Okay. There's a couple of microscopes on the table, there's ah, your slides, some books, a lot of dirty dishes, your jars of cockroaches…"

"My life. That's what you see. The confines of these walls in this tiny trailer, that's my life. I don't go shopping, I don't play golf, I don't even go outside—other than the rare occasion to save your ass. I sit in here and I do my work. It doesn't seem like a lot to ask for, does it?"

Martin just stared at his friend.

"Last week I got a notice from the owner of this property. It seems our illustrious city fathers want to raise the property taxes—actually, they want to double them—and of course the landlord, being the true American that he is, is passing the increase on to me. Do you know how much money I get every month from my disability? I'll tell you exactly how much: A paltry nine hundred and fifty dollars, a niggardly sum even for a man of my modus vivendi. That pays my rent, food—of which I grant I consume an inordinate amount; but all great fires need fuel—and leaves me a little extra for the appurtenances necessary for the continuation of my research, a research, I might add, taken on by yours truly with little regard for any recompense or commendation bestowed upon me for my significant contribution to modern science. But I'm not one to complain."

"So you cut off your fingers."

Vern raised his mutilated hand before his face. "Why not? Hell, I never use them anyway. Besides, I only meant to cut off one. I got interrupted"—he cast an accusing eye toward

Martin—"and had to rush the job. Damn saw sucked the others in." He brought the hand back down to his side. "Actually it turned out for the better. I'll get more money now."

"Vern, you could have asked me, I could have—"

"You could have what?"

"I would have thought of something."

"Look, kid, you're a nice guy and I think you're a decent writer, when you write, but you're not exactly—"

"What do you mean, 'when I write'?"

"What do you mean, 'what do I mean'?"

"You know what I mean, Vern. What are you implying?"

"Just that you're not exactly prone to prolificacy."

"It's just a temporary block, it'll pass."

"Well, so will a gallstone, eventually, but it's best to get rid of them while their small."

"Meaning?"

"Meaning, you keep waiting for some sort of…inspiration or something, some divine signal. It's so romantic…so…sophomoric."

At the word (sophomoric) Martin poured himself another shot and quickly downed it, then wiped his lips with his sleeve. Vern had frustrated him before, he could be obstinate and pig headed but he had never managed to get Martin angry. Not until now. "Well, maybe you're right, maybe I'm just dodging it, or maybe I don't have it, but what you're doing is nothing less than self-mutilation. It's sick."

Vern chuckled. "Oh, please. What do you call inhaling those obnoxious paint fumes everyday, or cleaning your hands in paint thinner? You don't think that stuff is going to catch up to you?"

"That's different. I at least try to wear protective gear. I mean, I don't lock myself in a bathroom and inhale lacquer."

"Listen, Martin, take a look at me, look at my life. I get up every morning at ten o'clock, I eat a little breakfast—okay, a large breakfast—I work at my desk for three or four hours—

hell, I don't even have a decent lab—I watch a little Oprah or Phil, have some dinner, if I'm lucky maybe you drop by for a couple drinks, and I go to bed. None of those activities requires the manipulation of any (or all) of the unfortunate missing digits. In fact, I probably haven't used them in ten years. Now I can use the money I'll get from them to continue my work. That's all I have. It's all I want. That's the difference between you and me. I'm committed."

"Is that what it takes, Vern, to be committed? You have to surrender parts of your body?"

"It takes what it takes."

Martin glanced at the mangled hand then quickly shifted his eyes down to the vacancy below Vern's knee, the words stacking up behind his lips like ammunition. It was the obvious question, the appropriate accusation, but he couldn't do it, didn't have the heart, didn't want to know.

FOURTEEN

When Marvin Sukowski turned up the alley behind Curtis Chang's house and saw what looked like Curtis's van parked alongside the garage, he thought he had finally got his man. He parked his car two doors down from the Changs and he and his partner, Jerry Bradley, got out. It was only seven-thirty but the temperature was pushing eighty and Marvin was already beginning to sweat.

Sukowski pulled his pistol from his holster; Bradley grabbed the shotgun from the car and cocked it. "You cover the front," said Sukowsi. "And remember, I want him alive."

Sukowski crept through the back yard like a cat burglar. He had waited a long time for this moment; he didn't want to make any mistakes. He reached the back door and tried the handle—unlocked. The smell of fresh coffee leeched through the walls, but it was not a welcome aroma to Sukowski; it only made him more aware of the heat. He waited another thirty seconds to make sure his partner was in place, and then he turned the knob, gave a kick on the door and burst into the house.

———

Juanita Chang had gotten up at six o'clock, made breakfast for her and Hector and then drove him to his job in Santa Monica; she hated driving the old clunker, but it was better than nothing. Carlos had spent the night with a friend and Juanita looked forward to having the house to herself.

She got back around seven-fifteen, put on a pot of coffee and started in on her daily chores. She was starting to worry about Curtis—she hadn't heard from him for three days—

and wanted to keep busy to keep her mind from imagining what horrible thing might have happened to him. She'd been through this dozens of time before; it never got any easier, still, she never complained; after all, he'd brought her into the country the same way.

She had gotten her laundry separated, the whites, the coloreds, permanent press, and had piled them by the washer just inside the back door. She counted six full loads, plus a few items she would have to wash by hand; it was going to be a long day. She poured herself a cup of coffee—she liked it black, and strong—and had just stepped through the entry way from the kitchen to the back porch when the door flew open, smacked into one of the larger piles of laundry, the darks, and then abruptly swung back into the man's path.

When the door hit him in the face, the man immediately dived into the room, rolling onto his back as he landed in the pile of white laundry, his gun held tightly in both hands, pointing up toward the inside of the door. There was nobody there.

The sound of the door busting open had startled Juanita, but she couldn't help but laugh at the sight of the large sweaty gringo lying in a pile of dirty towels and underwear. Then she heard the front door open and before she knew it Juanita was surrounded by two unattractive white men, their guns pointed in her direction.

The one with the shotgun spoke first. "Where is he?"

"Who?"

"Your husband. Su esposa."

By now the man on the floor had untangled himself from the laundry and had gotten to his feet.

"He's not here."

"Check the bedrooms," said the man with the pistol.

Juanita recognized the man with the smaller gun. He had been there before, poking around outside, peeking in the windows. Curtis had warned her about senor Sukowski. "Ay, Dios mio. Pinchi gringos dejennos en paz."

"I speak Spanish, bitch, so watch your mouth. Where's your husband?"

"I don't know. He doesn't live here."

"Oh, he doesn't live here, huh." He took a step back, reached down to the pile of clothes and pulled out a pair of men's underwear. "I suppose these are yours."

"Those belong to my son, but you can keep them if you want."

Sukowski approached the attractive woman. She was wearing a housedress and the top two buttons were open, revealing a small portion of her ample breasts to the agent. She instinctively reached up to button one of the buttons but he pulled her hand away. "Woman like you shouldn't be left alone. It's not safe."

He loosened another button on her dress, then put the tip of his pistol along the inside edge of her collar and moved it slowly toward her nipple.

His partner came out of one of the bedrooms. "Nobody here, Marv."

Sukowski pulled his gun away from Juanita. She was breathing hard but she was more angry than frightened. He pushed himself up against her and whispered in her ear. "I've had plenty of Mexican pussy, sweetheart. Maybe I'll come back and try you out."

"Si vienes otra vez, voy a cortarte los huevos."

"Good, get angry. Turns me on."

Juanita spit in his face. "I hear you prefer little boys."

The agent slowly wiped the spit away, and then he slapped Juanita's face with the back of his hand. "I'll be back. And when I'm through with your husband, you and I are gonna settle up." He motioned to his partner and the two men left out the back door.

Sukowski still had the underwear in his hand when he got outside. When he realized he was carrying it, he tossed it onto the ground.

"Think she knows where he is?"

"All that matters is he knows where she is. He's not gonna stay away from that stuff for long. I'll give him credit for that. I want somebody on this house, twenty-four hours a day. I want his ass."

"Looks like our John Doe is a painter after all," said Kate Mallory.

Frank was holding the phone away from his mouth so he could keep eating his sandwich without being rude to Kate. He hadn't had any breakfast and he had just gotten out of a three-hour meeting about the President's forthcoming arrival when she called. He swallowed a large bite. "You got a positive I.D.?"

"Well, we got a missing person report, filed by a Mr. Clint Stoner. His painting foreman has been missing since Monday and it sounds like our guy."

"Has he seen the body?"

"He came in about an hour ago, said he wasn't a hundred per cent certain what with his face all smashed in, but the good news is, the last time he saw him was Sunday night and he says there were a couple of suspicious looking guys watching them."

Frank's mouth was full. "So what do you think?"

"What?"

Frank had to spit half his bite out into his hand in order to talk. "I said, what do you think?"

"I think this could be our guy. Stoner is with a sketch artist right now trying to come up with a picture of the two men. I thought maybe you could go to the job sight and talk to the other men on Stoner's crew."

Frank set the remainder of his sandwich on his desk. "I just remembered. The guy from the barbeque place. What's his name?"

"Leroy?"

"Right. He told me a white guy, a painter, had tried to buy a gun from him. Do you suppose our vic was tied in with this terrorist group and somehow crossed them up?"

"It's a thought. Stoner brought in a picture of his friend. His name is Tim Liddell. I'll stop at Leroy's and show it to him and meet you at the job site, say in any hour from now."

Frank got the address from Kate, told his secretary not to take any more calls, then sat back to finish his lunch. He had less than a week to secure Los Angeles for the President's visit and the funny part was he couldn't figure out why in hell he would even want to come here.

"I sure would hate to be underneath that thing when they fill it full of bug spray," said Dudley. He was sitting on the edge of the roof with his feet dangling over the side, watching the men wrap the building next door with a huge colorful tarp. Martin and Hank were both sprawled out on the roof, shirts off, basking in the hazy sunshine.

"I'd say you've been caught under one of those tarps once too often already," said Hank.

"Uh, uh," said Dudley, "that's one thing I won't get near to is bug spray. I just kill em with my shoe at home. Hate that stuff."

Martin said, "Dudley, do me a favor, will you, and come away from the edge before you fall and break your neck."

"I ain't gonna fall."

When the door opened the three men assumed it was Spike returning with their lunch, but instead a tall blonde man in a dark suit stepped out onto the roof and made his way tentatively toward them, coming to rest about six feet from the edge. Martin's first thought was 'white Spike.'

"Who's in charge here?"

Martin pulled his sunglasses up on his forehead and propped himself up on his elbows. He was beginning to get annoyed with all these men in suits showing up asking questions. "Who wants to know?"

The man pulled his I.D. out of his jacket pocket. "Frank Noble. Secret Service."

Martin stretched his neck and squinted but he was too far from the agent to read the badge, and the man seemed hesitant to accommodate him by moving any closer to the edge; he was sweating profusely and his face had turned grey like the sky. Martin was afraid he might become ill at any moment. Then, the agent buried his left hand in his pants pocket and almost instantaneously the color returned to his face. He took a deep breath and leaned a little toward Martin, who reached out for a closer look at the ID.

Frank had never expected the hypnosis to work. In fact, he placed it right alongside Tarot cards, faith healing and reincarnation, all age old phenomena revitalized by nineteen eighties pop culture in a desperate attempt to romanticize the mystery of life and death, a mystery that to Frank was all too simple: you're born, a lot of shit happens to you, and then you die.

When he stepped into his step-father's office that evening, the first thing he had noticed was the preponderance of degrees plastered across the walls: B.A.'s, M.A.'s, P.H.D.'s, you name it. "Looks like you spent a lot of time in school. I didn't know it took that long to become a hypmotist."

"That's hyp-no-tist, Frank, with an n."

"Oh." Frank thought that was what he had said.

Jerry directed Frank to an overstuffed reclining chair. Frank sank into it and leaned back. He felt like a kid in a dentist's office. He didn't want to be there.

"The truth is Frank, none of these degrees have anything to do with hypnotherapy."

Frank wondered why anyone would take so much time to go to school for all those degrees if he didn't need to, and Jerry, as if he were reading Frank's mind, had explained.

"All these degrees are gotten through the mail, Frank. I don't normally tell my patients that, but you're family so I guess it's okay. You know what they say, `blood's thicker than mud.'"

And much more sticky, thought Frank.

Jerry put his hands on the arms of Frank's chair and leaned into his face. "I've been in this business twenty years, Frank, and I've been very successful while others have fallen by the wayside. Would you like to know why?"

Frank started to answer, wanted to tell Jerry that he really didn't need to explain, but he didn't even have time to separate his lips, let alone speak.

"I understand human nature, Frank. It's that simple. And would you like to know one of the most fundamental truths about human nature? Just this." He pulled back from the chair and pointed at his plaques on the wall. "Perception." He paused momentarily to let Frank absorb the full measure of the word. "The truth, reality, is only what we perceive it to be. If a client—notice I say 'client,' not 'patient.' I'm not a doctor, I make no claims to be one—if a client comes into my office and sees a dozen degrees on the wall, his faith in me is immediately heightened, he perceives in me a certain, shall we say, authority, an authority he has been indoctrinated to respect since early childhood. I call it the Authority of Paper—in fact, some day I intend to write a paper on that very subject, maybe submit it to the AMA; they don't think very highly of us, you know—anyway, like I was saying, the same principle holds true in all areas of life. In the case of your acrophobia, somewhere along the line, you came to believe—to perceive, Frank, to perceive—that high places were dangerous, and so heights took on a certain authority over you, a negative authority, granted, but an authority nonetheless. Rather than confront that authority you've chosen to avoid it, and the accompanying danger; the way you do that, of course, is, you make yourself ill, and, because none of us wishes to be ill, you simply stay on the ground, thereby avoiding the diversion of illness, which you created to protect you from the authority of heights. Any questions, so far?"

Frank stared blankly into Jerry's eyes.

"No? Good. Now, what I am going to do for you is the same thing these degrees do for most of my clients. I'm going to change your perception of reality. We don't have to waste time trying to discover why you are hypsophobic. It really doesn't matter. I'll simply put you into a hypnotic state then plant a suggestion into your subconscious mind, something as innocuous as pressing two fingers together or placing a hand in your pocket every time you feel threatened by your phobia. We'll just make it go away. Okay?"

Frank leaned back in his chair. His mother had married yet another nut. Yet, sitting there listening to him talk, Frank had felt himself drifting further and further from the scene until at last it seemed as though he were at the bottom of a well and Jerry's words were like drops of water splashing all around him.

———

Frank placed his ID back in his jacket pocket.

"We sure are getting popular up here," said Hank without opening his eyes.

Frank motioned to Martin. "You mind getting up and stepping over here?"

Martin got to his feet and moved closer to Frank. "If this is about that INS guy…"

"You know a man by the name of Tim Liddell?"

"Yeah, sure. He's the foreman here. Why?"

"A man fitting his description was found murdered a few days ago."

"Gee, who would want to hurt Tim?" said Martin. Hank got up and moved into the shade of the building. "Who wouldn't, might be a better question," he said.

"You want to come away from the edge so I can talk to you?" Frank was talking to Dudley, but Dudley was more interested in what was going on next door.

"Dudley," said Martin.

Dudley spun around and hopped down from the short wall.

160

"Somebody killed Liddell?"

"You fellows don't seem very upset about it."

"We're just not real surprised to hear it," said Martin. He glanced down at Frank's pocket; the government man looked very odd standing there questioning everybody while he appeared to be playing pocket pool. "You'd have to know Liddell. What happened to him?"

"We think he might have been involved with a terrorist group. Any of you ever see him hanging around with any suspicious looking people?"

Hank started to laugh. He pulled a cigarette from his shirt pocket and lit it. "Didn't he used to date Patty Hearst?"

"No," said Martin, "Jane Fonda."

"What's the joke?" asked Frank.

"Look Mr…"

"Noble."

"Tim Liddell liked to drink bourbon and complain. Would that about sum him up, Hank?"

"That's Tim."

"Even if he were to get political, I doubt any group would have him. What makes you think this, anyway?"

The door to the roof opened and Spike came through, pouring sweat and out of breath. He had taken to running up the four flights of stairs instead of using the elevator; Spike was proud of his physique and wanted to remain so. When he saw Frank, he dropped one of the bags of chicken and just stood there staring, oblivious to Hank's pleading for his food. The two men stood staring at one another and Martin was awed by their likeness. The door opened again and an attractive woman came through. She had a manila folder in her hand. She bypassed Spike and went straight to Frank. "Got the drawings of those two guys. Anything here?"

Her voice broke the spell that had come over Spike. He picked up the bag of chicken and moved toward the rest of the crew, all the time watching Frank. Frank tried to manipulate the folder with one hand but as it flopped open, the pictures spilled out onto the rooftop, one of them coming to rest at Spike's feet.

"Hey, Spike," said Hank. "Give it up." Spike handed a bag of chicken to Hank.

Martin had his eye on the attractive woman. "Let me guess," he said, "C.I.A.?"

She pulled out her badge. "L.A.P.D."

Frank took a few steps over toward Spike then bent over to retrieve the picture. For just an instant, the two large men were standing eye to eye, not more than six inches apart and a quiet fell over the crowd, a thick, caustic silence, hovering above their heads like smog. Frank turned away from him toward the attractive detective. "You know who this looks like? That guy, the janitor I questioned."

She grabbed Frank by the arm in an attempt to move him away from the crowd. "Dubois?" she whispered.

"Could be."

"Let's go," she said. "You finished here?"

Frank looked over her shoulder at Spike who continued to stare across the rooftop at him. "Yeah, for now," he said, and the two of them eased their way toward the exit. "Thank you for your cooperation, gentleman," said Frank and he and the woman bolted out the door, Frank's hand deeply immersed in his pocket. As soon as they were gone, Spike made his way toward the exit. "Where you going?" asked Martin.

"Left something in the car. I'll be right back."

Spike got to the ground floor just in time to see the two officers drive away. Then he ran down the street to the liquor store. A young boy was using the pay phone right outside the door. Spike grabbed him by the arm, hung up the phone and pulled him away from the booth.

"Hey, man..."

Spike just glared at the boy who mumbled a few incoherent

complaints and walked away. Spike lifted the receiver off the hook, put a quarter in and dialed a number. A voice answered.

"You better get the little fag out of there. The heat is on its way."

A month before he came to L.A., Spike was living a rather normal life in Memphis. He had moved in with his mother to help her with the mortgage on her house while she returned to school. His mother, still very attractive at forty, had been going part time, but now that her senior year was about to start, she wanted to plunge in full time and get it over with. So she quit her full time job as a clerk at the Bank of America and took a part time night job waiting tables. Spike, whose real name was Ronnie Davis, had just left the service a month earlier and was uncertain what he wanted to do, so it seemed only natural that he would move in with her, get a job and cut both of their overheads in half. His mother's name was Jackie.

One evening, as they sat watching the news together, the President of the United States came on to tell of his upcoming visit to Los Angeles where he would survey the reconstruction following the riots of the previous year. Standing a little behind and off to one side, was an attractive blonde haired man. Jackie Davis got off her seat and moved closer to the television, blocking her son's view.

"Momma, I can't see through you."

But Jackie couldn't hear her son's voice. She seemed in a trance. "Oh, my God!"

"What? Get out of the way, will you?"

Jackie pulled back from the television.

"What's wrong, momma. You look whiter than those crackers on TV."

"It can't be," said Jackie.

"Are you going to tell what you're talking about?"

"Turn up the volume, Ronnie."

Ronnie turned up the volume. The President was speaking.

"And I have all the confidence in the world in my long time friend, agent, Frank Noble..."

"It *is* him," said Jackie. "Oh, good Lord."

"Momma..."

"Sit down Ronnie, I need to tell you something. You remember I told you your father died in Vietnam. Well, you're old enough now to know the truth. I've been wanting to tell you for a long time but I haven't had the opportunity..."

"Momma, what are you talking about?"

"I'm talking about that man on the TV, the Secret Service agent. His name is Frank Noble. Ronnie, he's your father."

"What!" Ronnie studied the face closely. There was no denying the similarities between himself and the man on the screen. "He's white!"

Jackie told Ronnie how she and Frank had met at a club—she left out just what kind of club it was; no sense in getting him any more upset than he already was. She told him about their romance and how he had left for Vietnam. Ronnie sat silently as if in shock.

"Let me show you something," said Jackie. She got up and went into the bedroom. When she returned, she handed her son a gold watch. "He gave this to me on our last night together."

Ronnie inspected the watch. On the bottom were the initials, F.N. and an inscription. Ronnie had to squint to read the tiny letters. 'Happy birthday, Frank.' Ronnie put the watch in his pocket and got up from the couch.

"What are you going to do?"

"I'm going to L.A."

"Ronnie, don't. It was a long time ago. Don't go making trouble for yourself. Oh, I shouldn't have said anything."

"No, momma, you should have told me a long time ago. I'm going to return this watch to the man."

"But Ronnie, I have to start school."

"This won't take long. I'll be back."

FIFTEEN

Russ Holloway was working on his third jelly donut, chasing it down with a large cup of black coffee. The clock in the studio of KNOW radio said seven fifty-nine and Russ's assistants were busy preparing for the start of the show. Shirley, Russ's favorite, set a stack of papers next to the box of donuts on his desk. The top sheet had Russ's notes on the next topic of the day: homosexuals in the military. Russ stared at Shirley's crotch. She had a great body and her tight slacks accentuated every crevice.

"Yum, I love the filling," he said, and then licked the cherry gelatin from the middle of the donut.

"Be careful I don't sue you, Russ."

"Fellows," Russ yelled out to no one in particular, "you're my witnesses. I'm simply eating a cherry filled donut here and Miss Sexual Innuendo is trying to pull an Anita Hill."

A couple of the men in the studio laughed and Shirley grabbed the donut away from Russ. "Fifteen seconds, hon; better swallow your last bite."

Russ patted his large belly, wiped his mouth with his sleeve, let out a loud burp and smiled at his non-existent audience.

"Four, three, two, we're on," came the voice of his producer.

Russ started singing into his microphone, a cappella. It was a song from Jesus Christ Superstar, and Russ was doing his best impression of a homosexual. "I don't know how to love him..."

He sang the first two lines then went into his introduction for the program. "Aa-boo-nye, America, your hero is back, and no, I'm not gay, but we're going to talk about those fellows today, in particular about some of the legislation a few good Americans are trying to get passed into law that will stop giving the ho-mo-sex-u-als special treatment.

"But before we get into that, I have a special treat for you all. As you probably all know—and if you don't, you should—I have become very close friends with our great President during the past year, uh, I've been up to the White House for dinner on numerous occasions." This was a stretch, he was there once at a fund-raising dinner. "And, of course, I've had the President on my show." A five-minute interview over the telephone. "Well, I got a call last night from one of his staff who asked me if I would be interested in riding with our President when he comes to Los Angeles. For those of you who have been laid up in the hospital and haven't had access to your radio, the President will be arriving in a few days to tour the rebuilding of the riot torn areas and he, understandably, wants someone by his side who knows Los Angeles. Who better qualified than yours truly?

"So, I'll be there and if any of you have any questions you'd like me to ask him, you can call in during our next segment today and I'll be happy to jot down your request. Remember, I am first and foremost, your humble servant.

"We're going to take a small break right now, and when we come back, we'll be talking about the more gentler sex, and I don't mean women."

Martin got out of his Vega and stretched. The drive to L.A. everyday was beginning to wear him out and he had awakened that morning from a bad dream. And this thing with Liddell. Murdered? Not just killed in a fight but murdered and branded; the story was all over the news. Next thing he knew, reporters would be coming around asking a bunch of stupid questions. He wondered if it was somehow connected to his vision. He certainly hadn't seen Liddell in it; now that would be a nightmare. And what was the connection between Tim and these terrorists? Could it possibly have something to do with this job, this building? He couldn't wait to get it finished and get the hell out of there. Of course, he was free to quit at any time, but that just wasn't his style, never had been. He had always thought of himself as being the last one off the sinking ship and had always considered that to be a good trait. Now, as he stood there in the parking lot staring at the buildings around him, half of them still just burned out shells, he wasn't so sure.

As he headed for the door, a young boy came around the corner of the building. The boy kept looking nervously over his shoulder, as if someone were following him. Martin put his key into the lock, keeping one eye on the boy who was now just feet away.

"Are you Martin?" The boy looked vaguely familiar. "I am Carlos." Martin waited. "Chang," he added, almost as an afterthought. "My father works with you."

"I'm Martin. Where's your father?"

The boy moved closer. Once again he glanced over his shoulder. "I have a message for you. My father said to tell you to bring the ninos here on Sunday."

"Where is he? Did he find their mother?"

"I don't know. I have to go now. Sunday at twelve o'clock." Then Carlos ran off before Martin could get in another word.

He should have been relieved to get the message—June was getting a little impatient as a babysitter—but he'd had that dream last night, it had started out with his vision then quickly slid into a series of bizarre events. But one thing was definite: there were children in the dream. They didn't have faces, only voices, far away voices, voices filled with fear. And there was blood in the dream, puddles of blood, and the taste of blood. All this had horrified him but at least there had been a semblance of reality about it. The part that completely puzzled Martin came just after the shotgun was fired. There was a sensation of weightlessness and a panoramic view of bright colors, and music, far in the distance—a harsh, somewhat dissonant sound. No, he'd just as soon the kids didn't come anywhere near the building, not after that.

A car pulled up out front, Spike got out and the car quickly drove away. He had left the job the day before, right behind the two officers, and hadn't bothered to return. Martin figured he better talk to him; with Liddell gone, Stoner had put him in charge of the job, and although Martin didn't like the idea of being a boss, it was definitely a step up from having Clint around.

He waited at the front door for Spike, who moved slowly, staggeringly, toward him. His painting clothes were wrinkled, as though he had spent the night in them. He carried a brown paper bag in his hand.

"What happened to you, yesterday?"

"I had some business to take care of."

"Don't you think you could have said something?" Martin looked at the bag. He knew the shape of a half-pint when he saw one. "You had any sleep?"

"You ain't a bad guy, for whitey, but don't push it, okay?"

"What the fuck does that mean? And what was all that shit between you and that secret service guy?"

"It means, I know who Nat Turner is. Sum us niggers do read, you know?"

Martin wasn't sure if Spike was about to cry or commit murder. He didn't want to bear witness to either and he was wise enough to drop the matter right then and there, in case it was the latter of the two. Spike reached into the bag, unscrewed the cap and took a huge gulp from his bottle, then pushed his way past Martin and into the building. Something big was coming, Martin was sure of that. He was also reasonably sure there wasn't a damn thing he could do to stop it.

It had taken Frank Noble and Kate Mallory fifteen minutes to cut across town the previous afternoon from South Central to Raymond Dubois's apartment in West Hollywood. When they arrived, two uniformed officers were waiting in a patrol car. The four of them entered Raymond's apartment, guns drawn, but Raymond was already gone, along with his clothes and some of his personal possessions. There was one picture still up on the living room wall—the one that had bothered Frank so much—and taped to it was a note. Kate Mallory pulled the note from the picture. This is what it said.

'To the handsome blonde officer—is it Frank?—to remember me by. Hope to see you again. Love. Cervante.'

She handed the note to Frank. "It's for you."

Frank read the note and blushed. He pointed to Raymond in the picture. "That's our guy," he said.

Kate took the picture off the wall and handed it to one of the officers who just shook his head in disgust. "Have the lab blow up some photos of this guy's face," she said, "and get an APB out on him, right away." She turned to Frank. "Looks like you scared him away." She was slightly irritated.

The second officer came out of the kitchen. "He must have left in a hurry, stove's still warm."

Frank looked at Kate. "Maybe somebody tipped him off."

"Maybe," said Kate. She pointed to a package in the uniformed officer's hand. "What's that?"

"I found it in the kitchen. Looks like some kind of diapers or something. Says Depends. Think there's a baby…"

Kate glanced over at the picture. "I don't think so. Go ahead and tag it."

The officer shrugged his shoulders. "This apartment sure gets a lot of action."

"What do you mean?" Kate asked.

"I was here a few years back on a rape and assault case. Some guy took a baseball bat to this queer's head, then raped this chick, uh, woman, and…"

"And then killed himself," said Kate. "I knew I'd heard that name before. Dubois published a gay magazine…"

"Well, I guess that makes sense," said Frank.

"Yeah, nothing slick, newsprint with art and gay culture. Anyway, he exposed this guy—some actor—as a homosexual and the guy flipped out."

"Who was the girl?" Frank asked.

"I don't remember her name. I think she was a model. That'll be easy enough to check. In the meantime, why don't we talk to some of the neighbors, see if anybody saw our friend leave." Kate paused and looked around the room. "Hard to imagine."

"What's that?" asked Frank.

"It's just, well, everyone's so open about their sexuality these days, it's hard to imagine someone being so frightened he'd actually kill himself."

"It's even harder to imagine someone actually intruding in other people's lives like that. It's a rotten thing to do."

"I guess Mr. Dubois hasn't dealt too well with the guilt," said Kate.

"We're going to help him deal with it."

———

After she was raped, Wanda Moore had bought a house in Malibu Canyon and let Two-ton live there as part of their deal. Two-ton had proven to be a loyal protector and when Wanda changed her name and told him of her plans, he went along, not out of any political persuasion but out of care for her; and of course he had been late getting to her house that fateful night. It wasn't guilt so much as a debt he felt he owed her. For this, he would stay by her side till the end. So when she told him he had to let Cervante come and stay with him, he hadn't uttered one word of protest. In fact, he rather liked having Cervante around. Of course, Cervante thought Two-ton was a Philistine, and absolutely abhorred his personal habits, yet he couldn't deny the feeling of safety he had in Two-ton's presence. Two-ton was without fear. Cervante, well, Cervante slept with a light on.

The first thing Cervante did when he got to Two-ton's

house was start cleaning; the place was a disaster—Two-ton was not big on cleaning—and Cervante wasn't about to spend one night there in those conditions. He sent Two-ton to the store for some cleanser, paper towels, sponges and plenty of disinfectant. He had also added an item that had completely stumped Two-ton and had caused the checkout girl to blush. When he asked Cervante what the diapers were for, Cervante replied that in his younger days he had been a real "two-fisted" kind of guy. Two-ton had no idea what he was talking about and dropped the subject.

Two-ton also picked up a keg of beer while he was out and had just tapped into it when Cervante started work on the kitchen.

"Are you going to drink that whole thing?"

"I need the empty."

"What for?"

"For a bomb. You didn't think we were going to blow up the President's car with one of those little land mines, did you?"

"How would I know? Before you get too drunk, I could use some help."

"I'd like to help you Cervante, but I'm allergic to the chemicals."

"Well, you could sweep the floor or something."

Two-ton poured himself a beer. "Too much dust," he said. Then he walked into the living room, turned on the TV and sunk into the couch.

"How about the dishes then?" Cervante had followed him into the living room.

"Sure, soon as this show is over. You should watch this, Cervante, it's all about women who used to be men."

Cervante started to respond to Two-ton's last remark but quickly let it go; why was it so many people had this idea that all homosexuals wanted to be women? Besides, first things first. He needed to devise a game plan for attacking the kitchen. There was a huge pile of dirty dishes that had obviously been sitting there for days—mold was beginning to form on a few of the plates, a spider had weaved a web in one of the glasses—and Cervante didn't want to do the floor until the dishes were done; that would mean waiting for it to dry and all that time the mold would be spreading. Just the thought of that gave him the creeps.

He donned a pair of plastic gloves and started relocating the dirty dishes from the sink to the counter top, grabbing each one by his fingertips, holding it as far away from his person as possible. He missed his apartment already.

―――――

"Are you sure I can't get you something?" asked Wanda. She took a huge bite out of her cheeseburger. She had two of them on her plate along with a large portion of french-fries, and close at hand, to wash it all down, was a large bottle of Pepsi-cola.

"No, thank you," said Kate. She and Frank were sitting on the couch in Wanda's apartment. Frank found Wanda very attractive, but thought her hair was too short, and her clothes too masculine. She wore a drab brown shirt and slacks and heavy looking hiking boots that looked new and uncomfortable. And she was overweight.

"I don't really know Mr. Dubois. I just moved in here a year ago, and I keep to myself most the time."

"So you didn't notice him leaving his apartment this morning?" asked Frank.

"No, but I was out for a while. I went to the store."

"Do you mind if I look around?" asked Kate. She had gotten to her feet.

"Well, what for? I mean, you don't think he's here, do you?"

"No, of course not," said Frank. He looked suspiciously at Kate. He felt sorry for Wanda, who was obviously just a lonely, simple girl. With some new clothes and a diet she could be quite a looker.

"If there's a problem…" Kate started to say.

"Oh, no, go ahead. I have nothing to hide."

Kate left Frank and Wanda and made her way down the

hall toward the bedroom. Frank wondered just what it was she thought she was going to find, but he was happy nonetheless to be left alone with Wanda. "What kind of work do you do, Wanda?"

"Well, I'm unemployed right now," she said and smiled.

"You know, it's funny, but you look familiar to me. Ever been to Memphis?"

"No."

Wanda kept glancing down the hall toward where Kate had gone. Frank tried to cover. "Sorry about that. She's a good detective but not a very good judge of character, I'm afraid."

"Well, she has to do her job, doesn't she?"

There was an edge to Wanda's voice, as if she were defending Kate. Frank found that somewhat odd. "Well, I think this terrorist business has got us all a bit jumpy. I've been in the Secret Service a long time and I can tell you, terrorists are the hardest to figure. If you saw the guy we pulled out of the back of this Cadillac. Brutal."

Wanda seemed to stare right through him. "Well, I suppose there are many types of terror, Mr. Hogle."

Frank started to correct her pronunciation of his name but was interrupted by Kate, who had returned to the living room and seemed eager to leave. She and Frank thanked Wanda for her cooperation and let themselves out.

"Fucking idiots," Wanda said to herself as she closed the door behind them. Then she went to the phone and called Two-ton's house.

———

Two-ton set his beer on the floor and answered the phone. "He's cleaning the kitchen. Okay, I'll tell him." Two-ton hung up and walked into the kitchen. "That was Wanda on the phone."

Cervante was bent over mopping the floor. He looked up at Two-ton. "I just mopped that!"

Two-ton looked down at his feet. "Oh."

"What did she want?"

"She's coming over. She wants you to write another letter."

Cervante perked up. "Really?"

"That's what she said. I need some more beer."

"I'll get it. Just get off my floor. Is she bringing the type-writer?"

"I don't know. Can you hand me some chips, too?"

Cervante grabbed a bag of chips from the cupboard and filled Two-ton's glass with beer, then tiptoed over to Two-ton and handed them to him. Two-ton ripped open the bag with his teeth and spit the piece of torn bag onto the floor. Cervante looked down at the small bit of trash and then up at the awkward giant.

"Sorry," said Two-ton. Then he took a huge swig off his beer and the foam rushed down the side of his mouth and onto the floor. Two-ton burped and headed for the living room.

"You don't actually believe that girl is involved with the likes of Raymond Dubois, do you?" Frank fastened his seat belt as Kate pulled away from the curb.

"If I remember correctly, you thought Raymond Dubois was clean, too."

"Well, yeah, but, come on, you saw her. She's so timid, she's practically a kid."

Kate reached behind her jacket and pulled a small paperback book from her jeans and threw it in Frank's lap. "Well, maybe you can explain her taste in literature."

Frank picked up the book. "*The Anarchist Cookbook*" he said. "This was in her house?"

"That's right."

"You took it, without a warrant?"

Kate shook her head. "If we had gone for a warrant, Frank, it wouldn't have been there when we got back."

"Yeah, but..."

"Look inside the cover."

Frank opened the book. Down in the left hand corner were the initials, R.D. "What about it?"

"R.D., Frank. Raymond Dubois."

"That could stand for anything, Kate. Maybe she bought the book used, or maybe it was there when she moved in."

"She had other books, too."

"Yeah, so?"

"Ever heard of a book call *Backlash*, by Susan Faludi?"

"Can't say as I have."

"I'm not surprised. It came out a couple of years ago. Ms. Faludi used to be a model. Anyway, the basic thrust of the book is that models are exploited by advertisers in order to create their image of women."

"You sure spend a lot of time reading."

"I realize that makes me a bit of an anomaly, Frank, especially for a cop, but it does help me with my job."

"Well, just because she reads women's lib books, doesn't make her a terrorist."

"Not by itself, no. But I have a feeling about Miss Blade, if that's even her real name. The girl that was attacked in Dubois's apartment was a model, and look at the targets of the two bombings."

"You don't think this girl was a model, do you?"

"I admit she doesn't quite fit the bill. But something's not right. That much I know."

"If you're so sure she's involved, why don't we just arrest her?"

"I'm not sure. But I want to put somebody on her and do some checking."

"Fine with me." Frank tossed the book onto the seat. Then he took a deep breath and slowly released the air.

"Something wrong?" said Kate

"Ever get tired of it, Kate? Being a cop?"

"You sound like my partner. The answer is no. I like my work."

"Yeah, I guess you still would at your age. And before you get worked up, I don't mean that in a bad way, it's just, you're still south of thirty so I can understand the attraction to the work. But for me, all I'm seeing is an ugly world that just gets uglier every day."

"Sounds like you need a vacation."

"Yeah, a permanent one. My grandfather has a cabin in the woods above L.A. I used to go there every summer when I was a kid. It's funny. A lot of what Pop taught me about tracking animals and surviving in the woods helped prepare me for this job. He's been gone for years now; place is just sitting there empty. Sometimes I think I'd like to live there, just drop out, let somebody else catch the bad guys. Maybe do some fishing."

"You can fish right here, Frank. And it's a much bigger catch."

"Yeah. But it's too big a pond. Too many fish."

Kate laughed. "That's true. And very few of them ever hit the frying pan. But when they do, you have to admit, it's a beautiful sound."

Frank smiled. "Yeah," he said softly. "I suppose it is."

Sixteen

The note on Officer Wade Parker's locker read: Report to watch commander before you check in. Wade couldn't imagine what he might have done to receive such a note; he was never late, rarely missed a day's work, and his productivity was beyond reproach. But the fact was, such requests usually meant some form of chastisement, and of course everybody in his row of lockers had already read the note before Wade and were now busy giggling and whispering just loud enough for Wade to hear their snide remarks. Wade was not well liked among the other officers. He was a loner with a one-track mind: write tickets.

Wade took his time dressing, doing his best to ignore the chatter in the dressing room. He had just gotten his uniform back from the cleaners, and checking himself in the mirror as he buttoned his crisp brown shirt, he couldn't help but feel a strong sense of pride, and at the same time, a surge of anger. He had probably made some technical error on one of his citations, some bullshit mistake that resulted in a dismissal, and now some fat sergeant who could no longer remember what it was like out there in the trenches was going to read him the riot act.

Helmet in hand, his leather gloves nestled within the cavity, boots pounding out a steady rhythm against the hardwood floor, Wade paraded down the hall toward Sergeant Jack Anderson's office. He'd heard all about Anderson, had seen him in passing, but the two men had never met. The sergeant had spent twenty-five years on the street before taking a bullet in the spine that had left him partially crippled and just recently stuck behind a desk. However, word around the station was he had not let it affect his good sense of humor. He was always quick to make a joke about his gimp leg, lest anyone feel they had to tiptoe around him.

When Wade reached the office the door was slightly ajar. He tapped lightly, then stuck his head inside.

"You wanted to see me?"

"Yeah, come on in Parker, shut the door."

Wade entered the smoky office. Anderson set his pencil on top of the stack of papers before him, leaned back in his chair and ran his hands through his still thick grey hair. The butt-end of a cigar discharged a thick stream of smoke into the sergeant's chubby face, but he seemed to pay it no mind. "Got a call about you this morning," he said, his eyes transfixed on the spit and polish officer.

Wade shifted his weight and cleared his throat. "Is there some kind of problem?"

"Problem? No, no, not at all. Have a seat, Parker." There was something about his voice that bothered Parker. It had a monotone quality, as though the man were deep in thought— about Parker?—trying to solve some puzzle.

Parker sat down and set his helmet in his lap.

"How long you been on the force?"

"Twelve years."

"Twelve years, huh. Traffic?"

"That's what I do best."

Anderson brought his chair down on all four legs and took his hands out of his hair. Then he picked up his pencil and began tapping it on his desk. The single window behind him was shut and now with the door closed the smoke was beginning to fill up the room. "I looked through your file. You've issued more citations than anyone on the force. You aware of that?"

"I try to do a good job."

"Yes, I should say you do. Well, evidently you've impressed

a few people." He took a draw off the cigar and set it back in the ashtray.

"Sir?"

"Did you know the President is arriving this weekend and is planning a tour of our fair city, in particular, the riot areas?"

"I heard rumors."

All kinds of thoughts were racing through Officer Parker's mind. Was he being warned not to issue any citations to the President or his staff? Because, if he was, they'd be in for a big surprise. The law is the law, and violators got cited in Parker's territory. He looked down at the cigar. He wanted to say something about it, the smoke was making him nauseous, but it was almost finished so he kept quiet.

"Well, Parker, the rumors are true. And, I won't beat around the bush, you've been hand picked to lead the tour. Quite an honor, I might add."

Did he really mean that, about it being an honor? Parker couldn't tell. There seemed to be a touch of irony in everything the sergeant said, plus all this smoke was beginning to make Wade dizzy. "I see. When would that be?"

"This Sunday."

Parker bowed his head. He was deep in thought. The first three hours of the Sunday beat were the best. Plenty of drunks who had passed out in their cars after the bars closed on Saturday would be on their way home early Sunday morning, half-drunk and half-asleep. Easy targets. Big stats.

"You don't look very pleased."

"Oh, I am. It's just…I hate to miss work. What time is this tour?"

"You'll need to report here at nine o'clock." Anderson grabbed what looked like a schedule from the desk. "Now, according to this, you're scheduled for first shift this Sunday, so it looks like you'll get to sleep in a little later." He snuffed out the butt and pulled a fresh cigar from his shirt pocket, bit off one end and lit it. Parker coughed. "Smoke bother you?"

"No, that's, fine. If it's all the same to you, sir, I'd…"

"Don't call me sir, son, I'm just a sergeant." It was the first time he'd changed the tone in his voice.

"If it's all the same to you, sergeant, I'd just as soon patrol my beat for three hours and then report for the tour."

"Well, we can't do that. Then you'd have to be paid overtime and I'd have to fill out a bunch of papers." He motioned toward the stack on his desk. "I need that like a fucking hole in the head. You just show up here at nine."

"But…"

Anderson stood up from his chair, supporting himself on the edge of the desk. He obviously favored his right side. He extended his hand to Parker, who now also stood. "That'll be all, Mr. Parker. Congratulations."

Parker shook hands with the older officer and left the office. He wasn't sure what angered him more, the stench of smoke on his clean shirt, or the bullshit duty. There had to be a way to be on the beat those first three hours and he was damned if some peg-legged, smoke-stack of a sergeant was going to keep him from it.

"That's it? That's the whole thing?" Two-ton was standing over the stove about to flip a couple of hamburgers.

"You know how Wanda is, she likes things concise," said Cervante.

Two-ton flipped his burgers and then slapped a couple of slices of American cheese on each one. "Sure you don't want one of these?"

Cervante shook his head. "The idea of a blood vessel is for it to transport blood, not grease. Especially not at ten o'clock in the morning." He leaned up against the refrigerator. He had a small notebook in one hand and a pencil in the other, which he was now tapping against his chin. "Maybe you're right. Maybe I should add something else."

"I don't know nothing about writing, so you shouldn't probably listen to me. Let me hear it again."

"You've forgotten it already? It's only five words long."

Two-ton pushed the button on the toaster and two buns disappeared into the wide-mouth contraption. He loved to shop for food and anything else equated with cooking, and his toaster was his prize possession. He also had a twenty-two-cubic-foot General Electric refrigerator (complete with ice-maker and swivel shelves), two electric can-openers, three waffle irons (one Belgium, two regular), half a dozen non-stick frying pans, custom made hardwood cutting boards, backup sets of dishes, glasses and utensils assuring him of never actually having to clean anything if he didn't want to. He rarely wanted to. "I just want to hear it out loud again. Indulge me."

"Okay." Cervante pushed off from the refrigerator. "YOU PEOPLE ARE FUCKING STUPID!"

Two-ton's bread popped up and the big man wiped his hands on his apron and pulled the warm buns from the toaster. "It sounds good…"

"But."

"Well, it sounds like something Wanda would say when she's angry. It doesn't sound like you. Maybe if you told them why they were stupid. I mean, if they are stupid, how else will they know what you're talking about?"

Cervante watched with disgust as Two-ton squeezed puddles of mustard and ketchup onto his buns then plopped the cheese covered greasy burgers on top, causing the excess condiments to squeeze out and drip down the side of the bread. Then he smashed a handful of sliced pickles into the melted cheese and topped it all with a thick slice of tomato and a few crisp leaves of lettuce. He squeezed more mustard and ketchup onto the top half of the bun, spattered it heavily with salt and stuck it onto the lettuce. Then he repeated the entire process for his second burger.

"Tell them why they're stupid? They're stupid because they think they can catch us. They're stupid because they have peo-

181

ple like that cute Frank fellow in charge who couldn't find his asshole with a four-pack of Charmin."

"Oh. What's Charmin?"

"It's toilet paper. Haven't you ever seen that ridiculous commercial? With all the television you watch, I would think you'd know them all by heart."

Two-ton had taken a large bite from one of his burgers. A thick slime composed of grease, mustard and ketchup was dribbling its way down his chin. "I always mute the commercials," he said. "Except for the food ones."

"I better work on this. Do you have everything ready for tomorrow?"

"I just need to install the detonators. I sure hope Wanda's maps are right."

"Don't worry about Wanda. She knows what she's doing. And come Sunday you and I will make history."

Two-ton opened a beer and took a swig. "Just remember, Cervante. I ain't going to jail. I hear the food there sucks. I'd rather die first."

But Cervante wasn't concerned with any talk about prison. He was busy trying to figure out what else to put in the letter. It had to be succinct but not bland—he was, after all, a writer—angry but not hysterical, and most of all, it had to have poetry. Two-ton was right. His first effort was his attempt to write the letter Wanda would want, but Wanda was not a writer, Wanda was not a poet. Why, if it hadn't have been for his slight case of misjudgment regarding Perry Griffin, who knows what success he might have had as a writer. But that damn steel plate had fucked up his thought processes, making it difficult for him to concentrate. True creative genius required extensive powers of concentration. Who knows, he might have become the next Tennessee Williams, or Truman Capote. They had so much in common, had suffered for their individuality.

But all that was gone now; now there was only the letters. The first one was good, had even surprised him, but Wanda had been a big part of it—didn't she trust his talents?—but this one, this one would be his and his alone to write, perhaps his last, and millions of people would read it. It was a chance to show the world just how deep his talents ran, a shot at immortality. A shot at immortality, he repeated to himself.

Wanda Blade pulled her red Corvette into the parking lot of the Long Beach Holiday Inn and drove around to the far side of the building where her car couldn't be seen from the road. She had received the Corvette from Electra Bras in 1986 as part of a bonus package, which also included a time-share in Hawaii and a ten thousand dollar gold necklace. She sold the time-share shortly after the rape. The necklace had been ripped off her during the attack and eventually pocketed by one of the police officers that had responded to the emergency call that evening.

The Corvette was all that remained now from that other life and it had gone through a metamorphosis not unlike that of Wanda's. The convertible top was torn in several places, the once bright red paint had oxidized to a shade of dirty orange, much of which had chipped away, exposing a patch work of rusty metal. The interior reeked of mildew during the winter, thanks to the leaky top, and was bleached out in spots where the sun blared through during the summer. Wanda had no idea if the top could even be made to come down, for she had not attempted to do so since that fateful night. She had never once during those years really felt like letting the wind blow freely through her hair, which was too short now for that kind of thing anyway.

She went into the building through a rear door and took an elevator up to the third floor, making sure all along that nobody was watching her. When the elevator doors opened on the third floor, Wanda just stood there, her eyes closed, one hand on her forehead. She had felt a little weak that morning and now all of a sudden there was an awful headache and a bit of a fever. When she looked up again the elevator was at the fifth floor and a couple of women were getting on.

One of the women started to push seven and Wanda grabbed her arm. "This elevator's going down."

The woman looked up at the arrow pointing up. "But the arrow..."

"Fuck the arrow, lady. I said it's going down."

The two women quickly exited and Wanda rode the elevator up to the sixth floor where a man stood waiting to get on. The arrow changed to down. Wanda told the man the elevator was being repaired, and then she shut the doors before he could get in and proceeded back to the third floor. She felt like shit.

She was about to give the familiar tap on the door to room 308 when it opened and a strong hairy arm reached out and grabbed her by the neck and yanked her inside.

"Where the hell have you been?" The man shut the door. Wanda pushed his hand away from her.

"I've been busy entertaining."

He tried to grab her around the waist; she pushed him away again.

"What's with the cold shoulder?"

"I don't like being mauled. You got anything to drink around here?"

"Yeah, sure. What do you want?"

"You got any Coke, and some aspirin?"

The man, Charles Kramer, walked over to the small table and poured himself a scotch and grabbed a Coke from the fridge for Wanda. He was fifty-five, thinning on top, but still in good shape at six-two, one eighty-five.

"Your co-worker paid me a visit this morning."

"Noble?"

"Yeah, Noble, and some bitch Detective from the police department. I thought you were gonna take care of these people?"

"Those morons you got helping you aren't making things

184

any easier," he said. "Who authorized that second bombing, and what's with this fucking painter?"

"The painter was an accident, things got out of hand."

"Oh, really. Tell me Wanda, just exactly how does someone accidentally carve PTA in a guy's forehead?" He handed Wanda her drink. "Sorry, no aspirin. Sure you don't want some bourbon in that?"

Wanda grabbed the soda and took a huge gulp. "Look, everything is under control, but you gotta do something about these people, Charles. They're getting too close."

"We've only got a few days to go. I'll try and steer Noble in the wrong direction, but you have got to pull the reins in on your people."

"Don't worry about my people. We'll do our part. Did you bring the money?"

Kramer pulled Wanda toward him. "Yeah, I brought it. We got plenty of time for that." He kissed her on the lips, but she kept her mouth closed.

"What's wrong?"

"Nothing. I just want to take care of business."

Kramer let her go. "Jesus, Wanda. What's with you anyway? Every time I touch you lately you recoil like I'm some kind of monster or something. And look at you. You're getting fat, your hair's a mess…you're dressing like a guy. You going lesbo on me or something?"

"Well maybe you should find yourself a nice slim girl. Maybe that's what you need. Some little play thing."

That's just what Kramer thought he had when he first met Wanda. He was assigned to the L.A. branch of the Secret Service but was expecting to be promoted to Washington right after the election. Of course, all that changed when Frank Noble got the call. A bitter Kramer stayed in L.A., chasing petty, would be terrorists or guarding visiting dignitaries, while Frank Noble—a man not worthy to shine Kramer's shoes—

paraded around the streets of Washington, rubbing shoulders with the upper echelon, getting his picture in the paper with the President of the United States.

The PTA was just getting started then. They weren't even called the PTA, yet. Just Wanda and Raymond throwing rocks through department store windows and torching a delivery truck now and then. When they bought some guns with counterfeit money, Kramer got assigned the job of busting up the operation. It only took him a few weeks to put together the dossier on the two amateurs.

At first all he wanted from her was sex—back then, Wanda still looked pretty good. He showed her the dossier and explained prison life in detail. The choice was hers. Wanda chose Kramer; better to sleep with one sweaty pig than every guard in Leavenworth. The vandalism stopped and once a week for six months Wanda met Kramer in some hotel for a few hours of boring sex.

Then the riots happened and shortly after that word came down that the President would be coming to L.A. and that Frank Noble would be coming with him. That's when Kramer hatched his plan. When he first mentioned it to Wanda she had laughed in his face, and told him he had better pull out the file on her and put her away, because there was no way she was going to kill the President of the United States. Then he told her about the President's holdings in Electra Bras. He even showed her copies of the stocks. But the clincher was the money. Kramer promised her a half million dollars to do the job. Half of it upfront.

"Where are you going to get half a million dollars?"

"You think I'm the only one wants that SOB dead?"

"I'm sorry, Wanda. I guess I'm just a little bit nervous. You know how I feel about you. Once we get rid of Noble, everything will be fine, you'll see."

Wanda sat on the bed and looked up at the big man. It was

bad enough when he was forcing himself on her, but now he was acting like some love-struck kid. She despised him. Little did he know that every time he opened his mouth he stuck the knife a little deeper into his own back. When this was all over she would deal with Charles Kramer, but for now she needed him. "Let's make love," she said. "Then you can show me the money."

Kramer sat down next to Wanda and put his arms around her. "Jesus, Wanda!"

"What?"

"You're pouring sweat. What's the matter with you?"

"I don't know. I must be getting a cold."

"Another cold? It's the middle of summer."

"It happens, Charles. Does that mean you don't want to fuck?"

"Hey, I'm just worried about you. You been sick a lot lately."

"Yeah, well, it's a sick world, isn't it?"

Kramer tried to pull Wanda's shirt over her head but she stopped him. "You know the rules." ß

SEVENTEEN

The pile of used tissues on the couch next to Wanda was driving Cervante absolutely nuts. He couldn't understand why she couldn't at least keep a bag next to her, try and contain her germs. But he wasn't about to say anything to her, at least not while she was reading his letter. He sat across the room on a rocking chair, trying his best to keep still, but every minute or so he'd shift his weight or cross his legs and the chair would squeak, and Wanda would shift her eyes from the paper to him—sometimes she'd even sigh and slightly shake her head— and he'd whisper a soft "sorry" and she'd continue her reading.

After about fifteen minutes—she must have read the thing five times—when he thought he'd reached his end and was about to explode in his chair, she set the letter down on her lap and looked over at him. There were tears in her eyes but none got out. Cervante scooted up to the edge of his chair. She glanced quickly back at the letter, then turned her attention to the window. Cervante turned to see what was so interesting but there was nothing unusual out there, just an empty canyon, brown with shrub, and a stand of oaks, motionless in the still afternoon. He had the feeling she wasn't even seeing that; she seemed to be somewhere else, someplace faraway, and for a moment he feared he had lost her, that she had abandoned his work.

"It's beautiful, Cervante. Beautiful." She was still looking out the window. Then, she blew her nose, tossed the tissue into the pile, lit a cigarette and left the room.

Cervante didn't know what to say. Wanda was obviously

moved by the letter—she'd even called him Cervante—and for this he was grateful, but he wanted more; he wanted specifics. This was his masterpiece, his moment. She should have mentioned his genius, the poetry, his enormous talent.

He got up from his seat and picked up the letter, and then he followed Wanda into the kitchen where she stood hunched over the open refrigerator door gazing into the box like some disoriented explorer before a frozen tundra. Cervante cleared his throat but Wanda didn't budge. "So, do you don't think it's too long or anything?"

Wanda pulled back from the fridge empty handed and shut the door. Then she slowly turned around. The soft look on her face reminded Cervante of a long time ago—another life?—when a beautiful young model sat drinking wine in her brand new evening gown, laughing and full of excitement about the evening ahead. "No, Cervante, it's perfect."

"Oh." More, he wanted more. "I thought the second paragraph was…"

"I have to go lay down. Wake me up when Two-ton gets back, will you?" She turned and walked away, leaving the genius alone with his masterpiece.

Not too far from El Centro there's a stretch of empty rolling hills and a narrow stream running through the middle of them that separates the U.S. from Mexico. Every evening Mexicans and South Americans would gather by the shoreline waiting for the sun to go down to try their luck crossing the border. On most nights there would only a handful but on some occasions the number would swell to fifty or more. On the U.S. side, Border Patrol officers would sit in their trucks drinking coffee, swapping stories, waiting for the evening roundup to begin.

It is a crude and often times dangerous way to get into the country, especially during the winter when the stream can become a raging river, but in the summer if there are enough people brave enough to give it a go, a certain amount are bound to get through. There just aren't enough officers and trucks to handle them all. Most of the ones who do manage to make it usually get picked up further down the line on the interstate, but there is always that small percentage who make it to their destination, find work, even change their lives.

Curtis had been across the border a hundred times. He knew all the routes, the tunnels, the guards who could be bought. Each way had its downside but for Curtis none was worse than rushing the border, especially with women and children. You had to be quick and strong; plenty of people had broken their legs or fallen and cracked their heads open, or been run over by a Border Patrol truck in pursuit. It was a brutal, desperate method, often times a last resort for those who had no money to pay a coyote, or no connections to a better route.

Curtis found Conchita Cortez holed up with some relatives just outside of Tijuana. She was a strong woman but her nerves were beginning to wear thin after all she'd been through. Curtis assured her the children were safe but said he hadn't heard any word from her husband. Then he explained his plan. He knew of a tunnel not far from TJ; it was used mostly by drug runners, but for a price he could take her through it. The price was a thousand dollars. Conchita told him it may as well be ten thousand; she had no money left and her relatives had maybe two hundred between them. Besides, she did not approve of drugs and did not feel right about using the tunnel. Curtis explained that he couldn't use his regular routes right now, that the police were looking for him. If she wanted to cross that night they would have to leave immediately and try to cross by El Centro, but that he didn't recommend it.

"I want to see my children," she said. "And I want to be with my husband. We go now to El Centro. I am a good runner."

———

There were close to a hundred people down at the river's edge when Curtis and Conchita arrived; it was going to be a busy night. Curtis checked the other side through his binocu-

190

lars. He counted only five trucks but he knew there would be others further from the river to pick up the stragglers that made it through the first assault. Still, the large group would work in his favor.

Looking around at the gathered crowd, Curtis was struck with an immense sadness. Half of the people there were mothers with their small children. They would not make it a hundred yards past the river. Many of them had probably tried it a dozen times and still they returned for another try, always full of hope and dreams. Curtis wanted to share his knowledge with them all, wanted to deliver them all safely to America, to a better life, but the sad part was, he needed their innocence, their naivete, to increase his chances of getting Conchita across.

Conchita was lucky, she had Curtis; nobody knew the game better than he. The others: a few would make it, would carve out a life in El Norte, would break their backs doing menial labor to feed and cloth their children, give them an education, some opportunity. But the majority would watch their dreams fade with each failed attempt until eventually they would no longer return to the river. Perhaps, some day, their children would cross it for them.

The sun set early behind a thick wall of clouds toward the coast and there was little moon that night so the dark came quickly. Conchita inched toward the river but Curtis held her back.

"We stay at the back of the crowd and watch the trucks. Don't be too anxious."

A silence fell over the crowd as everyone grabbed what few belongings they had brought with them. Parents gathered their children together. All watched the sky as if someone, something, would send them a message.

And then, it started. The crowd had grown to over a hundred and they were in the water now working their way across, spreading out as they approached the other side. If they could keep the trucks busy chasing one or two at a time their chances

191

would improve. Curtis noticed a young boy, a teenager, was sticking close to him and Conchita. He didn't have the heart to chase him away.

Curtis moved through the crowd like a star end on a football team. When a truck started moving in his direction, he would duck behind the nearest group of people, putting them between himself and the truck. Before he started across the river he had noticed a small stand of trees about three hundred yards away. He made that his goal but he hid not head directly for it but rather swung first to the west with the bulk of the group until he was sure most of the truck drivers had committed themselves to that direction. Then, he pulled Conchita down to the ground and waited. All hell had broken loose: women screamed, children cried in terror; men in trucks spoke distorted orders over their speakers; hi-beam lights burned through the cloud of dust, so thick now that many of the runners lost all sense of direction. Still, they kept moving.

Curtis was up again now as he and Conchita cut back to the east and then turned north toward the trees. He couldn't see them but he knew he was headed in the right direction. He had counted every step they took. He had blazed a trail in his head long before they ever set foot in the water. And close behind them was the boy. Curtis looked back at him and smiled. "We can make it," he said. "We can make it."

———

Martin had been sitting in his underwear gazing into the blank computer screen for over an hour, time enough to down three double bourbons and run through every trick he could remember to help jump start his imagination. Nothing was working. He was no longer trying to work on the novel he had started months earlier. He had left that one for dead now. He had made the mistake of jumping into it too soon back then; the concept had not germinated long enough to sustain him. He had tried to force it along, to breathe life into it, knowing all along the best ideas were the ones that haunt you, that keep popping up in your mind week after week until finally you have no choice but to sit down an extricate the story, those characters, from the confining gray walls of the brain, and relocate them onto the world of paper and ink and a shot at immortality.

Why hadn't the vision come through for him? Instead of delivering a story, it seemed to be catapulting him toward some reality, some large event, much bigger than any story. It seemed to say, this story you have to live, not write.

He grabbed some books from a shelf. He would try another approach, one he hadn't used since college. Back then, when he had to write a paper or a short story for class, he would open a novel and randomly select a sentence and use that sentence to set the tone and the theme for his work. He picked up a book, *The Confederacy of Dunces*, opened it and blindly ran his finger down the page. This was the sentence:

'His nose rebelled against the very noticeable odor of fresh enamel.'

Enamel, thought Martin. I'm back to the building, back to the vision. He tried another. This time it was a James Cain novel, *Serenade*.

> It flashed over me, that mob at the novelladas, pouring down out of the sol, twisting the tail of the dying bull, yelling at him, kicking at him, spitting on him, and I tried to tell myself I had hooked up with a savage, that it was horrible...

Martin read the paragraph over and over. The writing was good, but there was something else. That character, Juana, she was so involved, so engaged, in life. She had met John, the narrator, in Mexico. She was a whore and he was an opera singer who had lost his voice and with it, his manhood. She had given them both back to him. Was there something here Martin could use?

He set the book down and went once again to the screen.

He was beginning to feel the bourbon, now, and instead of loosening him up like he had hoped, it only managed to sink him into a state of depression. What was wrong with his brain? It wasn't like he'd never written before; he had piles of manuscripts, some not so good, but some that were the real thing— he was sure of that.

A tack fell from the wall and a rejection slip glided slowly toward his desk, as if to taunt him. Had he come to believe that they were right without consciously admitting it? Why else would he keep them up there? How long could he continue joking about his own failure? No, worse, he was worshipping it. He had tacked these paper icons to his walls, building a shrine from his own disappointment. He let out a quick sardonic laugh as the thought of his brother, the real estate tycoon, flashed through his mind. He had sent Martin a book on positive thinking. It arrived one drunken afternoon shortly after June and he had split up, and Martin had immediately frisbeed it up against a wall. Positive thinking was lame; but negative thinking, what was that, noble?

Martin glanced half-heartedly around the room but didn't see the book. Then he put his hands on the keyboard.

Lars sat staring into the blank screen...

"That's brilliant," he said out loud. "Just what the world needs: another book about a drunk writer's block. And a Viking at that! All he needs is the hat."

He poured another drink. As he raised the glass to his lips he thought he heard something outside. He set the glass down and leaned in his seat toward the door. Someone was definitely out there. Martin got up quietly—at least he thought he was quiet, but he was drunk and actually quite noisy—and moved closer to the door. The shotgun was propped up in the corner. He leaned over and picked it up. The image of Juana with the saber passed through his mind.

"Okay, motherfucker," he whispered. "Here I come."

Martin took a deep breath and then kicked open the door and stumbled into the night.

"Jesus Christ, don't shoot!" It was Vern. The shotgun was about six inches away from his nose and Vern quickly raised his left arm and pushed it aside.

"Vern? What are you doing sneaking around out here?"

"I wasn't sneaking. I need to talk to you. Are you drunk?"

"I've been drinking, yeah. What of it?"

"Nothing. Nice underwear. Help me inside."

Vern had to get out of his chair and lean against the trailer on his good leg while Martin lifted the chair up the stairs. Then Vern put his arm around Martin's shoulder and tried to hop up to the first step, but Martin—in his drunken state—had not braced himself properly and quickly collapsed under the big man's weight. The two men toppled to the ground, trapping Martin under Vern's huge stomach.

"I can't breathe. Get off."

"What do you think I'm trying to do?"

"How do *I* know? Collect more money from your insurance, probably."

Vern reached up for the trailer door, grabbed hold of the bottom edge, and began pulling himself up. But he had grabbed with his bad hand, and with only a thumb and forefinger was unable to maintain his grip. He plopped back down onto Martin again.

"Ow! You're killing me."

The two men lay there criss-crossed at the bellies, squirming and heaving like they were engaged in some bizarre mating ritual.

"Try rolling me toward your legs,"

"What?"

"Push me toward your legs."

"God, I gotta piss, so bad. You're crushing my bladder."

"Push!"

Martin reached up with both arms and placed his hands on Vern's blubbery stomach, but when he tried to push, his hands just disappeared into the fat man's flesh. "I can't...I can't budge you." Martin was running out of breath.

"Okay, okay, I've got an idea. I'll count to three. When I get to three I'll push off the ground with my arms and you pull yourself out from underneath. Okay?"

"Anything. Just hurry."

"Okay. Here we go. One, two, three!"

Vern raised up about three inches but his stomach just continued to sink into Martin's body.

"Higher. You gotta get higher."

Vern's arms were shaking violently as he pushed down harder onto the sidewalk until finally his elbows locked and Martin felt the huge mass of weight lift from his body.

"Hurry up. I can't hold this for long."

Martin was pretty drunk but he had probably never moved any faster his whole life, and it's a good thing he did, for the instant his feet cleared Vern's belly, the big man plopped back down to the earth. At least it was a short drop.

They lay quietly next to each other for a moment, and then Martin turned to look at Vern. "Mind if I smoke?"

"That's funny. Help me up."

Earlier that summer a baby minke whale had washed up on the beach and Martin had helped get him back in the water. The image of that beautiful creature brought a smile to his face now as he rolled Vern over onto his back and helped him into a sitting position.

Then, with Martin's help, Vern managed to scoot along on his butt up the short flight of stairs and into the trailer and the security of his wheel chair. Vern was pouring sweat and there was a small amount of blood coming from the scratches on his arms.

Martin grabbed his robe from the bedroom and put it on. When he got back to the living room, Vern was sitting, drink in hand, in front of the computer.

196

"So, I see you're writing."

"You said you wanted to talk?"

Vern read the sentence on the computer screen out loud. "Perhaps we should discuss this first."

Martin reached over and erased the sentence with the cursor. "End of discussion. What's on your mind?"

Vern turned away from the desk. "Very well. I seem to have found myself in a rather…shall we say, awkward situation, which I believe can be easily rectified with the assistance of a minor benignant gesture on your part; for which of course I fully intend to recompense you."

"Ah, and here I was thinking you came over to dance. This is about your hand, isn't it?"

"I had a visit from the insurance adjuster, yesterday, a prickly little feme sole, all buttoned up from her chin down to her bony knees; you know the type, thinks her job is some sort of religion, probably has her office set up like an amen corner. Anyway, she started in about some 'minor inconsistencies' in my story. Wanted to know why there were two calls to 9-1-1 and why some of the neighbors said they heard what sounded like a saw running as the ambulance arrived."

"Sounds like very astute observations. And just exactly how do I fit in?"

"You have to be my witness."

"Your witness?"

"All you have to do is call this woman." Vern began rummaging through his pockets. "I have her card here somewhere. Ah, here it is. Notice how the layout is perfectly symmetrical."

He handed the card to Martin. "I need you to serve as my attestator."

"Vern…"

"Don't worry, I've already worked it out, I'll tell you precisely what to say."

"Isn't there some other way?"

"I already gave her your name."

"You did what!"

"I'm sorry, Martin, but I had no choice. She started in about withholding my ten thousands dollars and quickly segued to the punishment for filing a false insurance claim. I had to think quickly. I'm telling you, this, this Joan of Arc took one look at me and decided to do me in. She's probably avenging her decrepit mother who was no doubt deserted years ago by some poor soul whom I have the distinct misfortune of resembling."

"Yeah, or maybe she's just good at her job, Vern, and knows a fraud when she sees one."

"I see. So, you're aligning yourself with the enemy. And not just any enemy, but an insurance company at that. And all for a measly ten thousand dollars. Do you have any idea how much money these companies make? Well, allow me to enlighten you."

"Vern, stop. I'll do it, okay. Just tell me what to say. But you have to promise me you'll never do this again."

"Listen, I don't want you to compromise your integrity. Of course, I wouldn't be in this predicament if you hadn't barged in on me that day."

"Just, get on with it."

"We'll need a pencil and some paper. And another drink. So, you're working on some Nordic Tale, I presume?"

Hector Chang was beginning to get nervous. He had been sitting in the old van just outside of El Centro since nine o'clock and it was now almost midnight. Curtis had told him not to wait past twelve and Hector was anxiously counting the minutes. Everything had gone smoothly up to now. He had driven the van to La Mesa. Curtis had left a list of things to do and the first was to check on the second car. It was right where it was supposed to be. He had started it up, made sure there was plenty of gas and checked the CB. Everything was perfect. Then he had gotten back into the van and headed for El Centro.

As long as he had had plenty to do he was fine, but sitting here in the middle of nowhere for three hours not knowing what might happen was a bit unnerving for a sixteen year old on his first run. Where was his father?

He thought he saw a light flash up ahead. He watched closely for a few seconds but to no avail, simply a case of wishful thinking. No, there it was again. He flashed his headlights three times in quick succession and the light up ahead followed suit. Hector took the first good breath he'd had in two hours and when he saw his father step out of the bushes he couldn't contain the smile that erupted across his pimply face.

Curtis wasted no time in ushering the woman and the teenage boy who had followed them, into the van. As they headed toward La Mesa, he explained to his son why they were so late.

They had made it across the river to a stand of oak trees and had planned on waiting there until things settled down, but on their arrival there were already six others hiding there including a mother with an infant child who had proceeded to cry. Curtis did not like the situation so he had quickly moved Conchita and the boy away from the group to the edge of the stand of trees. When he heard the distant sound of a motor moving toward them he ushered the boy and the woman up the tree.

Shortly after, a truck arrived, then another, and Curtis could hear the group of immigrants scattering through the trees. A third truck arrived now and border patrol officers seemed to be everywhere. The headlights from their trucks illuminated the miniature forest below Curtis and his frightened companions who watched in silence as the trespassers scrambled in and out of the bright lights like blinded deer.

One of them, an older man, had tried to climb Curtis's tree but an officer managed to jump up and grab him by the foot and yank him down hard onto the ground. Curtis thought for sure their hideout would be exposed but the man managed to break free and the officer quickly set out after him.

The three of them had sat up there for two hours, not a word spoken between them, until Curtis descended to the ground and after carefully perusing the area, signaled the others to join him. The only evidence that remained of the evening's drama was a patchwork of tire tracks and a red bandanna, most likely dropped by a fleeing immigrant. Curtis bent down and picked it up and wrapped it around his forehead. It was half an hour's walk to El Centro, but at least the worst was behind them. Or was it?

EIGHTEEN

Martin had never been fond of funerals, had only gone to one in his life (his father's), and was still trying to understand, as he turned into the driveway at Rose Hills, exactly why he was bothering to come to Liddell's. The two men had not been close, although Tim had actually tried to establish a relationship when they first started working together. "Come by and have a beer sometime, you asshole," he'd say, or, "I'm going fishing Sunday with Clint; you should come with us. Get out of that fag-infested town you live in." He had even offered to help Martin paint his car.

Martin would respond with a "maybe" or an "I'll try and make it," knowing full well he had no intention of showing up. And it wasn't that he totally disliked Liddell—not like June, who thought he was repulsive—it was more like if he went and had a beer then there would have to be a second time and another beer, and then there would be bowling or fishing or hunting, or maybe even a little golf; time consuming events that occur among friends and eat up your life, hour by hour. He didn't need it, didn't want it, especially with a redneck.

And so what he refused to give him in life he was now donating this hot smoggy Saturday afternoon after death. A neighbor had been kind enough to loan him a jacket and tie and Martin had washed his best pair of Levis in an effort to make himself presentable. He was surprised to see so many people there, about twenty, and half of them women. This (the presence of women) seemed somewhat contradictory to Martin, for he saw nothing attractive about Tim; he was crude, spiteful, misogynistic, still living (well, not anymore) in a man's world, and so it seemed odd—bizarre—that women would not only be attracted to him, but would come to mourn him; the attraction during life might be explained by intimidation, or low self esteem, but the mourning, how would one explain that mystery? It made Martin wonder who was more naive, these women, or himself.

The only person he recognized was Clint, who had gone to the trouble of donning a black golf shirt and slacks and was now busy helping lower the casket into the ground. Then, he actually gave a short eulogy, wherein he extolled the virtues of Tim, how he could drink a pint of bourbon and still stand on his feet, what an artist he was with an airless, how he was there for his friends when they needed him. A couple of the women paused between tears to check Clint out—perhaps there was something to live for after Tim. Of course, Clint welcomed the attention of any woman, but these gals were way too far down on the scale for him to give them any play, and besides, an hour or so from now he would undoubtedly be teeing off at some nearby course, all thoughts of Liddell, and his girls, dead and buried.

And what about Martin's thoughts? An older woman—Tim's mother?—gently poured a handful of dirt into the hole and Martin wondered whether or not he would manage to publish a book before he was put in the ground, and if he did, would that make his bones dissolve any slower than Tim's? And if they did, so what?

As he walked away from the grave, somewhat in a trance, Clint's last sentence about Tim's enormous capacity for life still echoing in his head, Martin felt a hand on his shoulder, and having just seen a man laid to rest, it naturally caused him to jump a little.

"I'm sorry. I didn't mean to startle you."

Martin turned to face the attractive woman. He hadn't noticed her in the crowd but he recognized her now from that day on the roof. She looked great in black. "Not the best place to be sneaking up on people."

The woman reached inside her jacket. "I'm Detective Mallory."

"LAPD, I know. I've already seen it. Do you always come to your—what do you call them, clients, victims?—you always come to their funerals?"

"No, not always. But you'd be surprised who shows up at these things. Take you, for example."

"Hey, you know, the guy was pretty much of a schmuck, but I figured somebody ought to be here."

"That's it?"

Kate Mallory took off her sunglasses. She had the darkest brown eyes Martin had ever seen. He couldn't understand how those eyes could witness the brutality of Los Angeles's streets day after day and still have so much life in them. Or was it just a matter of time? "What else would it be? Unless you think maybe I had something to do with Tim's murder."

"From what I hear, you weren't too upset about Mr. Liddell's death."

"Well, I have a closeness problem. You can ask my ex-wife."

"Listen, I'm not accusing you of anything. A man's been murdered, we think he was tied to terrorist activities and it's my job to follow up any possible leads. That's what I get paid for."

Martin wondered what it was that motivated this woman, possessed her to take on this most thankless of jobs. To him, having women running around with guns and badges was just about the saddest thing imaginable. And of course he realized that this attitude made him somewhat of a relic. What a piece-of-shit world this was. "I hope it's a lot."

They reached his Vega. The back was full of paint supplies and the car was filthy. June was always on him about that car, wanting him to get rid of it or at least put a paint job on it. Martin had always laughed at her. "We may be what we eat, June, but we are definitely not what we drive," he'd say. But now, standing here next to this woman, this cop, he felt somewhat embarrassed, somehow immature, as if telling himself, you are not necessarily what you do, was not enough anymore, that this belief system only existed in his head, and that the outside world saw his true reality, that of a forty year old housepainter who didn't clean his car or his house and didn't even own a suit; a loser hiding behind a delusion he calls art. The attractive officer didn't give the car a second look.

"You want to know if I know anything about Tim's death," said Martin. "Let me ask you a question. Do you believe in premonitions? No, it's more than that. Do you believe some people can see into the future and predict what's going to happen?"

She smiled. "You mean like fortune telling?"

"Call it what you will."

"I think there is usually some scientific answer for most things, but I suppose anything's possible. Why, have you seen the future?"

Martin reached into his pocket and pulled out his keys. A couple of women from the funeral passed them by. One of them was crying uncontrollably. He watched them for a few seconds then turned his attention back to Kate. He was attracted to her, there was no getting around that, but she was a cop and he was having a hard time picturing that scenario. Then he had to laugh to himself, and he could feel a smile breaking out over the thought of the two of them together.

"What?" she said.

"Nothing. I was just trying to picture something."

"Oh. Another premonition?"

He sunk into those deep brown eyes. "Actually, I was just trying to picture the two of us, you know…together. Pretty crazy, huh?"

"Well, I don't know. I suppose stranger things have happened. So, you were saying something about the future."

"I'll tell you what I've seen," he said. "You can take it for what it's worth."

It was Charles Kramer's job to secure the area of the President's intended visit, with particular attention paid to the six-block section picked to showcase the refurbishing progress since the riots. The President was inclined to get out of his limo now and then or pull a Kennedy and travel in a convertible, with the top down, so every window, man-hole, doorway in the area had to be checked.

Kramer passed out checklists to his agents. They would do their preliminaries today (welding man-hole covers shut, posting no parking signs along the route, stationing agents at strategic locations), and then early Sunday morning swoop down on the area like a minor invasion. Nothing would be left unchecked. Well, almost nothing.

The new community center, the keys to which had cost Tim Liddell his life, was on Kramer's own personal list; no other agent would be checking it. (Still, Kramer had insisted on the keys, just in case some nosey cop wandered by and noticed a busted lock on the fence.) And he had marked off a hundred yard stretch on Normandy Avenue where Dubois and Two-ton would be setting their explosives. Of course, for the record, the Center and that small stretch of road would be on another agent's list, an agent destined to be one of the unfortunate victim's of the terrorists' attack.

Yes, Kramer had thought of everything. The maps he gave Wanda specified the exact manhole for Two-ton and Dubois to exit after the attack, and he would be there to tidy up that loose end when the time came. By Monday morning, the President and Frank Noble would both be dead, the Vice President would be sworn in and Charles Kramer would take over Noble's position with the Secret Service. Life would be great.

Wanda Blade had good reason to be upset. She'd been fighting that damn cold for over a month and had finally decided to see a doctor. She needed something to get her through the weekend. She was running a fever and had almost passed out a couple of times, which would never do in the middle of a gun-fight. The doctor had prescribed some generic antibiotics for her until the lab results were in, then he would hit her infection with something more precise. He felt confident he could help her. Then he saw the lesions on her back.

"How long have you had these?" he asked. He was an older man, and very soft spoken, and Wanda, sitting there half-naked, her breasts exposed to a man for the first time since the rape, felt oddly at ease around him. He hadn't even mentioned the scars.

"I don't know, a couple of months, I guess. I eat a lot of junk food, I figured maybe they were cysts."

"Let me ask you a question, Wanda. Now, don't be alarmed, it's just, with the lingering cold and the lesions…have you ever been tested for AIDS?"

Wanda thought back to the hospital, after the rape. They had wanted to test her but she said no. But that was so long ago. There was no way she had aids. Unless Kramer…"No. No, I haven't. But I'm sure I don't…I mean I haven't been very active."

God, she felt like a child. Sounded like one. She was blushing, she was sure of it, could feel the heat in her face, and then a welling up in her chest. Why was she thinking about him, about that night, the crazy glare in his eyes as he slashed at her chest with the knife? And the sex; not sex really, just a different kind of stabbing, a more painful kind, a kind that bores so deep you don't know where the weapon ends and you begin. What had she done to deserve that? Why was he taking away her life?

Got to hold it down. Have to try. But it was no use. She'd been shoving it down for years, layering it with anger and denial. Spitting it out with a wicked tongue through a false face. But there was so much there, so much pain, such a gigantic festering wound; it needed an eruption, a rebirthing, and sitting their naked with this kind old man who now gently touched her cheek with his hand, she finally let it go.

The doctor let her cry for five minutes before he spoke. He had sat down next to her and wrapped his arm around her shoulder. "There now, it's okay. We're just going to run the test to be sure. You're probably right, probably just cysts." He had no way of knowing what the tears were really about.

She had left the doctor's office and gone straight back to Two-ton's place, hoping to spend some time alone, to think things out. Was it any wonder she was less than attentive to Cervante and his letter?

———

Frank Noble got to the airport two hours before the President's scheduled arrival, made sure all his men were clear on the transporting procedures, then tossed down a day old pre-packaged turkey sandwich. He was still hoping to talk the President into getting back on Airforce One and returning to Washington. The two men had been through a lot together, there had been some close calls, and Frank knew better than anyone that luck had played a big role in their good fortune more than once. But how long would the luck last? It had been a strange week, to say the least: bombs going off; weird messages coming in about Jackie Davis; Dubois and his pornography; the body in the trunk; and just the appearance of the city, itself, especially South Central, particularly since the riots. Parts of it resembled a war zone, and Frank supposed there had been a war of sorts. It was not the place, and definitely not the time, for the President to be sticking his neck out.

The entire situation was just too damn depressing, and once again he found himself actually considering retirement. He'd have twenty years in by the election. Maybe that would be a good time to get out, take his pension, find some quiet place; settle down.

The press had amassed in full force, and was in the President's face before his shiny black Florsheims hit the ground, polite and reverent, smiling right through the innuendos. If only once, one of them would come straight out and ask it.

"Mr. President, isn't it true you care nothing about the residents of South Central L.A., and that your only motivation for making this trip is the upcoming election?" The funny part was, it bothered Frank much more than it did the President. "Frank," he'd say, "if you want to get downtown, take the subway, if you want to bypass the press, use the subterfuge."

Frank wanted him in the limo and out of harm's way as soon as possible and after about two minutes of bantering with the press, he opened the car door and virtually shoved the President inside.

"Boy, these guys out here in L.A. are real animals," said the President, still waving to the gathered crowd. "They oughta get themselves a real job."

"Yes, sir, Mr. President," said Frank. He was dripping wet with sweat. How was it the President managed to stay so dry?

"Frank, please, when it's just you and me, you can dispense with the formalities, okay."

The limo pulled away. Frank wiped his forehead with a hanky. "I can't get used to that, sir. I just don't think it's right."

"Well, what if I make it an order?"

This one temporarily stumped Frank.

"Oh, never mind. You do what makes you feel more comfortable. Now, tell me, how do things look out here? Spoke with Kramer yesterday. He doesn't seem to think there'll be any problems."

"Well, sir, overall I'd say he's right. I'm still worried about this PTA group, though."

"Have there been any threats?"

"No, not directly, but there have been two bombings, and there was a fellow murdered who works in one of the buildings we had planned on visiting."

"Well, that's simple enough. Just change the itinerary."

"I've already seen to that."

"Then I'm sure everything will be fine." The President let out a quiet laugh. "You remember that time in Detroit, that young woman pulled a revolver out of her hair. Had one of those big beehive hairdos. Looked like that gal from the Black Panthers…"

"Angela Davis."

"Right. She still in prison?"

"Angela Davis?"

The President laughed. "No, the gal with the gun."

"I believe she is, sir."

"Thank God the gun got caught up in her hair, or you might not have gotten to her in time."

Frank put his hand on his side. "Still hurts now and then."

As the limo left the airport, Frank consistently watched the road for any possible signs of trouble. He felt pretty secure inside the steel plated limo. If he could just keep the President from getting out and wandering around he figured he could keep a handle on things.

"Oh, Frank, there is one other thing. This radio disc jockey, Russ Holloway. Someone on my staff scheduled him to ride with us but I've been reading some of the transcripts from his show and I'm not so sure it would be good for me, politically, that is, to have him along."

"He is pretty extreme, sir, but he has a large listening audience, and from what I gather if you pull the rug on him now, he could make life pretty miserable for you while you're here."

Frank looked past the President and out his window just as a man with long hair riding a motorcycle flipped them off. How in the hell had he managed to get so close? Frank pulled the President down onto the seat and pulled out his gun, but the man was quickly surrounded by three CHP who forced him to the side of the row. "All clear," he said and the President sat back up and straightened his tie.

"That fellow needs a haircut. So, what do you suggest we do, about this Holloway?"

"Wait until it's time to depart, then we'll stick him in with the Chief of Police. That way he can still say he rode in the procession, but he won't be able to come on like you and he are best of friends."

"I like it, Frank. You're a real life saver."

Frank stuck his pistol back into its holster. I hope that won't be necessary, he thought.

———

Curtis Chang sat in the van just outside of Oceanside with Conchita and the teenager, waiting for a call on his CB from Hector. This was the plan: Hector was to go ahead in the rental car and drive through the border patrol just south of San Clemente. If it wasn't being patrolled he was to call Curtis immediately and he would head north with his passengers. If it was being patrolled, Hector was to proceed to Basilone Road—the closest off-ramp—and turn around. Then he was to proceed southbound to within a couple hundred yards of the station, pull to the side of the freeway and pretend to have car trouble, all the time keeping his eyes on the checkpoint. The minute it was clear, he would call Curtis and give him the word.

It was only a fifteen-minute drive from Oceanside and Hector had been gone over an hour, but Curtis had done this many times. Sometimes you had to wait all day. After three hours—around four p.m.—the call came through. In another twenty minutes, they would be home free.

When they got within three miles of the checkpoint, Curtis had Conchita get down beneath a false floor. There wasn't room for the boy down there but Curtis had rigged up some empty boxes and blankets while they waited in Oceanside, which the boy now pulled over himself. It looked pretty good, but Curtis knew he was risking everything for this hitchhiker. But how could he say no?

They were only a mile away now; Curtis could see the structure up ahead. Then the CB came on. It was Hector. He sounded panicked. "Papa, go back. They've opened up again."

"I can't turn around, now. It's too late."

The young boy popped out of his hiding place. "Que pása?"

"Nada, no problemo. Get down."

Curtis could see the guards now as the traffic began to slow up; they were only a couple hundred yards away. Curtis heard a loud clicking noise and when he checked his mirror he saw the back doors to his van pop open and the boy about to jump out. "No! Get back in."

But it was too late. The boy jumped from the slow moving vehicle and began running across the freeway. Curtis stopped the van and watched in his side-view mirror as the boy attempted to cross the lanes. Most of the cars were moving pretty slowly and for a moment it looked as though he might make it. Then, in the far right lane, a car—it seemed to come out of nowhere—clipped him and sent him flying a good ten feet. The boy came down on his knees, rolled over and grabbed his legs. He tried to get up, but his legs were obviously broken and he quickly collapsed.

There was a long empty space now between Curtis's van and the checkpoint. Curtis wanted to go to the boy, but he knew it would be bad for all three of them. In the confusion of the accident, with so many of the guards running down to where the boy lay grasping his legs in pain, Curtis slid through the check-point unmolested by the guards. Tears in his eyes, he made a promise to himself. He would come back another day for the brave young boy who had sacrificed himself for his new found friends in America.

NINETEEN

Wade Parker woke up around eleven o'clock Saturday evening, as was his routine, took an ice-cold shower, shaved, then sat nude in his tiny kitchen taking in a small meal of orange juice, Cheerios, and dry white toast. This was normally Wade's favorite time of day, a time when he could fantasize about the adventures before him—a record breaking ticket-writing day, perhaps, or maybe a couple of DUIs—but instead his mind was preoccupied with this special assignment with the President. Of all the cops out there, why did they have to choose him? He couldn't care less about the President, including any alleged prestige one might gain from leading the procession. As far as Wade was concerned, absolutely nothing good could come from this assignment.

He finished his breakfast, tidied up the kitchen, and then went into the bedroom and took a freshly laundered uniform from his closet and laid it out on his bed. He was itching to get out there. In just a few hours the bars would close and the streets would be full of drunks speeding down to the nearest liquor store to grab another bottle before the two o'clock closing time. Only tonight, Wade wouldn't be there to write them up. Tonight, some other cop would be on his beat, some other cop would be nosing around in Wade's territory. What if this cop liked his new assignment? What if he had some pull downtown and managed to wrangle the shift away from Wade? This kind of thing happened all the time. Who would be there to fight for Wade? Who would protect his territory?

Wade had a blown-up poster of Erik Estrada over his bed. As a teenager he had watched his show, C.H.I.P.s, religiously, and although he hadn't made it into the Highway Patrol, he still rode a motorcycle, and as far as Wade was concerned, that was close enough. He stood there now wondering just what Erik would do in this situation. What harm would it cause if he went out and wrote a few tickets before going to the procession? It would even be a good idea to let his fill-in see him out there. Let him know who was in charge. He wouldn't clock in, so it wasn't like it would cost the city any money, and that fat has-been, Anderson, wouldn't have to worry about paperwork. I'll never take a desk job, he thought; I'd rather be dead.

Wade paced back and forth from the window, where he watched the early morning activities begin to unfold, to his bed, where his pristine uniform lay waiting. He checked his watch: quarter till twelve. He sat down on the bed and began to gently pat the pressed cotton shirt. It was more like a skin to him than just a piece of material. He reached across the uniform and grabbed his underwear, stood up and slowly pulled them on, followed shortly thereafter by his t-shirt, and before he knew, he was completely dressed, standing in front of the mirror checking himself out. Nobody wore that uniform better than he did. He took good care of himself, no alcohol or drugs, no fatty foods, plenty of time at the gym. He wasn't some pork-chop, cruising around all day in a black and white, wallowing in hot dogs and donuts. His discipline and pride, his absolute devotion to his work were traits not often found and rarely understood. You take an individual like this and try and squeeze him into some kind of box, force him to toe some arbitrary line drawn by someone way beneath his level and you eventually destroy him. Well, that wasn't going to happen to this cop, not today. He had to get out there, had to do what he knew he did best. There were people making illegal turns, people speeding, and running red lights. Somebody had to stop them.

Wade strapped on his gun, grabbed his helmet and gloves and looked over at the poster. Erik was straddling his bike; he had his sunglasses on and wore a stoic expression that seemed to contradict his boyish good looks. "You understand, don't you, Erik," said Wade as he flashed him the thumbs up sign and then quietly left the apartment.

Wanda had been sleeping, too. She woke up around midnight with a very heavy feeling in her chest, a feeling she couldn't put her finger on at first, and then she recalled her visit to the doctor. She wondered if he had called with the results. She switched on the light next to the bed. The floor was covered with weapons and ammunition. In addition to her Makarov Pistol (her favorite), there was a Scorpion VZ 61 Czech-made machine pistol, capable of 840 rounds a minute—a particular favorite of South Africa urban guerrillas—an M1 Carbine she had gotten from a former IRA member, a box full of hand grenades—mostly M26s—and an extremely nasty piece of work called the RPG-7 Portable Rocket-launcher.

Wanda stared down at her arsenal. Sitting there in their crates they were completely innocuous; they just needed somebody to pick them up and put them to work. It still wasn't too late to call the whole thing off, and Wanda began to wonder if she could do it, just walk away. She'd have to deal with Kramer, but she figured she could handle him—in fact she looked forward to it. Raymond might be upset, but Two-ton would back her up. Spike, he was the loose cannon, but he would most likely just carry on by himself; he'd never really been part of the team, anyway. Yeah, to hell with all this. She could leave Los Angeles, go somewhere new, start over; there was still plenty of money in the Swiss account.

She jumped out of bed and went into the bathroom and washed her face. There were large bags under her eyes and her hair was filthy. She tried washing her face again, and then another time. Each time she kept seeing the same tired look, especially in her eyes; something was missing, a sparkle from long ago had now gone dark so that she seemed to be peering into a deep cold pit. She thought about putting on some makeup, and began rifling through the cabinet, but there wasn't any to be found. She turned to the side and checked the sores on her back, then she pulled her bra down and ran her fingers across the light pink scars; they felt like silk. She examined her hands; the skin was dry and cracked and there was grease under her nails from cleaning her guns.

"Who are you kidding?" she said to her own reflection. She threw on an old robe and went out into the living room. Spike was sitting in the dark, nursing a bottle of whiskey, and watching television.

"Where are the guys?"

"They left already. Two-ton said he had to pick up a few things and drop off the letter, then they were going to get to work."

"Any calls for me?"

Spike seemed a little confused by the question. "Not that I know of," he said and chuckled.

It was the first time Wanda had seen Spike smile.

"You shouldn't watch TV in the dark, ruin your eyes," she said, but there was no irony whatsoever in her voice. Spike just stared at her, didn't say a word.

"You all set for tomorrow?"

"Yeah, sure."

"Got all the signals set in your mind?"

"Yeah, I know 'em. Ain't that hard."

"Let's go over them one time."

Spike took a deep breath. There was something different about him. He seemed, well, somewhat deflated. Something, some part of him, was missing.

"Humor me, okay."

"Jacket over the left shoulder is number one, right shoulder is two, left hand, three, and right hand, four."

"And…"

"If you drop the jacket, I clear out."

"Good. Now, one more question. You sure you want to go through with this?"

Spike took a hit off his bottle then turned his attention back to the TV. Wanda recognized the movie. It was one of *The Thin Man* series with William Powell and Myrna Loy. Nick (Powell) was drunk (again) and was speeding recklessly down the street. "I remember that scene," said Wanda. "It's funny." But she didn't laugh. "So what do you say? It's not too late to back out."

Spike stared straight ahead at the TV. "I came here to settle an old debt. I ain't backing out of nothing."

"Well, you better go easy on that stuff, then."

Spike turned up the volume with the remote and took another swig of booze.

"It's weird, Vern, because it was a dream this time, and not a vision, like before."

"So maybe that's all it is."

"No, I'm telling you, it was too real. I mean, I was standing up on that roof, I was there."

"Okay, let's say you're right. You're up on the roof, bombs are going off, people are dying, you've got the shotgun, etc. All you have to do is not go there tomorrow and the dream doesn't come true."

"Or maybe it comes true, but without me."

"Then call the cops. Tell them what you see."

"I already did, sort of. Let me have a hit off of that."

Vern slid the bottle of bourbon across the table and Martin took a huge swig. He picked up a newspaper article from the table. "What's this?"

"I haven't read it yet. Looks rather interesting, though. So, what did they say?"

"Who?" Martin had begun reading the article.

"The cops. You told them about your vision?"

"I told this woman detective. She didn't come out and say it but I know she thought I was some kind of nut."

"You told her everything?"

"You sure you haven't read this?"

216

"I think I should know what I have and haven't read."

"There's this ant in the Sahara, called the silver ant, and it says here it can withstand temperatures up to 128 degrees. But the interesting part is, its main predator is a lizard, and the lizard retreats to its lair when the temperature reaches 116, and that's exactly when these ants emerge from their burrows to forage for food. So they've got this small window of opportunity everyday to get out and eat."

"It's nice to see you're finally taking an interest in my work. Now, about the cop."

"It's not so much that I'm taking an interest. It's just a little odd, knowing you, that it's going to be over a hundred degrees tomorrow and now I find this article on your desk."

"Martin, sometimes a cigar is just a cigar, okay. Tell me what you told the lady detective."

Martin set the article down on the desk. "Well, I wasn't about to tell her about Chang or the kids, or the fact that I'm holding a shot-gun in the dream and that I shoot it. I may be crazy but I'm not stupid."

"And?"

"Well, first she cracked some joke about Oswald. Then, she realized I was serious and she said the President wouldn't even be visiting our building but that she was sure the Secret Service would give it a thorough going over, anyway."

"Well, there you go, nothing to worry about." Vern's tone seemed a little too flippant.

"I guess your right. I'll just stay away. I wish there was some way to get hold of Curtis. He's going to show up there tomorrow and I won't be there."

"He can call you."

"Yeah, I suppose. I better call June in the morning, let her know we've changed plans."

"And don't forget, you have to call a certain female insurance agent."

"I doubt if she'll be in her office tomorrow."

"Are you kidding? This one is a descendant of Scylla, herself. She's got six heads and they each take turns sleeping while the others strike terror into innocent citizens like myself."

"I think you might be overstating the situation just a little, Vern." Martin picked up the article again. "What's this?"

"What?"

"I didn't notice this before. Somebody underlined this part right here, about the lizard." He handed the paper to Vern.

"Oh, well, I might have skimmed through it. It's possible."

———

Cervante and Two-ton had gone over their checklist a dozen times. They had flak-jackets, helmets, mines, grenades, a couple of pistols, extra clips, lamps, rubber boots, gloves, various ropes and strips of velcro, flash-light, back-packs and the maps of the sewer system. It seemed like everything was there but Cervante was certain they were forgetting something.

"Just go over it with me one more time."

Two-ton was driving the Olds. "We've got everything, Cervante. I'm sure of it."

"No, something's missing. I just know it." Cervante was dressed completely in black, including a pair of leather gloves and a heavy leather jacket. He looked like an assassin from a James Bond movie. Two-ton wore a yellow Arrow shirt, with multi-colored pin stripes running through it, and a pair of old green slacks. He couldn't find any rubber boots big enough to fit over his shoes so he was in his stocking feet.

"You're just nervous. Hey, hand me a beer, will you?"

"You shouldn't be drinking while you're driving."

"I can't drive without beer. It calms me down."

Cervante reached down to the floor and grabbed a beer from the paper bag. It was a warm evening and both men had their windows down as they cruised up Western Avenue. Two-ton was surprised at the amount of traffic at one in the morning. "Where are all these people going?"

"It's Saturday night."

"Oh."

"It's Saturday night."

"I heard you the first time."

"What do you mean?"

"I mean you didn't have to say it twice."

"Say what twice?"

"It's Saturday night."

"I didn't say it twice."

Two-ton took a swig of beer and burped. "Yes you did. You been doing that a lot lately."

"What?"

"Repeating yourself."

"Well, this whole thing's making me nervous."

"Have a beer, forget about it. Did you give Wanda her message?"

"What message?"

"From the doctor. You said he called about some tests, that they came out negative."

"Oh, that's right. I forgot."

"Well, that's great, Cervante. Wanda's gonna love you."

"Well, this whole thing's making me nervous."

"God, Cervante, you did it again. What's wrong with you?"

"Nothing's wrong with me. Just leave me alone." Cervante switched on the radio and Two-ton turned off Western onto Adams.

They were getting close.

"It doesn't work."

"What?"

"The radio, it's busted."

"Oh." Cervante kept turning the knob from station to station, until Two-ton reached over and slapped his hand.

"It doesn't work, Cervante. Man, I hope I can depend on you to keep it together."

"That's it!"

"What?"

"My Depends. I forgot my Depends. We have to go back."

"We can't go back now. There's no time."

"Find a store, then. A market."

"Can't you just go without them?"

Cervante leaned toward Two-ton and took off his glasses. "No, I can't go without them. Can't you go without your beer?"

Two-ton thought about it for a minute, looked at his watch, then very calmly said, "Okay, we'll find a store."

They continued up Adams for a couple of blocks and then Cervante called out. "There. Turn left."

Two-ton drove on by the turn.

"You missed the turn. Turn around."

"I'll have to go up to the light."

"Just make a u-turn."

"It's a double-double line, Cervante."

"Just, make a u-turn."

Two-ton wasn't sure if Cervante meant to repeat himself that time or not, but he didn't bother to ask, he just drifted into the right lane and then swung the Olds into a u-turn without so much as touching the breaks. There was a fair amount of tire screeching, but with the power steering, the car had no problem negotiating the turn. "How's that?"

"Fine. Just hurry. They could be closing any time now."

"Oh, oh."

"What. What's wrong."

"Don't look back, but we've got company."

Two-ton kept his eyes on the rear-view mirror. He was hoping the flashing light wasn't for them, that the cop would just pass them by, but then the siren came on and the motorcycle pulled up along side of them.

"What's he want?" asked Cervante

"He wants me to pull over. What should I do?"

"What's he want?"

Two-ton looked over at Cervante, then back at the cop. He

wasn't used to making decisions but it didn't look like he had much choice. He took his foot off the accelerator and slid the big V8 over to the curb. "You better hide the beer," he said and turned off the ignition.

Kate Mallory tried to reach Frank Noble at his office but they said he had gone back to his hotel to get a few hours sleep. She rang his room at the hotel. It rang a few times and she was about to give up when he answered.

"Yeah...who is it?" He sounded half asleep.

"It's Kate, Mallory. I'm sorry to call so late. Were you sleeping?"

"What time is it?"

"It's a little after one."

"Just a minute."

Kate waited a couple of minutes before Frank returned to the phone. She was still at the police station, sitting at her desk, hard at work on her computer.

"What's up?" he asked. He sounded more cognizant now.

"Remember the innocent Wanda Blade?"

"Yeah, what about her?"

"Well, for starters, her real name is Wanda Moore. She used to be a very famous model until some wacko sliced her up a few years ago. After the attack she kind of fell off the map for awhile."

"Okay, so she changed her name, so what?"

"So, she lied to us. She said she just moved in to that building last year and hardly knew Raymond Dubois."

"And?"

"Frank, she owns that building. She and Dubois were together the night of the attack. They were partners in the magazine."

"The actor..."

"Frank..." Kate took a deep breath. "Listen, it gets better. Wanda had a huge contract with Electra Bras which they abruptly canceled after her accident."

"Why would they do that?"

"I guess they thought a woman with scars across her chest might not be the best person to represent their product."

"Jesus, he did that to her?"

"That and more."

"So you think she's been blowing up those department stores?"

"Frank, I'm sure of it. There's more. Guess who owns twenty-five percent of Electra Bras."

There was a long silence on the other end of the phone.

"Frank?"

"You're not going to tell me what I think you are, are you?"

"I'm afraid so. Our beloved President is one fourth owner of Electra Bras, and unless I'm completely out of my mind, I'd say she's going for him, tomorrow."

"Well, you've got somebody on her. Pick her up tonight."

"We don't know where she is."

"What!"

Kate pulled the receiver away from her ear until Frank finished yelling. "She must have left the house right after you and I were there. I've got an APB out on her and I'm checking out some other leads but for the time being she is out there and I'd say extremely dangerous. You have to talk to the President. Get him to call off the tour."

Frank scoffed. "You don't know him. There's no way he's going to stop this tour. The guy thinks I'm some kind of lucky charm or something. Besides, Kate, I'm going to have two hundred men out there tomorrow. She'll never get close to him."

"She may not have to."

"What do you mean?"

"This is going to sound crazy, but, you remember the painters in that building, the new community center? I talked to one of them yesterday, a Martin Sheppard, and he says he's been having nightmares about tomorrow. Says he hears explosions..."

222

"Whoa, wait a minute. What are you saying, the guy's a psychic?"

"I just, I've got a real bad feeling, Frank."

"Listen, we've been over that entire area with a fine toothed comb. There's no way anybody's going to get a bomb in there. Look, I'll talk to the President, see if I can at least get him to stay in the limo for the whole trip. You find that girl."

"We're trying. She used to have a bodyguard name of Perkins. I'm trying to run down an address for him. Maybe he's still with her."

"Good. I've got to get some sleep. Call me here at six o'clock, let me know what's happening. Thanks Kate, for the good work."

"Sure."

Frank hung up the phone and then got up from the bed and walked to the window of his hotel room. He drew back the curtains and gazed out at the night. From his room there on the tenth floor he couldn't hear a sound from outside. Millions of city lights spread out below as far as he could see and in the distant sky an occasional blinking light from a passing plane seemed to wink at him. It all seemed so peaceful.

"Where are you?" he said. "Where in hell?"

TWENTY

Wade Parker had been waiting over an hour for somebody to give him an excuse to write a ticket that Saturday night, and he had begun to wonder if he had made a mistake. There would be hell to pay if that smokestack of a sergeant found out he was out here, plus, he was going to be dog tired on Sunday with his Presidential duty; so far he had absolutely nothing to show for his efforts. Then he saw the Oldsmobile make the u-turn and before the car had gotten completely straightened out he had his light on and was in pursuit.

Wade started to call in the license plate number but quickly remembered he wasn't supposed to be on duty and would only complicate matters by calling in. It looked like a pretty nice car. Odds were there wouldn't be any warrants on it; he was willing to take the chance.

"Let me do all the talking, Cervante." They had pulled to the side of the rode and shut off the motor.

"Since when are you giving orders?"

"I'm not giving orders. You're all screwed up lately. Must have been that hit on the head."

The officer tapped on Two-ton's window and he slowly rolled it down. "Evening officer."

"Can I see your license, please?"

Two-ton carefully slid his license from his wallet and handed it to the officer, who examined it closely, then flashed his light in Two-ton's face. "Jimmy Perkins. I know that name."

Two-ton looked over at Cervante. There was probably an

APB out on them and now this cop was going to ruin everything. And all because of some stupid diapers.

The officer flashed his light at Cervante, who was staring straight ahead. "Something wrong with your friend?"

"He has a medical problem."

"Uh, huh. That was quite a turn you made back there."

"I know, officer, you're right, this 88 has an incredible turning radius…"

"Well, unfortunately, that's an illegal turn."

"Oh, sure, I understand, but we had a bit of a medical emergency." Two-ton breathed directly into the officer's face, who quickly pulled back from the window.

"Jesus. How much have you had to drink?"

"Drink? Oh, I think I had a beer or two with my dinner, but that was hours ago. I'm perfectly sober." Two-ton's chubby hands gripped the steering wheel tightly as he spoke. Beads of sweat began to drip from his forehead.

"Uh, huh. I need you to step out of the car, please."

"Since when are you giving orders?"

The officer flashed his light at Cervante. "What did he say?"

"Don't pay any attention to him, officer. He's not well."

"There's nothing wrong with me," said Cervante. "Don't kiss this guy's ass. Although I'm sure it's a cute one."

Two-ton wanted to strangle Cervante. He grit his teeth and stared over toward him and then forced a smile onto his face as he glanced back toward the officer. "I really should get him to a doctor."

"We'll see about that. Right now I want both of you out of the car."

Two-ton wiggled his way out of the car and leaned up against the door.

The officer placed his hand on his holster. "Move back a little and put your hands up on the roof of the car."

Two-ton did what he was told. The officer started to pull his pistol from his holster but as he did, Cervante shot out of the passenger side and stuck both arms across the top of the car. Cocked and pointed right at the officer's head was .357 Magnum. "Now I'm giving the orders. Put your hands up on top of the car. Get his gun, Two-ton."

"Two-ton Perkins! I knew I recognized the name. You played with the Cowboys."

"Yeah, that's swell," said Cervante. "Get his gun, Two-ton."

Two-ton took the officer's gun as Cervante worked his way around the car.

"I used to watch all your games. I'm originally from Dallas. Name's Wade Parker."

"You did?"

"That's enough out of you," said Cervante.

"You see that tackle I made in the playoffs in eighty-six?"

"It was beautiful…"

Cervante smacked Wade Parker in the face with his gun. "I said, shut up!"

Wade reached up and grabbed his face. Blood was dripping from his nose.

"What did you go and do that for?" asked Two-ton.

"That's enough out of you," said Cervante and then he stared up at the sky as if he were searching for something.

By now, Wade Parker was getting nervous. His voice began to break up as he spoke. "You better talk to your friend, Two-ton. You guys could get in a lot of trouble for this."

Two-ton had Wade's gun in his hand. He casually lifted it up high enough so that it was pointed right at the cop's heart. "Just don't do anything stupid." Then he grabbed Cervante by the arm and shook him. "Hey, Cervante, what are we gonna do with him?"

Cervante came out of his reverie. "Shoot him."

"Hey, wait a minute," said Wade. "Are you crazy? I'm a cop. You can't shoot a cop."

"I don't think we should do that, Cervante."

"He knows who you are. What do you suggest we do, let him go?"

226

"Can't we just tie him up?"

"What if somebody finds him?"

"Who's going to find me at this hour. You could put me in the trunk."

"Shoot him."

Wade Parker looked like he was about to pee his pants.

"He's just repeating himself," said Two-ton. "I told you, he's not well." He shook Cervante again. "Let's put him in the trunk and gag him."

"What if somebody finds the car?"

"We'll take him with us."

"In the sewer?"

"What sewer?" said Wade. "I'm not going down in any sewer. I just had this uniform cleaned."

"Mind your own business," said Cervante.

"Yeah, we'll take him down there and tie him up."

"Shoot him," said Cervante, and for the first time since this whole thing started, Two-ton began to question the wisdom of it all.

———

The sun was just about to come up over the hills in Malibu Canyon as Spike gathered all his things together and prepared to leave for the city. He really didn't have much to take with him, just a few detonators, a couple of hand grenades and a Browning High Power Pistol. He had brought nothing with him to California other than a few changes of clothes, and these he would not bother to take with him now.

He walked out onto the rear deck of the house. He'd been up drinking all night; in fact, he'd drunk himself right into sobriety. A thin sheet of mist hung over the rolling hills and for a moment, Spike was back in Tennessee, hunting rabbit. A sparrow chased a blackbird in and out of the low fog. Spike never could understand why such a large bird would let such a little pest intimidate it.

He reached into his pocket and pulled out the gold watch

he had brought with him from home; the watch Frank Noble had used to try and purchase his way out of a sticky situation with Spike's mother all those years ago. Spike could feel the rage bubbling up through a belly full of liquor; for years he had imagined this moment, had taken comfort in the possibility of revenge. Now that his opportunity was about to present itself, the picture was not so clear. His mother had been wronged, that much he was sure of, but she harbored no anger; she had even pleaded with him not to go to Los Angeles. So just exactly who was it he was revenging? This quandry had kept him in a half drunken stupor for days. The alcohol had kept him moving forward, had pushed the nagging doubts to the back of his mind, but even it was losing its grip on him.

"Just a few more hours," he said softly as he stuffed the watch back into his pocket.

He went back inside and called out to Wanda that it was time to go, but she didn't respond. He went to the front door, opened it and stood in the entry for a minute, listening for some sound from her room. It was quiet. He called out to her again. Still no answer. It was still dark outside and Spike was anxious to get on the road. He walked out to the garage, opened the overhead door and threw his pack into the red corvette. What the hell was she doing?

Damn women, he thought, as he left the garage to go back into the house. Then he saw the headlights approaching up the road. He didn't pay them much attention at first, not until they went dark. There was a second car and its lights also went off, and then a third and a fourth. The cars moved closer until at last Spike was able to recognize them. He sidestepped behind a tree, keeping his eyes on the lead car, as it advanced fifty yards past their driveway and then turned left into the driveway across the street. The other police cars followed. There must have been a dozen of them.

Spike waited until the last car had made the turn up the drive, then he crouched down and crept slowly back to the house. Once inside, he called out to Wanda. "Wanda! Jesus, girl, where are you?"

Wanda came out of her bedroom. She had on a nice pair of green slacks, a light yellow blouse, and a floral scarf wrapped around her neck. Spike did a double take.

"What's the problem?"

"Man, there's cops across the street. Tons of them."

"What?"

Wanda rushed past Spike and into the front yard. He couldn't get over the change in her appearance. She actually looked like a woman.

"They must be looking for us," said Wanda. "Get your things, let's get out of here."

"I'm way ahead of you, girl. My stuff's in the car."

"Then help me with mine."

Spike helped Wanda load her weapons into the trunk of the Corvette then she jumped in behind the wheel, started the car and pulled down the driveway and onto the street. The house across from them was set way back off the road but Spike could see in the distance as a couple dozen police officers gathered behind their cars, weapons drawn and pointed at the front door. Spike laughed out loud. "Boy, somebody's gonna get a rude wake-up call."

Kate Mallory expected to find a large gathering of police when she arrived at Two-ton's house—she had gotten a judge out of bed to issue a warrant and had sent the SWAT team on ahead to secure the area—but when she got there, she was all alone. She got out of her car and stood motionless before the front door, her hand on her pistol, all her powers of concentration focused on the house. There were lights on inside but no sounds of life. All her years on the force, every instinct she had pointed toward the same conclusion: She was too late. And then a distant noise, a noise both familiar yet indistinct, began to filter through to her consciousness. Nausea swept over her as she turned toward the street and slowly began running down Two-ton's driveway. When she reached the street her fears materialized before her eyes. They were at the wrong house.

Kate ran down the road and crossed the street, waving her badge as she went. When she reached the house she saw a group of officers surrounding a man and woman, both elderly, on their knees in the dirt, hands clasped behind their heads. The woman was sobbing and the man kept repeating, "Don't shoot. Just don't shoot." From the sounds coming from inside the house, Kate figured they were tearing the place apart. Kate was furious. "Where's Bentley!"

"He's inside, ma'am...sir," said the young officer who was standing with his rifle pointed at the old man's left ear.

"Put that gun away, you idiot. You got the wrong house. And get these people up off the ground. My God."

Kate stormed into the house. The front door was no longer on its hinges. "Bentley. Where are you?"

After explaining Officer Bentley's mistake to him, Kate and a group of officers went back across the street. There was little hope of finding anything of use there; still, they had to go through the routine. One of the officers broke out a couple of canisters of tear gas but Kate just glared at him like he was insane and he quickly put them aside. Kate walked up to the front door, turned the knob and slowly pushed open the unlocked door.

What they found inside was a cluttered mess of empty beer cans, potato chip bags, a sink full of dirty dishes and a TV still turned on (with the sound off), sitting on the living room floor. A cop came out of a bedroom carrying an empty kerosene can in one hand and a large bag of Depends in the other.

"What do you suppose these are for?"

"You don't want to know," said Kate. She walked to the front door and stared out into the night. She was hoping that maybe the group had given up on their idea. After all, nothing had happened since the second bombing; there hadn't even been another letter. Maybe they just packed it in and headed south. "Fat chance," she said aloud and then she turned to one of her men. "Peterson, I want you to go over every inch, see if you can find something, any kind of clue that might tell us where they are. If you find anything, I don't care how incidental you might think it is, call me."

"Will do. Where will you be?"

"Looks like I'm going to a parade."

———

Russ Holloway showed up at the Bonaventure Hotel in a chauffeur-driven limo. Russ was wearing a black tuxedo that was too tight around the chest and way too warm for the weather. The minute he stepped out of the air-conditioned car, tiny beads of sweat began to form on his forehead and neck. Close behind Russ, squeezed into a bright red mini-skirt and matching halter-top (the top managed to cover about half of her generous bosom), was a shapely redhead who, in her four-inch heels, stood about six-two. Russ was five-seven.

Russ helped his lady-friend out of the limo, pulled her close to his side and then began waving to the crowd of gathered photographers. A couple of Secret Service agents swept down to the curb to greet them and quickly ushered them inside the building.

"What I want to do," Russ was saying as they entered the elevator with the agents, "is broadcast part of my show right from the limo. I've got a crew waiting right outside, we can set it all up in twenty minutes."

The two agents stared straight ahead, sunglasses intact. Russ's date tugged at the top of her blouse, and Russ shot a dirty look at the agents, thinking they were copping a look through those dark shades.

"To think," said the girl, "I'll be riding in the very same car as the President of the United States."

"What did old Russ tell you?" He gave her a light pat on the rear, and then he winked at the agents. One of them pulled his shades down to the tip of his nose then peered over the top directly at the girl's breasts. He shot a glance toward Russ, and then he pushed his glasses back up and turned his head away.

"Eat your heart out pal," said Russ as the elevator came to a halt and the doors pulled back.

Russ and his date were led to a room where four other VIPs waited for the President's appearance. Russ recognized the Chief of Police, Harold Swatter, a slim, good looking middle-aged man—he'd been on Russ's show—and the Mayor, of course. The others he hadn't seen before today. All the men wore suits and ties but only Russ had on a tux. The only other woman present was an older, very refined looking lady. She was sitting on a couch talking to the Mayor, but she was having a hard time keeping her eyes off Russ's date, as was everybody else.

It didn't take long before all the men in the room, except for the mayor, were gathered around Russ and his date, who hadn't let go of each other since they left the limo. Harold Swatter was suggesting to Russ that it was time he came back on the show, said he wanted to discuss the issue of the 'moral and social responsibility of the entertainment industry.' Russ said he'd be happy to have him back on, and told him of his idea to broadcast from the President's limo.

Harold looked at the tall redhead. "Gee, Russ, I was kind of hoping you'd be riding with me."

Russ chuckled. "Love to accommodate you, Chief, but after all, I was requested by the President, himself. You understand?"

Before Harold could respond, the door to an adjoining room opened and a tall good looking man with blonde hair came in. "Excuse me, ladies and gentlemen. If I could have your attention for just a moment. My name is Frank Noble; I'm in charge of security. I just wanted to let you all know, we'll be ready to depart in about half an hour. I have the seating arrangements here. I'd like to go over them with you real quick if I could."

Russ and his girl squirmed their way to the front of the group.

"There will be three limos. The lead one will carry Mrs. Rampaul, from the DAR." Frank looked toward the older woman. "Are you Mrs. Rampaul?" She nodded. "Riding with Mrs. Rampaul will be Fire Chief, Gustauf Miller."

"Call me Gus," said Mr. Miller as he stepped forward and shook Frank's hand. Gus looked to be in his late fifties, solidly built, a full head of hair and a thick grey mustache.

"Okay, Gus. The middle car will carry the President…"

At the word 'President' Russ gave his date a nudge. Frank continued. "…and his honor, the Mayor, Mr. Hugh Atkinson. And in the last car we'll have the chief of police, Mr. Swatter, and Russ Holloway, the radio disc jockey. And of course, each car will carry two secret service agents. Are there any questions?"

"I thought we were riding with the President, Russ." Russ's date's voice had a high-pitched shrill to it and when she spoke the whole crowd went stone silent and turned to stare at them. "Honey, are you alright?" The redhead was staring at Russ like maybe he was in the middle of a heart attack. "You're turning red, Russ."

Russ was furious. Not only had he been demoted to the number three car, but now this upstart agent had referred to him as a 'radio disc jockey.'

Russ's date reached over and tried to unbutton Russ's top button of his shirt. "You need to get some air, sugar."

Russ pushed her hand aside. "Just a minute, Mr. Goble."

"That's Noble, sir."

"I need to speak to you. Alone."

Frank looked at his watch and then agreed to go into the next room with Russ. Russ left his date alone and went with Frank to try and clear up the mistake. "I'm sorry to spring this on you so late, Mr. Holloway, but you see, we have a very touchy situation here. You see, quite frankly, the mayor refuses to ride with you. Now, we could have put the mayor in the lead car but the Chief of Police refuses to ride with the mayor."

"Well, why can't the mayor ride with the fire chief?"

"He could, and we suggested that. Believe me, the President is very upset by this whole thing. The problem is, that would put Mrs. Rampaul in the rear car, which is totally unacceptable with her. I'm sure you can understand that. After all, the DAR organized this whole affair."

"Then put the Mayor and the Kraut in the rear car."

Frank put his arm around Russ. "I've listened to your show Mr. Holloway, and it's apparent to me, and I'm sure all your listeners, what an intelligent, articulate man you are. Now, can you imagine, what would happen, politically that is, if the Mayor of Los Angeles were forced to ride in the rear car? It would be disastrous. Listen, the President asked me to ask you as a personal favor to him to go along with this arrangement. And please, feel free to bring your friend along."

Then Frank excused himself and directed Russ back into the waiting room. Somebody had turned on some music and when Russ came through the door, his date was in the middle of the room doing the cha-cha with the Mayor. Russ tore off his bowtie and stuck it in his pocket. Somebody was going to pay for this.

––––––––

When June didn't answer her phone, Martin got a little nervous. He waited about half an hour and then tried again. Still no answer. Where the hell was she? It was a quarter till nine. He decided to wait fifteen more minutes and try again. He paced the floor for ten minutes, imagining the worst. Something had happened to one of the kids; Sukowski had found them and taken them and June away. He picked up the phone and dialed her number. Nothing.

Martin stared at the shotgun leaning against the wall in the corner of the room. He didn't want to take it with him, didn't want to contribute to the vision, but, for some strange reason, he felt better with it around. He grabbed his car keys and the gun and ran out to the Vega. He told himself he was only going to June's apartment, nothing in the dream about that, perfectly okay to take the gun.

When he got to June's apartment, he found a note tacked to the door. It was not what he wanted to find.

Martin, in case you didn't get the message on your machine, I've taken the kids to L.A. to see the President. Will meet you at your job at noon.

Martin used his key—he had conveniently forgotten to return it to June—and let himself into her apartment. He needed to sit down and figure this whole thing out. There was a little wine in her fridge, which he quickly downed. She went to L.A.? This was bad, very bad. He went through the bedroom to use the toilet and on the way back out he spied the stuffed Mickey Mouse next to the bed. He reached over and picked it up. "Come on Mickey, let's go for a ride."

He threw Mickey into the passenger seat and sat there for a moment pondering the unfortunate turn of events. The shotgun was in the trunk. All he had to do was drop it off at his trailer on his way out of town. He started the car and pulled out onto the road, but instead of going north, toward his place, he went directly to Laguna Canyon Road and headed inland toward the freeway. There was a painter's cap between the two front seats. Martin grabbed it and stuck it on Mickey's head. "Liddell rides again," he said to his stuffed companion. It was a quarter till ten. With any luck he'd be in L.A. before eleven, especially now that he was free to use the car pool lane.

TWENTY-ONE

Two-ton and Cervante had quite a walk ahead of them. Kramer had marked an exact manhole for them to enter and it was a good six blocks away from the target area. They had planned on tying Wade Parker up and leaving him inside the entrance but then Two-ton came up with a better idea: With so much stuff to carry, why not put the young officer to work? And so the three of them set off on their trek through the sewers of Los Angeles, Parker loaded down with a backpack, and a beer-keg now filled with kerosene.

It stunk pretty badly down there and Wade Parker was up to his calves in muck (Cervante had boots). Two-ton led the way, flashlight in hand, his giant steps splashing even more filth onto Parker, while Cervante brought up the rear, prodding Parker along with the tip of his pistol.

"How much farther is it?" a tired Parker asked.

"Just keep moving and don't ask questions," said Cervante.

"This keg's heavy. What are you going to do with all this beer down here, anyway?"

"I said, shut up." Cervante gave Parker a shove and the soiled police officer dropped the keg. Muddy water splashed up onto Two-ton and Parker. Two-ton stopped and turned around. "Now look what you did. I'm soaking wet."

"He pushed me," said Parker.

"Pick it up," said Two-ton, holding the light down on the keg. "And cut the rough stuff, Cervante."

"Tell this pig to keep his mouth shut."

Parker retrieved the muddy keg and cradled it in his arms.

The stench was overwhelming so he heaved the keg up onto one shoulder hoping to get the fumes away from his nose, but it was just too damn awkward up there and he soon dropped it back down into his arms. His freshly laundered uniform was now completely splattered with sludge.

The threesome proceeded ahead and after another hundred yards they came upon a section that was closed off by a thick steel-mesh grating, making any forward movement impossible.

"What's that?" said Two-ton.

"We must have come too far."

"I better check the map. This isn't supposed to be here."

The three men stopped and Two-ton pulled the map from his backpack and opened it up. Cervante nudged Parker. "Get down on your hands and knees."

"What?"

"You heard me. I don't want you getting any ideas."

"Look, I'm not gonna try anything. It's filthy down here."

"Give the guy a break, Cervante."

"Well, then, put your hands up against the wall where I can keep an eye on them. You make one false move and you're dead meat." He sounded a little like Edward G. Robinson. Two-ton was going to say something about it, but with all of Cervante's other strange behavior he figured it was best left alone.

Parker set the keg down, then he leaned up against the wall while Cervante and Two-ton checked their map. "We've still got a block to go," said Two-ton.

"We'll just have to turn here and go around."

"Left or right?"

"What difference does it make? Go left."

The three men continued on to their left. When they got to the next corner, a bigger surprise awaited them. Not only could they not turn right to make up for their detour, they could no longer move in the direction they were headed. "We'll have to go left again," said Cervante.

"Hey, I just noticed, you're not doing it anymore."

"Doing what?"

"Repeating yourself."

"I don't know what you're talking about. Let's get moving."

"Hey, how about one of you guys carrying this keg for awhile. My arms are about to fall off."

Cervante stuck his pistol right up into Parker's face. "Listen, pig, you just keep your mouth shut or I'll shut it for you. This ain't no policeman's ball."

"I'll carry it," said Two-ton. "Here," he said to Parker, "you take the flashlight and lead the way."

"I don't believe this," said Cervante. "We should have shot him, like I wanted."

After two more detours and another forty-five minutes of dredging through the sludge, they finally arrived at what they believed to be the correct location. It was getting close to ten o'clock. Two-ton busily prepared the bombs while Cervantes kept a silent vigil over the worn out motorcycle cop who was now sitting on the keg.

"You don't have to point that gun at me, you know," Wade said to Cervante.

"You talk too much."

"So, Two-ton. What happened to you? Why'd you quit playing ball?"

"I got suspended. You're gonna have to get off that keg now."

Parker got up from his seat. "You were the best. Too bad"

The first two bombs Two-ton had set up were small ones, not unlike the variety used in the shopping centers. These he attached to the manhole covers with tape. The third one, the one destined for the grand finale, was the keg. Two-ton had to rig up a swing to support it directly below the man-hole, which took some doing (there weren't a lot of places to tie off a rope) but he finally managed to get it together, and then Cervante and Parker heaved the keg into place.

"Okay, all set. Let's get out of here. I'm starving," said Two-ton.

"What about him?"

238

"Well, we'll take him with us."

"Where?"

"What do you mean?"

"I mean, we can't just keep him with us forever, Two-ton."

"Well, we can't just kill a man in cold blood."

"What do you think is going to happen when these bombs go off? A lot of people are going to die."

"That's different. I won't have to watch."

Cervante pulled a knife from his belt. "You don't have to watch now. You go ahead and I'll catch up with you."

Right about that time, Parker must have realized his luck was running out. He still had the flashlight in his hands and when Cervante turned to face him, he switched off the light and began running down the dark sewer.

"Hey, he's getting away!" Cervante raised his gun to shoot him but Two-ton grabbed his arm. "They'll hear it up there."

"We can't just let him go."

"By the time he finds his way out of here, it'll be too late. Let's go."

"He's got our flashlight."

"I've got some matches, and I've got the map. We'll be fine."

"I don't believe this," said Cervante. "We should have shot him, like I wanted."

———

It cost June ten dollars to park her car in some black guy's driveway—she wasn't even sure he lived there—and she still had to walk half a mile with the kids through a pretty rough looking neighborhood. She had lived in Southern California all her life, yet this was the first time she'd ever been to South Central. Well, she'd driven through on the ten, but she'd never walked the sidewalks before, and it made her nervous today.

Groups of young black men gathered about on broken down porches, many of them drinking beer and whistling as she passed by. She was struck by the inconsistency of the neighborhood. She passed a house that was completely dilapidated, weeds overrunning the yard, newspaper taped over broken windows, graffiti covering the walls, and then, right next door, stood a completely renovated cottage complete with a picket fence and manicured lawn. The only thing the two houses had in common were the iron bars on the windows.

Juan and Maria did not seem the least bit bothered by their surroundings. Perhaps they were so excited about seeing the President, they didn't notice. Or maybe it didn't look that bad to them. And after a few blocks, June began to relax, too. People passing her on the sidewalk smiled and said hello, and there were small children gathered together in yards, playing games. Thousands of people ate and slept here, raised families and went to work. It couldn't be easy, June was sure of that, and she couldn't help but respect them for their efforts, but her strongest feeling was one of embarrassment, not only for her ignorance, but for her fear; mostly for her fear.

It took them about fifteen minutes to make the walk. June had stopped for a minute to show the kids where Martin worked but they really weren't very interested aside from the colorful tent wrapped around the building next door. June tried to explain what the tent was for but she couldn't find the word (extermination) in her book.

When they finally arrived at the parade area, there was already a large crowd jockeying for position along the street. Vendors had set up corner stands, hawking everything from t-shirts with the President's image embossed on the front, to sodas in flag-painted paper cups. June bought some sodas for the kids, then she stopped a police officer to ask how long it would be before the President arrived. "Stay on the other side of the ropes and please keep moving."

———

Spike had no problem getting through the gate with Liddell's keys but it had taken him a few tries to get the card to open the front door. Once on the roof, he had situated himself behind the utility shed so that if anyone were to come up there he would be out of sight, yet still have a clear view of the action below him.

He had taken his remotes from his pack and checked each one, making sure the batteries were in place. Then he lined them up on the ground in the intended order of detonation. He checked the area with his binoculars, paying particular attention to the corner where Wanda would be standing. (She hadn't gotten there yet, but it was only seven o'clock. Nothing to worry about.) The place was thick with cops and for the first time Spike wondered if he would actually be able to get away when this was over.

He thought about Cervante and Two-ton, somewhere under the street right now, setting their bombs. They were so incompetent. When he came to L.A., Spike had planned on getting to Noble, face to face, let him know exactly why he was dying, and then he ran into Two-ton, and now here he was, about to wipe out a bunch of strangers. He felt bad about that, he really did; he'd never killed anyone in his life, even in Panama. He kept telling himself that Noble had to pay for what he had done, but now, as he watched the crowd below him growing in size, women and children crossing back and forth over the very spot where the explosions would be, he wished there were some other way. He was tired; he needed some rest. He set the alarm on his wristwatch for nine o'clock and lay back for a nap. Maybe, when he woke, he would think of something.

———

They brought out the Fire Chief and Mrs. Rampaul first. The crowd that had gathered outside the Bonaventure gave them a token round of applause. The couple got into their limo, along with the two Secret Service men, and the limo pulled forward enough to allow the other two limos to move into position. Russ Holloway came out with his date, arm in arm, followed close behind by the Chief of Police, who seemed strained trying to keep up with them. Russ did not wave to the crowd or bother to smile, but rather kept his eyes fixed on the ground before him. He had one arm around the redhead and the other wrapped around his own middle, as if he were carrying something inside his jacket.

No sooner had Russ and the others entered their limo than the crowd burst into a thunderous round of applause as the President and the Mayor exited the hotel and made their way down the short walk to their car. There were a dozen agents on either side of them, with Frank Noble leading the way.

The President smiled and waved generously to the crowd, and he and the mayor stopped just short of the limo and shook hands as photographers pushed and shoved their way into position for the best shot. Frank opened the back door to the limo and helped the two statesmen in. So far, so good.

"Let's get this show on the road," said the President.

"We'll be taking off in just a moment, sir. We're still waiting for the lead cyclist."

Officer Parker was supposed to arrive an hour ago and still had not shown up. Frank closed the President's door then went back to the third limo to speak to the Chief of Police.

"We're still waiting on your patrolman, Chief. You assured me a responsible officer would be chosen." Frank made no effort to disguise his anger regarding the absent cop.

"Officer Parker is one of our best. Something must have happened to him."

"Well, we can't wait any longer. I'm putting somebody else up front."

"But nobody else knows the route."

"I'll have to give him directions from the President's limo."

"I have a better idea. Why don't I guide him? After all, I know this city like the back of my hand. We don't want any mistakes."

Frank did not appreciate the chief's remark. It seemed impertinent, to him. "I think I'm capable of reading directions off a sheet of paper, chief. Thanks anyway."

He slammed the limo door shut, then went to the front of

242

the caravan, picked out an officer at random and explained the plan. "Do not," he said, "under any circumstances, sway from my directions. Understood?"

"Yes, sir," said the officer. "Loud and clear."

"Good. Let's get moving."

Frank walked back to the limo and stood by the door, one hand on the handle, and stared into the horizon. It was coming; he could feel it. But where? When?

―――――――

There was a lot of traffic on the freeway, but with Mickey by his side, Martin made it to L.A. in just over an hour. He went directly to the job site. The streets were packed with people and blockades had been set up at the corner, just three buildings away. He got out of his car to unlock the gate but found the lock hanging open from the chain. He was sure he had locked it on Friday, but he thought perhaps the electricians had been in on Saturday and had forgotten to lock up. He opened the gate and pulled his car inside the grounds then closed it behind him so as not to encourage anyone else to park there.

Next door, the exterminators were busy unwrapping the building. It didn't look to Martin like all that tarp could fit in the back of one truck, but he guessed they knew what they were doing.

He had no idea where to begin looking for June. There had to be a couple of thousand people out there. It was a quarter till eleven and the President would be arriving any moment. Maybe it was best to just wait here for June to arrive with the kids, rather than fight that crowd. He left the shotgun wrapped in a blanket in the back seat, grabbed Mickey Mouse and headed for the front door. Can't very well shoot the gun if I don't have it, he thought as he entered the building.

Once he got inside, he left the door unlocked so June could get in, then he got into the elevator and headed for the roof. Now that he was actually in the building, he was no longer nervous, and in fact, he felt a little ridiculous about all the worrying he had done over his vision. And he had even told that cop. The look she had given him.

The elevator reached the top floor and Martin got out to take the stairs to the roof. The place was looking pretty good. Talbert's enamel work really was exceptional. It was a shame most people didn't appreciate the difference, didn't give a man like Talbert his due. He was a true craftsman, a vanishing breed.

He pushed open the door to the roof and stepped out into the bright sun, the Disney character tucked under one arm. It was a good ten degrees warmer up there than it was on the ground. He walked to the edge of the roof. He could see the barricades at the end of the street and hear the distant roar of the crowd, anxiously awaiting the President's arrival; and there was music— it sounded like Dixieland, but it was hard to say for sure with all the noise. Next door, the men busily folded the tarp and began stuffing it into the bed of the truck. Martin laughed to himself, realizing he had probably created the infestation with Vern's roaches. Then he thought of June and the kids, and recalled his most recent dream. He was starting to worry again; he should be down there now, looking for them, and he resolved to do just that, and then he heard a noise, a clicking sound, and turned around. There, not ten feet away, stood Marvin Sukowski, his gun drawn and pointed at Martin.

"We meet again," said Sukowski. "Only this time, I don't see your fat friend with the shotgun. But, maybe your little Teddy Bear can help you."

Martin glanced down at the stuffed Mickey Mouse. Just how stupid was this guy? "What do you want?"

"I want your wet-back friend. But first, you and me have a score to settle."

"Yeah, well, he ain't here, so you're wasting your time." Martin gazed around the roof looking for an avenue of escape. Right now he was wishing he had brought the shotgun with him.

"He'll be here."

"What makes you so sure?"

"Because I got ears, and you make stupid phone calls. I have to admit, though, your girlfriend sounds sexy. I might have to pay her a visit, myself."

"Yeah, you should do that, if you ever get off this roof."

"You and I are both getting off this roof, only you're taking the fast route. Now move over by the edge."

Martin just smiled.

"I'm glad you think that's funny."

"You were half right, my fat friend's not here. Unfortunately for you, the shotgun is."

"Drop the gun, señor."

Sukowski slowly turned around. Directly behind him, with shotgun in hand pointed at his head, stood Curtis Chang, and he looked very pissed off.

TWENTY-TWO

Frank had argued for half an hour with the President, trying to get him to call off the tour, but he just wouldn't hear of it. "If I backed out now, Frank, I wouldn't have to worry about an assassin; the press would do the job for them. And what have you got, really? A dead house painter and a bitter model that goes around blowing up underwear displays. There hasn't been any threat on my life, and you know as well as I, these people always make their threats. They crave the publicity."

"There was the letter. And you do have substantial holdings in Electra Bras."

"The letter was two weeks ago and there wasn't any direct threat mentioned. Now, as far as those stocks are concerned, we had to dump some other holdings on account of an alleged conflict of interest, so we bought into Electra. It seemed innocuous enough, at the time. I can assure you, I never even heard of this Wanda what's-her-name."

"Blade. That's what she calls herself, now. Her real name was Moore. She did all their ads for a couple of years. You don't remember the slogan? 'I get a charge out of my Electra.'"

The President laughed. "I'm afraid I don't watch much television."

"Well, I got the information from a detective working on the case."

"It's a catchy slogan, but, unless you've got something else to tell me, something more substantial, the tour is on. And that's my final word on it."

And so they loaded up the limos and proceeded toward

South Central L.A. As they drove along, Frank went over the procedure with the President one more time. In the case of an emergency, he was to hit the floor and put his hands over his head. Frank would then throw himself on top of the President.

"What about me?" asked the Mayor.

Frank looked over at the Mayor. He was a small, fragile looking man. Frank wondered how he ever withstood the rigors of campaigning. "There's only room on the floor for one. Just get down in your seat and Mr. Carter, here, will take care of you." Frank was referring to the other agent riding along with them.

The light on the phone lit up and Frank picked up the receiver. It was Kate Mallory. She explained the foul-up at Two-ton's and said they hadn't found anything substantial at the house, but she was sure Dubois had been there.

"One other thing. We found a police motorcycle—what was left of it anyway—not far from the tour area. Belongs to a Wade Parker."

"Parker. That's the guy who was supposed to lead the procession today. That can't be good."

"You're probably right, Frank. They found the bike around six this morning. The guy wasn't even supposed to be on duty until nine. This whole thing is getting weirder by the minute. I'm at the tour sight now. I'm going to park my car and go on foot, see if I can spot anything."

"Okay. Watch yourself out there."

"I'll see you when it's over. We'll have dinner. My treat."

Frank hung up, and rechecked his directions. They were close now, just a couple more blocks. He picked up a second phone; this one was a direct line to the motorcycle officer leading the procession.

"Turn left on the next street."

"Are you sure, sir?"

"Absolutely."

"Whatever you say."

Frank hung up the phone. Everybody wants to be in charge, he thought.

———————

Wade Parker had come to an intersection in the sewer and was trying to figure out which way to go. He had made a lot of turns, trying his best to evade the two terrorists in case they were following him, and had tried a dozen man-hole covers, but all had been welded shut. He was beginning to think that maybe he was going in circles. To make matters worse, the batteries in the flashlight were getting weak and his left arm had fallen asleep from carrying that damn keg for so long. Wade was starting to get worried. What if he lost his arm? What if those bombs went off while he was still down here? He could be killed. And what about his motorcycle? The big guy (Two-ton) had wheeled it into an alley and dumped it behind some trashcans; just pushed it over, like it was junk. What if some gang members found it and were stripping it down? The thought (the picture) of that was just too painful to consider. He had to get his mind right, had to concentrate, had to find a way out of this hellhole, and soon.

He was pretty sure he'd lost the two men by now, no need for anymore zigzagging, just head in a straight line, if possible. He had no idea which way was which so he just pointed himself in one direction and took off. The going was slow—the hike in with the beer keg had tired him out—and he ran into a couple of blockades, forcing him to make detours, but he managed to keep his sense of direction and after a while came upon another man-hole. He climbed up the metal steps on the side of the wall and gave a shove. It was heavy but he felt it move a little. He lifted his sleeping arm up and pushed as best he could with both hands this time and a stream of bright light poured through. Daylight!

Wade pushed the cover completely off the hole then carefully poked his head up. He was in the middle of a street but there was no traffic. He quickly climbed out onto the pavement. A couple of small children pointed at him and started laughing, but Wade didn't pay them any mind. He had to get oriented. He knew he couldn't be too far from the parade, but what direction?

"Hey, you kids, come here." Wade's voice was weak and scratchy sounding.

The two children shook their heads, no. He must have looked like some kind of monster to them, his police uniform was plastered with filth from the sewer, and his hands and face were caked with the now dried mud.

A voice called out from behind him. "What you doing there in the street like that?"

Wade turned around. An old black woman was standing on her porch, pointing a broom handle at him. She was a rather large woman with curly grey hair and she wore a house dress that hung all the way down to her heavy black shoes. "Go on away from here. Quit bothering them children."

"I'm a police officer. Do you have a car?"

The woman laughed. "A car. Now, that's a good one. I ain't even got no groceries, and even if I did have a car—which I don't—I most definitely would not give it to you. You got no business around here. Go on now, before I call the police."

"Lady, I am the police." Wade rummaged through his pockets in vain, trying to find his badge. "Can you tell me how to get to Normandie and Martin Luther King?"

"Martin Luther King? He's dead, fool."

"No, lady, the street."

"What you wanna go there for?"

"The President is in danger; I have to warn him. It's an emergency."

"The President. Ha! I got some things I like to say to him, myself. But he ain't gonna talk to me and he sure ain't gonna wanna talk to you. You must be some kind of fool, alright."

"Lady, please."

"What kinda danger?"

"I don't have time to explain. Please, just point me in the right direction."

The woman put one hand on her hip and shook her head in disgust. Then she pointed with her broom. "Go on up about six blocks, then turn left. But you better put that lid back on so them children don't fall in."

But Wade had already started running.

"Where are the ninos, Martin?" Curtis had the shotgun jammed right up into the small of Sukowski's back.

"My wife has them down there somewhere." Martin pointed at the door. "You better watch your back. Our friend here usually has a partner with him."

"I already took care of him." He slowly moved the barrel of the shotgun up to Sukowski's face. "What do you think I should do with him?"

"Go ahead you grease-ball; pull the trigger."

Curtis cocked both barrels. "My wife says you weren't very friendly."

"Curtis, why don't you go look for the kids?"

"What about him?"

"I'll keep him here. Give me the gun."

"Are you sure, amigo? I could easily shoot him, then you wouldn't have to get involved."

"I'm already involved. Give me the gun."

Curtis kept the shotgun pointed at Sukowski and moved carefully to the edge of the building, by Martin. "You know how to use this?"

"Just aim and squeeze, right?"

"You don't got to aim much."

"That makes it even easier. You better get going. If June shows up with the kids, I'll send her downstairs."

"Gracias, amigo. Oh, your wife, what does she look like?"

It occurred to Martin that he should explain to Curtis that he and June were no longer together. It also occurred to him

250

that he was still referring to June as his wife, which, he realized—perhaps for the first time—had a nice ring to it.

"You can't miss her. She'll be the only beautiful gringo out there with two small Mexican children."

Curtis headed for the doorway, stopping momentarily by Sukowski. "Till me meet again, pendejo."

"This ain't over yet, Mex."

Curtis laughed and then disappeared into the stairwell. Martin looked down at Mickey Mouse, still tucked under his arm, and called out to Curtis, but he must not have heard him. Sukowski took a step toward Martin. "That's close enough."

"You'll live to regret this day."

"Just seeing your face fills me with regret. Now why don't you just relax and watch the parade." Martin's mind felt clearer than it had in months. It was as though all the moves were being made for him; even his words seemed out of his control.

Sukowski looked down at his gun.

"Tell me something, Sukowski. You believe people can see the future?"

"Fuck you!"

"I never really did, either, but if you make a move for that gun, I'm going to have to reconsider my opinion."

———

As the crowd grew, June and the two children found themselves being squeezed further and further from the street and any chance of a good look at the President. She was searching for some kind of high ground, where they might have a better vantage point, when she noticed a small set of bleachers not far off, occupied by a group of young people; it was some sort of band. They were wearing bright blue uniforms and gold hats, and they all had miniature music stands either strapped around their necks or attached to their instruments. The bleachers only went four or five steps high, but most of the top step was empty.

June forced her way through the unruly crowd. She had placed Maria on her shoulders and had a death grip on Juan's

251

hand. Maria wrapped her tiny arms around June's neck, making it hard for June to breathe, while Juan bounced up and down with delight at all the activity. It was worse than Disneyland.

They reached the bandstand, but rather than ask the conductor for permission, she just handed Maria to a boy sitting in the top row and he obligingly set the young girl in the seat above him. Then she lifted up Juan who immediately started jumping up and down in the bleachers, his joyful screams lost in the chaos around them. June stayed on the ground, an arm's length from her two wards. The band started into a song. June recognized it immediately from her days as a flute player in the high school band. It was Hail To The Chief.

The crowd turned to the north, cheering and waving, and then there was a momentary lull in the noise as everyone dropped their arms and simultaneously turned to the south and raised them up again as though they were doing the "wave" at some sports event. Someone in the band mentioned something about the limos coming from the wrong direction. Not that it mattered to June. She couldn't see a damn thing.

Spike picked up his binoculars and checked for Wanda. The streets were thick with people and Spike figured he'd never be able to pick her out, and maybe that wouldn't be so bad. Maybe she hadn't shown up. That thought brought with it a slight sense of relief; this whole thing was getting a little too real. He looked back at the two men, and then down at his watch. He had slept right through the alarm and had not woken until they had shown up. He wanted off that roof, wanted to forget the whole thing and now he was trapped. That fat guy, Sukowski, would just love to bring down a terrorist, thought Spike. He keeps looking down at his gun. He's gonna go for it and blow Martin's brains out and then I'm gonna have to kill him. He turned his attention back to the street, and there was Wanda. She had her jacket in her hand, hanging down by her side. Let's see, he thought, left shoulder is number one.

There was a lot of noise coming from the street, most of it a block away, a jumbled mixture of cheering and music, but now a new sound caught Spike's attention, one more distinct and close. It was a man's voice, but alternately shrill and then raspy, as if someone with laryngitis were trying to scream. Spike looked through his binoculars toward the street directly below him. The sound seemed to be coming from a man dressed in some kind of dirty uniform, waving one arm over his head as he ran up the street. Spike couldn't make out exactly what the man was saying but he was obviously in a state of panic.

The man was running right along the side of the building now and people were stopping and staring at him. He looked like he had just climbed out of a swamp. Then Spike saw the pick-up truck—the one with the tarp—as it started to pull out from between the buildings and into the street. He looked back to the mud-covered man—there was not enough time to call out—as he raced around the corner and clipped the front fender of the truck. The driver hit the breaks and the man flew up onto the hood and smashed against the windshield. Spike watched in complete awe as the man rolled off the hood of the truck, hit the ground standing and continued running. He got about twenty feet—he was still waving one arm in the air— when he came to a complete stop, turned around and looked at the truck as though he had just realized what had happened, and collapsed in the middle of the road.

Spike looked over toward Martin, who was watching the commotion in the street, then he glanced back at Sukowski, who at that very moment was reaching down for his gun. Spike jumped up and called out. "Martin!"

Martin turned first to Spike, then to Sukowski, who now had his gun pointed at Spike, and then there was a large explosion as the shotgun went off. Spike flinched as Sukowski's legs were blown out from under him, and the big man went down hard on his knees; he didn't appear to have much leg left below them.

When Spike looked back toward Martin, he was gone. The

shotgun was lying on the roof, smoke billowing from the barrels. He could see the people in the street pointing up at the building and knew it wouldn't be long before the place was swarming with cops. He felt a stinging in his neck and reached up with his hand; it was warm and wet and when he pulled his hand away it was covered with blood. He checked his binoculars again. This time he could see Wanda (there were two of her) frantically flipping her jacket from shoulder to shoulder.

Spike set the binoculars down and wiped his eyes with his sleeve. There were two of everything now and the buildings were beginning to spin. He felt dizzy, like he was going to pass out. He searched for the detonators. Now there were six of them. He started to bend over, his intention was to push them out of the way, and then everything went black as he lost consciousness and fell hard onto the floor.

Russ Holloway hadn't said a word since they'd left the Bonaventure, which was okay with the chief. He had managed to get Russ's date to sit next to him and was having the time of his life sharing some of his most exciting police anecdotes with her. Swatter had never actually had to use his gun during his twenty-five years on the force, but he'd heard plenty of stories from the guys. All he had to do was pretend the incidents had involved him.

And Russ's date, Carla—she had finally introduced herself— had been around, too. She had taken a degree in Public Relations, but had not been able to find a decent paying job, so two years ago had started working as a stripper, and raking in a lot of dough in the process. "I could tell you some stories, Chief. Off the record, of course."

The chief was a conservative man, he did not frequent strip joints, but in his mind he had been undressing her all morning. "Quite a gal you got here, Russ."

Russ seemed preoccupied. "How much longer till we get there?"

"Couple more blocks."

Russ opened his jacket and pulled out a headset and a small contraption that looked like a transistor radio.

"What do you have there?"

"This, my friend, is my revenge." He put the headphone on and clipped the box to his jacket pocket. There was a small microphone attached to the headset and Russ began speaking into it. "Testing, one, two. Can you hear me, Nancy? Nancy, are you there? Good. I'm all set to go. Punch me in."

"Russ, did you clear this with security?"

"Don't you want to be on the radio, chief?"

"Well, sure, but…"

"Then don't worry about it. What's the harm? Carla, show the Chief what a good job those surgeons did on your tits."

Carla blushed. "Russ."

"It's not like you haven't shown them before. You wanna see them, don't you Chief?"

"Well, I, I don't want to embarrass the young lady."

"Oh, here we go. Aa-boo-nye, America. This is your humble servant, Russ Holloway, coming to you from inside the President's limo, in beautiful South Central, Los Angeles." As exuberant as Russ's voice started out, it now became equally full of remorse. "Oh, wait a minute, L.A. There's been a mistake. Let me apologize. I'm not in the President's limo. I know, I, I had promised you all I would be with him today, but it's nobody's fault but my own. When the President called me and asked me to ride with him, I took him at his word. After all, he's a Republican, and I'm a Republican. I was caught off guard. I should have remembered, he is first and foremost a politician, and it seems it is more politically correct to ride with our liberal mayor, than an insignificant radio talk-show host like myself."

Carla pulled one of her large breasts from her dress and the Chief turned his attention away from Russ. "Go ahead and touch it," she said. "You can't tell it's not real."

"I don't know if I should, Carla."

Carla reached over and grabbed his hand. "It's just a tit, chief." She placed his hand under her breast and the chief let it rest there like a potato, afraid to move one finger for fear of being accused of feeling her up.

"What they had to do," said Carla, "was make an incision right here at the bottom. If you look close, you can still see a light pink scar." She ran her finger in a half circle around the bottom of her breast.

The limo turned the corner and the chief glanced out the window. Hundreds of screaming fans squeezed up against the retaining ropes, hoping to get a closer look at the President. Now and then a daring soul would slip underneath it and approach one of the limos, only to be grabbed by the collar and yanked away by a secret service agent or a uniformed cop. Swatter wasn't sure, but it seemed to him they were going in the wrong direction. Across the seat from Swatter, Russ continued on with his speech.

"I suppose if I were of the darker persuasion, things might have turned out differently, but I'm of a different minority altogether. I'm white and employed, and—and this is the real stinger, good people—I'm wealthy. It's politically correct to snub..."

At the word "snub," there was an enormous explosion and the limo began to lift off the ground. The chief looked down at his hand on Carla's breast, then at the floorboard as a huge chunk of metal burst through. It looked like part of a keg of beer. It only took maybe a second for the limo to split in two and the Chief watched in horror as the front half flipped over and began spinning upside down before him. Each time the front half spun around he could see Russ grasping in desperation for something to hold onto, his mouth wide open, his eyes screaming in absolute horror. Then, something hit the chief in the head and he felt himself begin to lose consciousness. Later on, when asked by reporters what he had seen, Swatter would recall the last image before passing out was that of Russ Holloway being spit out onto the road like a battered Jonah.

Minutes before the explosion, Kate Mallory worked her way through the street, hoping against hope for some kind of clue that might help her abort whatever it was the PTA had in mind. She had her badge pinned on her jacket so she could move freely on the inside of the rope, away from the massive crowd that packed the sidewalks. It was probably eighty-five degrees out, but down on the street, surrounded by all these people it felt closer to a hundred.

She passed a set of bleachers where a small band started in to Hail To The Chief. The roar of the crowd was deafening. Then they stopped, just for a second, and quickly started up again. Only now, they were facing in the opposite direction. Kate turned to see the limos coming around the corner, headed her way. It caught her off guard; she had expected them to come from the other direction. And there was something else. In that instant when the crowd had quieted down, she had heard another sound, something familiar, yet foreign to the surroundings. It sounded like a gunshot; it had come from somewhere behind the limos. And there was something else, right after the sound; she had caught a glimpse of it out of the corner of her eye. It appeared to be a body, a body falling from the top of a building half a block away. Kate recognized the building; she had been there just a few days earlier.

Most of the people in the crowd either didn't hear the gunshot or chose to pay it no attention, but there was a woman across the street, on the corner, who was staring up at the building, swinging her jacket over one shoulder, then the other, then frantically back and forth.

"Wanda," said Kate quietly. She pulled her gun and started running across the street toward the woman. "Wanda Blade!" she yelled and the woman dropped her jacket, reached behind her back and brought out a pistol. Kate fired and Wanda grabbed her side as the bullet tore through her flesh. The crowd definitely heard that shot and began to scatter as the lead limo moved closer to the two women. The police tried to maintain order, but as panic set in the crowd began to trample over one another in a desperate attempt to flee the area. The bleachers that held the band began to shake and the music came to an abrupt halt.

Then there came a tremendous explosion that shook the buildings and knocked Kate from her feet. She landed hard on her back and her gun flew from her hand. There was a squealing of breaks, and when Kate turned her head, the front wheel to the limo came to rest just inches away. All around her were bodies, thrown to the ground from the concussion.

Kate quickly rolled out from under the limo as the second car plowed into the first. She jumped to her feet just in time to see a body come flying out of the front half of the third limo just before the severed car slammed into the rear of the one before it. The back half of the third limo rolled up onto the sidewalk and came to a stop not ten feet away from Kate. There were two people inside of it, an attractive redhead with her dress pulled down to her waist, and the Chief of Police, passed out with one hand cupped around her naked breast, the other still pointed at the gruesome sight before them. Having been spit out of the limo, Russ Holloway was now affixed at the stomach to a metal pole so that his body hung at half-mast like a human flag. On the ground, below the skewered victim were the broken remains of a sign that read: no parking any time.

Kate turned away from the disgusting sight. She was still feeling dizzy from the concussion, and now this had made her sick to her stomach. All around her, people were running and screaming; many were lying on the ground, wounded from the concussion of the explosion. Wanda had disappeared and the place was now swarming with men in black suits who had quickly surrounded the President's limo. Citizens trampled over one another in a frantic attempt to flee the area. Then she heard a familiar voice.

"Kate, are you alright?" It was Frank.

"Yeah, I think so. The President…"

"He's fine, but we have to get him out of here."

"I saw Wanda. I think I hit her but she got away."

"We'll get her, don't worry."

Kate pointed to the building down the street. "He's up there."

"Who?"

"Whoever set off the explosion. He's on the roof."

"I'll go. You better sit down, take it easy."

"I'm going after Wanda."

"Be careful," he said and took off toward the building. Kate grabbed a couple of uniformed cops who helped her squeeze her way through the frenzied crowd to her car, and went looking for Wanda Blade. She was wounded, Kate was sure of that. She couldn't have gotten far.

TWENTY-THREE

Frank came out onto the roof, one hand in his pocket and the other holding his pistol. He found a man lying close to the doorway in a puddle of blood, both legs ripped to shreds, a pistol still gripped loosely in one hand. Frank took his hand from his pocket and felt for a pulse but from the amount of blood on the floor, he didn't really expect to find one. He was right. Not far from the body, by the edge of the roof, lay a shotgun. Frank walked over and picked it up. Both barrels had been spent. He leaned against the edge and looked down to the street. There were cops and SS men everywhere, but few civilians left. Gazing over the edge made him dizzy and he quickly placed his hand back into his pocket. He wondered how many had died in the explosion; he'd only noticed one—the radio commentator—and the image of his twisted body gave Frank a start. He pulled away from the edge. Then there was a voice. "Okay, drop the gun and turn around, slow."

Frank turned around. He still had one hand in his pocket and he had yet to let go of his gun. A black man stepped out from behind a wall. His pistol was pointed at Frank, but his hand was shaking and he was pouring sweat. Frank recognized the face. He'd seen it right at this very spot just a week earlier. "Take it easy," said Frank.

"No, you take it easy, Frank, and drop that gun."

Frank looked across the floor to the dead man. "That your work?"

"That look like a pistol wound to you?" Spike raised his pistol a little so that it was now pointed directly at Frank's head.

"I'm not gonna tell you again. Drop the gun."

"Okay, okay. Just, be careful with that thing." Frank dropped his gun onto the roof. He still had one hand in his pocket.

"Now put your hands up where I can see them."

Frank raised his free hand over his head.

"Both hands."

Frank slowly removed the pocketed hand and lifted his arm above his head. He felt dizzy and weak in the knees and he could feel his body begin to sway. He was afraid he might pass out.

"What's the matter with you?"

"It's...I can't stand heights. If I could just put my hand back in my pocket."

"What? What are you trying to pull?"

Frank was getting weaker by the moment. "I'm going to pass out."

"Well, go on, put your hand down. But I'm warning you, you try anything and you're a dead man."

Frank stuck his hand back in his pocket. He immediately felt better.

"You don't know who I am, do you?"

"I suspect you're the person who just tried to kill the President of the United States."

"Wrong. I could give a shit about some jerk-off politician. Guess again."

"Look, whoever you are, I'm not very good at guessing games." Spike lowered the gun a bit.

"You look like you've lost a lot of blood," said Frank. "You should get to a doctor."

Spike took something from his pocket. "I've got something belongs to you." He tossed the item at Frank's feet. "Pick it up."

Frank reached down and picked up the watch. He recognized it immediately. "This is...my father gave this to me. Where did you get this?"

"From my mother. You probably don't remember her,

either. She was just a good time you had one night, just another white boy out for his black wings."

But Frank hadn't forgot. He had given her the watch hoping she would sell it and use the money. All these years she had held on to it. "Your mother's still alive?"

"Why, you want another run at her?"

"Look, it was a long time ago. I don't understand…"

Spike cocked the gun and his anger seemed to intensify. "Look at me! Take a good look."

Frank stared at the large black man, his neck and one side of his body covered with blood, his eyes filled with hate. Then he looked down at the watch and all of a sudden he understood. He spoke very softly. "I had no idea."

"You could have asked. You could have come back."

"I don't know what to say to you. I did come back. That night, after I dropped her off, I came back to find her, to tell her…well, that she didn't have to do it, that we'd figure something out. Anyway, she was gone when I got back. I had no idea where she lived. I left for boot-camp the next morning, I assumed she was going to have it taken care…that is, I didn't think…"

"You didn't think? You didn't care! You didn't care if she had an abortion, or, or me. She was just a piece of ass. A black piece of ass for some rich white boy."

"You're wrong about that. First of all, I wasn't rich, not even close. And second, I cared very much about your mother, but…things were different then. It was a different world." Frank thought back to those nights at the lake. Her image was still so clear in his mind. "I thought about your mother a lot when I was in Nam. I thought about trying to find her…you're mother was a beautiful woman."

"She still is, Frank."

"Of course. Of course she is." Frank lowered his eyes. "So, what do we do now?"

"I don't have much choice, do I? I either kill you or go to jail for the rest of my life."

"You shoot me, you'll never get out of this building alive. There are cops everywhere. Answer one question for me. Did you detonate the bomb?"

"What's the difference?"

"It makes a difference to me."

"What if I say I didn't? You're gonna believe me?"

"I don't know. Try me."

Spike stood silent for a minute trying to take in everything that had just happened. He was getting weaker by the moment and his hand with the pistol began to drop so that now the gun was pointed at Frank's knees. "I don't know. I mean, I came up here to do it, but then I saw all those people down there, little kids." He reached up to his neck. "I got shot, I must have passed out. Maybe I fell on the detonator. I don't know."

"What's your name?"

"Spike."

"Your Christian name."

"Ronnie. Ronald. What the hell do you care? It's a little late to be getting acquainted." He raised the gun back up at Frank's body.

"Okay, Ronnie, just, take it easy. What I want you to do is give me the gun, and then you and I are going to walk downstairs and get in my car. I'll take you to a hospital, and then I want you to get on a plane and go home to your mother."

"Right. You're gonna let me just walk out of here."

"It's up to you. But you better decide quick."

Spike raised the gun higher now toward Frank's head. "You're just trying to save your own ass."

"If you really believe that, all you have to do is pull the trigger. But before you do, think about your mother. I almost took you from her back then; don't you do it now."

The two men stood in silence staring at each other, Frank wondering if his life were about to end. Then, Spike pointed the gun above Frank's head and fired off a couple rounds. He walked toward Frank then stopped abruptly and dropped the gun at his feet. "This don't make things right," he said.

Frank was silent. He looked down at the dead man and then back at Spike. "We've got some work to do," he said. "Help me with this body."

When the large bomb exploded, the concussion knocked Two-ton and Cervante off their feet and ruptured one of Cervante's eardrums. They had been searching for a way out for over an hour but had somehow ended up less than a quarter mile from the explosion. Two-ton helped Cervante to his feet. There was blood trickling from his ear.

"Are you okay?"

"What?"

"I said, are you okay?"

"I think so. Your voice sounds funny. Everything is ringing."

"I think you ruptured your eardrum; it's bleeding."

"It's what?"

"Bleeding. Your ear is bleeding. Come on, we gotta get out of here."

They walked another fifty feet where they found another manhole, then Two-ton reached into his bag and pulled out a small package. "I'm tired of looking for an open one." He handed the package to Cervante. "Climb up the ladder and tape this to the cover. Set the timer for thirty seconds."

"How long?"

"Thirty seconds."

"Okay."

Two-ton started moving away from the area. "Soon as you set it, run like hell."

Cervante taped the small package up, set the timer, and then dropped down to the ground, twisting his ankle in the process. "Two-ton. My leg, help me."

Two-ton was already twenty yards away. He stopped and ran back toward Cervante. "What's wrong?"

"I twisted my ankle." Two-ton picked him up, threw him

over his shoulder and started running. For a minute there, he was back on the football field with the old Silver and Blue; he could almost smell the pigskin. He got about thirty yards before the bomb went off. Both men went down hard, Two-ton on top. When the smoke cleared away, Two-ton rolled off of Cervante. "You okay?"

"I think so. You?"

"I took some shrapnel in my back. Help me up."

Cervante helped the large man up. Blood oozed from the shrapnel wounds and Cervante quickly began pulling the pieces of metal out of Two-ton's flesh, but the large man stopped him. "There's no time for this, now, Raymond."

The two men hobbled back to the manhole and were pleased to discover the bomb had worked—sort of. The blast had blown away most of the man-hole cover but had left a small section about two inches wide, making the hole a little smaller than normal. Cervante climbed up the ladder and stuck his head through the hole. The street was virtually deserted. The other explosion had probably scared everybody off.

Cervante climbed through the opening then reached down to help Two-ton. The big man managed to get the upper half of his body through the opening but when he got to his middle he got stuck.

"Pull on my arms."

"What?"

"I said pull. I can't get through."

Cervante grabbed Two-ton's arms and began tugging. Two-ton didn't budge. "It's no use. Maybe if you get down below me and push."

"I am pulling."

A car came around the corner and sped past the two men, barely missing Cervante.

"Cervante, listen. You need to get below and push."

Cervante stared down at Two-ton, his fat body stuck in the manhole, blood still seeping from his wounds. It would be so easy to just walk away. Time was everything and going back down into that sewer just didn't seem like a good idea. Two-ton, suspended halfway to freedom must have read his mind for he quickly grabbed the smaller man by the ankle.

"Hey. You hear me?"

"Yeah, yeah, I heard you. Let go of my leg." He tried to free his leg but there was no way Two-ton was letting go.

"Sure I will. Soon as we get down inside again. Don't think I don't know what you're thinking."

"You don't trust me?"

"We're wasting time here, Raymond."

Two-ton slowly let himself down into the sewer, Cervante in tow right behind him. "Okay, now listen carefully. I'll get my upper body half through, and then I can push down on the street while you push up on me. Understand?"

"I am pulling," said Cervante. He seemed a million miles away.

"Oh, God." Two-ton grabbed Cervante by the shoulders and started shaking him. "Snap out of it. Cervante."

"What?"

"When I get half way through…"

"Yeah, I know, I push up."

Two-ton took a deep breath then started up the ladder. He got his head and shoulders out the hole, checked both ways for cars and then pulled himself out a little further. "Okay, start pushing."

Cervante had to step on the second rung in order to reach Two-ton's ass. He started pushing with both hands but almost fell off the ladder, so he switched to one hand, holding the bar to balance himself with the other. To make matters worse, blood from Two-ton's wounds kept dripping into his eyes and every minute or so he'd have to stop and wipe it away.

Two-ton pushed down hard on the street. The shrapnel dug deeper into his back and sent waves of pain through his body. But Two-ton was used to pain; he had taken plenty on the gridiron for twelve years, had played with the kind of pain that would put most men on their backs. He could feel his body moving ever so slowly. It would work, but it was going to take some doing. Up he went, inch by inch, first his chest, then the bulk of his stomach clearing the hole. It wouldn't be long now. Then he saw a flash of red come whipping around the corner and head his way. It was a car and it was moving fast, maybe a hundred yards away. Then another car, a cop car with siren blaring, appeared. "Oh shit. Pull me back. Cervante. Pull me back in!"

"I am pushing," said Cervante. "It's hard to get any leverage down here."

"No. Pull! Pull, not push." The car moved closer. It looked very familiar to Two-ton. It was so close now, he could read the license plate. It was a custom one and it read: 1htmdl.

"One hot model," he said in a whisper. "Wanda."

"It's no use," said Cervante. "I can't budge you." But something was very strange. Two-ton's body had gone into spasms for a few seconds and then become very limp, and it seemed to get even heavier. And there was something else, something wet and warm easing through the manhole and running down onto Cervante's hands and face. "Two-ton. Two-ton!"

Leroy Washington figured he'd make a bundle after the tour. He'd cooked up plenty of extra chicken and had brought in extra help to handle the customers. Hell, he might even sell a few shocks today. When he heard the explosion he figured it for some fireworks, part of the celebration, but then the sirens started and before long, ambulances were racing down his street toward the parade. Something had gone wrong.

He stood out front of the building staring after the sirens when a red convertible skidded around the corner a block away and sped up the road toward his shack. Directly behind the red car were three police cars in hot pursuit. When the car hit the dip in the road at Leroy's corner, the rear end dropped and the whole back of the car started dragging along the road, sparks shooting out from underneath. The driver spun the wheel, turned into Leroy's lot and screeched to a halt not ten feet from Leroy. A woman got out. She was carrying a rifle in one hand and a briefcase in the other.

Leroy recognized the car immediately. He had sold his first pair of shocks to the pretty young woman who owned it. But the woman who was standing there now didn't look anything like her. This woman looked much older, much harder. She came right at Leroy, her rifle pointed at his head.

"Don't shoot! I've got plenty more shocks. No charge."

"Get inside. Now!"

Leroy went into the small building, the barrel of the automatic weapon jammed into his lower back. The lot was filling up with police cars now and a couple of Leroy's girls were going into hysterics. The woman with the rifle pointed it at the ceiling and fired off a few rounds. "Everybody shut up!"

The place went dead silent. Leroy looked out the window. There were cops everywhere. Then he noticed the blood coming from the woman's side. "You're losing a lot of blood, sister."

The woman set her briefcase on the counter and put her free hand over her wound. Leroy turned to one of his girls. "Carla, get some water and bandages."

"Never mind," said the woman. "It's too late for that." The woman looked out at her car, then back at Leroy. "You sold me those shock absorbers, didn't you?"

"You hit the dip pretty fast. Ain't no shock can take that kinda treatment."

"Evidently. You're Leroy, right?"

"That's me."

"You remember me?"

Leroy looked her right in the eye. "Yes'm, I do. You're the model…Wanda."

"You remember me, but you don't recognize me, do you?"

"We all change. Looks like maybe you've seen some hard time."

Wanda laughed out loud. "You think?" She looked around the small restaurant. It was old and beat up, but clean, no trash on the floor, no food lying out. "You've done alright for yourself. These girls all work for you?"

"Yeah, yeah they all good girls. Why don't you let them go?"

Outside, one of the cops, a woman, started talking through a bullhorn. "Wanda Blade, this is Detective Mallory. Come out with your hands up."

"I need something to eat," said Wanda.

"I got tons of chicken. I made extra for today."

"Get me some." She pointed to one of the girls. "Come here."

The girl moved nervously toward Wanda.

"Go out there and tell the one with the bullhorn I want to talk to her." Wanda turned to Leroy. "You got a phone here?" Leroy pointed to the phone on the wall and Wanda turned her attention back to the waitress. "Give her the number and tell her to call me. You got that?"

The girl looked at Leroy who nodded for her to go, then she ran to the front door and started yelling. "Don't shoot. Don't shoot. I ain't Wanda. Don't shoot."

"Put your hands on top of your head and come out slowly."

The girl looked back at her friends. There were tears in her eyes but she still managed a small smile before stepping through the doorway and out toward the police.

Leroy set a plate of chicken in front of Wanda, and then she waved him away. "This place got a back door?"

Leroy pointed behind her.

"Lock it," said Wanda.

Leroy walked over to the door and turned the deadbolt. "Why you wanna do this to us, girl? We ain't done nothin to you."

"Hey, I didn't stop here for lunch. You're the one put the bad shocks on my car. I don't want to hurt anybody so just do as I tell you and you'll all be fine." She looked at the women. There were six of them, all ages. "He treat you good?"

"This is my family," said Leroy, but Wanda quickly interrupted.

"Shut up. I want to hear it from them."

One of the older women stepped forward. She was smacking on a stick of gum and didn't seem the least bit upset. "It's like he said, sweetheart. We's all family here. Now why don't you put that peashooter down and get your lily white ass outa here."

Wanda pointed at the briefcase with her rifle. "You'll all be leaving here soon enough, but I'm not going anywhere." She took a bite of chicken. "This is good. You got any coke?"

"Yes'm, I do."

"Get me some. I want three of your girls to gather up some of your chicken and take it out to the cops. People get itchy on an empty stomach. I don't want anything to happen quite yet."

When Kramer found out from Frank that there was one dead terrorist on the roof and another splattered all over the street, and that now they had Wanda trapped at some fast-food joint, and that she was asking for him, he began to think he might just get out of this mess unscathed. He abandoned his search for Cervante and Two-ton—they hadn't exited where they were supposed to—and headed over to Leroy's Shocks and Bar-B-Q. When he arrived he found over fifty police picnicking on a feast of fried chicken and coleslaw, served up by some tired looking waitresses in hot pants and bright pink halter tops.

An attractive woman greeted Kramer at his car. "You Kramer?"

"Yeah, I'm Kramer, and you are?"

"Kate Mallory, LAPD. We appreciate you coming over. Here's the deal. We've got a female inside, she's holding a couple of hostages whom she says she's prepared to release, and she's willing to surrender, but only to you. Any idea why she wants to see you?"

270

Kramer was viciously chomping on a piece of gum. "Hey, you tell me. Maybe she thinks I can do something for her. How many hostages?"

"She let them all out except for the owner and one of the waitresses."

"No chance at a shot?"

"I'd rather bring her out."

Kramer got out of his car. His future was waiting inside this little chicken shack. All he needed was one good shot.

"Well, sure you would. But right now, that's not your call. You've got a dangerous terrorist in there and you need to send in your swat team."

"I hate to disappoint you Mister Kramer, but it is my call. I've got two hostages in there with her and I'm not about to sacrifice them so you can be a hero. She says she'll surrender to you. You want to go in and bring her out, be my guest. You don't feel up to that, I'll see if I can get her to talk to me. It's your choice."

"I could have your badge for this."

"You can try."

Right now, Kramer's choices weren't too appealing. If he doesn't go in Wanda's going to spill her guts to this cop; he knew her well enough to know she wasn't going to take the fall alone. On the other hand, going inside with Wanda seemed like a sure recipe for suicide.

"Okay, I'll go in. But you pick out your best two shooters and tell them to be ready. I'll see if I can get her in front of that window.

"She says she wants to surrender."

Kramer ignored her. "I get you a shot, you take it. You see me in front of the window instead of her, you send in your team.

Are we clear on this?"

"Crystal."

"Good. Don't hang me out to dry. You got a vest for me?"

Wanda opened the briefcase. Inside were stacks of money and one small brown paper bag. She pointed to the briefcase. "There's two-hundred and fifty-thousand dollars in there," she said to Leroy. "As soon as he gets in here, you take the money and your friend and get out of here."

Leroy reached for the briefcase. Wanda stuck the barrel of the rifle in his chest. "Make sure you share."

"I told you…"

"Yeah, I know, you're one big happy family."

Leroy looked down at the paper bag. "Why don't you come out with us? You don't have to do this."

Wanda was growing weak fast. She was half bent over now, clutching the wound in her side. "You make good chicken, Leroy. But your shocks aren't for shit. Anybody ever tell you some things just don't go together?"

"Sometimes you got to work with what you got," said Leroy.

"Wanda Blade. This is Charles Kramer with the Secret Service. I'm coming in."

Wanda waved her gun at Leroy. "You, go to the door and open it slowly, tell me what you see."

Leroy did as he was told. "One white man with both hands in the air, walking this way."

Let him in and then close the door behind him.

The door opened and Kramer walked in. Wanda changed positions so she could keep her gun on Kramer and still not get sideswiped by Leroy. "Move out of the way. Let these people by."

Leroy grabbed the briefcase and he and the one remaining waitress slowly worked their way to the door. "We're coming out! Don't nobody shoot." The two of them stepped outside and closed the door.

"It's just you and me now, Charles."

"You really managed to fuck things up, Wanda. So what are you going to do now?"

"You're going to take me in. Be a big hero. Move over here."

272

Kramer moved to within a few feet of Wanda. "Hand me your cuffs." He took his handcuffs out and gave them to Wanda. "Now, give me your hand."

"What for?"

"I'm going to handcuff myself to you and then you're going to walk me out of here. You'd have a hard time explaining why you had to shoot a handcuffed prisoner."

"I'm not armed, Wanda."

"Sure. Take off your coat."

"What for?"

"Take it off."

Kramer removed his jacket.

"Now, turn around."

"Listen, Wanda…"

"Or I can shoot you. It's up to you."

Kramer slowly turned around. There was a pistol tucked into his pants at the small of his back. Wanda reached over and grabbed it. "No gun, huh. Turn around."

Kramer turned around and faced Wanda. "And what are you going to tell them? People are wondering why you asked for me."

"Don't worry, Kramer, I won't say a word about us. I'll tell them I read your name in the paper. The way I see it, you're my ticket out of this mess. Man in your position can get things done. Otherwise, I've got my story to tell. Now give me your hand."

"How do I know I can trust you?"

Wanda pointed the barrel right at his head. "This rifle says you have no choice."

"Okay, okay. Just let me signal them outside." Kramer made a move toward the window.

"Hold it. No one's going anywhere near the window. What do you take me for?"

"Wanda, you think…"

"I think there are a half a dozen sharpshooters out there right now, each one of them just dying for a chance to be the hero. Now, give me your arm." Kramer slowly extended his left arm. Wanda opened the cuffs, attached one end to Kramer's arm then quickly attached the other half to a thin post.

"Hey, what are you doing?"

"Did you really think I was going to walk out of here with you?"

"But, you…"

"Shut up. I lied." Wanda grabbed her wound and leaned over in pain.

"Looks like you've lost a lot of blood, Wanda. Take off these cuffs and I'll get you some help."

"I don't think I can handle anymore of your help, Charles. You like chicken? They say Leroy's is the best in town. Or maybe you'd like to have a little fun before we go."

"Wanda, listen, I'm your only hope here."

Wanda swung the butt of the rifle into Kramer's gut. Then she reached over to the paper bag, pulled the bomb out and set it on the counter and began setting the timer.

"You being my only hope isn't exactly what I would call good news. What do you think, Charles, one minute, or two? One minute's not a lot of time, I admit, but two minutes, that would be cruel, don't you think, Charles? All that time to ponder your own death. I've thought about mine a lot during the last few years. Best not to dwell on it. Yeah, I think I'll do you a favor and make it one minute, in memory of all the good times we had." She set the timer and then she walked over to Leroy's phone and dialed a number. "Get your people away from the building. And just so you don't think you sent an innocent man to his death, you should know Kramer was behind it all. You got thirty seconds to clear the area."

She hung up the phone and turned to Kramer. "Any last request?"

Kramer was down on his knees, sobbing. "Please, Wanda, don't do this. I don't wanna die."

"You're pathetic. I should have put a bullet in you two years ago and taken my chances with the law. Now here we are at last." She took a bite off a chicken leg and then a long swig of coke. "But I'll tell you what I'll do. You always wanted to see these." Wanda ripped her shirt off and pulled away her bra. "Go ahead," she said, "touch them. They used to be worth millions."

Kramer looked up at the large, perfectly shaped breasts. In the poor light of the building the scars were barely visible. He raised his right hand from the floor and reached up, but it never made it to Wanda's chest.

"I remember," said Martin, "the shotgun going off and then the kick from it knocking me backwards off the roof. I couldn't breathe. I guess the force of the gun knocked the air out of me. I think I must have done a somersault, because I remember seeing the ground and some bright colors just before I hit."

"That must have been the tarp," said Vern. "From the exterminators. You landed in the back of their truck."

Martin reached up to his face. "What happened to my eye?"

"You landed on something in the truck," said June. "I think it was Mickey Mouse's hand."

Martin pulled himself up in his hospital bed. "Is it gonna be alright?"

Vern laughed. "Well, if they ever find it."

"You mean…"

"It's gone," said June, and then she reached over and grabbed his hand.

"Gone!" Martin reached up to his missing eye socket.

"Small price to pay for being a hero," said Vern.

"What do you mean?"

"It's in all the papers. How you shot the terrorist with your shotgun."

"Terrorist? That was Sukowski, the I.N.S guy. I only have one eye?"

"Aye, Captain," said Vern

"Well, evidently he was part of the group," said June, "I think they called themselves the PTA. Anyway, he was already under investigation by the I.N.S., and they found his prints all over the detonators."

"No way. There was someone else up there. Somebody warned me."

June looked at Vern, who shrugged his shoulders. "Like who?"

"I don't know. But someone was up there on the roof. And whoever it was saved my life."

"Nothing in there about any third person on the roof," said Vern. They killed all the terrorists except for some guy named DuBois, or something like that. They're still looking for him. Oh, and, on a sadder note, you recall the establishment where you used to procure our barbeque chicken? Up in smoke."

"Leroy's?"

"That's the one."

"What happened?"

"I guess the woman, Wanda, blew herself and some government agent up along with the building."

"Is Leroy okay?"

"Evidently."

Martin rubbed his hand over the patch on his eye. He was still feeling groggy from all the drugs. "I forgot to call that woman about your accident, Vern."

"Not necessary. Soon as she found out who my witness was, she couldn't write the check fast enough."

"Man, this is crazy. What about the kids?"

"They're fine, Martin," said June. Curtis picked them up this morning."

"Now, you want the good news? There's a guy outside from Hardcopy, wants to pay you fifty thousand dollars for your story," said Vern.

"Hardcopy?"

"Yeah, the TV show."

"I know what it is, Vern. They probably want to get a close-up of my empty socket. You tell them to fuck off?"

"I figured you would want to do that yourself. I would like to be here when you do it, though. I want to see their faces when you reject their most generous offer. I'm sure you'll find some colorful way to express it."

Martin looked at June, then back at Vern. "Fifty-thousand, huh?"

"That's what he said, but I think they'd pay more. Course, it doesn't really matter, does it?"

"How much more?"

"If it were me, I would shoot for a hundred grand."

"You think so? That much? And all I have to do is go on TV and pretend I'm some kind of hero, that I saved the President's life."

"Simple enough."

"Except it's not true, Vern. First of all, the gun went off by accident, and secondly, I went there because of June and the kids, not the President." Martin laughed. "Aren't you the guy that told me I should shoot the President?"

"Well, we may have mentioned that option, Martin, but this is even better. You can be famous and not have to go to prison. Don't forget, you're disabled now. You have to think of the future. What kind of a painter will you be with one eye?"

"I'd be an honest one, Vern. Now, if they want to pay me for the truth, I'll be happy to go on their stupid show and take their money. Otherwise, hey, I'm pretty good with a brush. I won't go hungry."

Vern moved in real close to Martin. "Martin, nobody's that good with a brush. Take the money. Write your book."

"What do you say, June?"

"The truth isn't always black and white, is it Martin? I mean, even if you didn't intend to save the President, you still did it. What's wrong with taking a reward?"

Martin sat quietly for a moment. "I don't even know what to write, or even if I can anymore."

"Why don't you write about what happened?" said June.

"Great idea," said Vern. "You could tell all about your vision."

"You think people would want to read that?"

"Are you kidding? You've got terrorists, orphaned children, murder, and, lest we forget, our good friend Leroy Washington, who makes the best chicken in town and sells shocks to boot."

"Shocks and Bar-B-Q," said June.

"That's it!" said Vern. "That's your title."

"What?" said Martin.

"Shocks and Bar-B-Q," said Vern. "It's perfect."

"I think you better leave the writing to me," said Martin. "Shocks and Bar-B-Q," he said quietly to himself. "It actually does have a certain ring to it, doesn't it?"

"It's lyrical," said June.

"Of course, Leroy would probably want some money for using the name," said Martin.

"Would you have it any other way?" said Vern.

"What the hell," said Martin. "Shocks and Bar-B-Q it is."

℘

EPILOGUE

Kate Mallory received a citation for bravery for her role in thwarting the assassination attempt. She is still working as a detective for the L.A. Police.

Frank Noble also received a citation. It was determined that had Frank not made the wrong turn, the President's car would have been the one to take the brunt of the explosion. Of course, as far as the President was concerned it was just further proof of Frank's good instincts. Frank finished out the term then retired from the Secret Service and moved to a small house in the mountains above Los Angeles.

Although Wanda managed to swerve away from Two-ton, the cop directly behind her didn't quite negotiate the move. The impact killed Two-ton instantly.

The police never did capture Cervante. Residents of the area claim they still hear someone down in the sewers now and then, but nobody has ever laid eyes on him since the incident.

June had liposuction on her hips and cheeks and two months after the assassination attempt, signed a three-million-dollar deal with Electra Bras.

Spike returned to his home in Memphis. He lives with his mother and is attending college.

Wade Parker now patrols Chinatown where he continues to set records for citations issued.

Curtis Chang quit the coyote business and moved his family to Brownsville, Texas, where he found work as a foreman on a large farm owned by a Mister Miguel Garcia. From day one, there was something familiar about Curtis to the Garcias, and in fact, the wife was sure they had met before. One hot afternoon, as was her custom, she brought a basket of sandwiches and drinks out to the workers. Curtis had his shirt off and when he turned his back to his employer he heard her omit a quiet shriek. Mrs. Garcia grabbed Curtis by the hand and pulled him to the house, calling to her husband along the way.

When Miguel saw the birthmark on Curtis's back he dropped to his knees and wept. His son had come home.

Vern got his ten thousand dollars for the missing fingers and he also was paid five thousand to appear on Geraldo. The episode was entitled: People Who Have lost Parts of Their Body. He is currently writing a book on the Phoracantha semipunctata, an Australian beetle renown for its devastating impact on the eucalyptus tree in Southern California.

Martin is still living in his trailer in Laguna. After much consideration, common sense prevailed and he accepted the offer from Hard Copy to tell his story. He did however refuse—despite pleas from numerous lawyers—to sue Disneyland for the loss of his eye (supposedly caused by Mickey's hand); the maker of the shotgun; the owner of the building (for not having built a guardrail atop the roof); and the exterminating company (just for being in the wrong place at the wrong time). The exterminators did, however, sue and recover three hundred dollars from Martin for ripping their tarp when he fell. Martin published Shocks and Barbeque. It sold a few copies and then slowly went away like so many novels do.

Leroy's business was completely destroyed by the bomb, however, the girls contributed their share of the two hundred fifty thousand to help open a new shop at the same location. They no longer carry shock absorbers but you can get a t-shirt with Wanda and Leroy's picture embossed on the front for a mere ten bucks.

Three months after the assassination attempt a custodian for the Times found an envelope behind a desk in one of the editor's office. Upon opening the envelope, he discovered a letter dated three months earlier and addressed to the Times. He showed the letter to his boss, who promptly read it. "Gee," he said, "this is a beautiful letter. I wonder who this Cervante is?"

"Wasn't that one of those terrorists, tried to kill the president?" asked the employee.

"Oh, yeah, yeah. Too bad." He crumbled up the letter and set it on a desk.

"Aren't you going to hand it in?"

The employer shook his head in disgust. "Are you stupid? It's three months old. I hand it in now, who you think they're going to blame for losing it? Besides, it's ancient history. Nobody cares. Too bad, though. It sure was a beautiful letter. Funny, guy has all that talent and he chooses to go around blowing people up. Yes, sir, that's a real shame," he said as he picked up the crumbled letter and tossed it into the trash.

અ